Maryam & Son

Praise for Previous Books

'*The Collaborator* is a tour de force of urgent political observation, filtered through the gaze of a timid adolescent narrator, about a subject unimaginably macabre and surreal. It is a great accomplishment to hold all this in balance with a tender, convincing story of human relationships. Waheed does it brilliantly and the effect is riveting.'

—*Financial Times*

'I loved it. The voice is lyrical, to match the beauty of Kashmir, and yet is tinged with melancholy and grief. I was shaking at times, was livid at times and was moved to tears ultimately.'

—Nadeem Aslam

'*The Collaborator* transcends the banal evil of the Captain to provide us a moving, universal story, and one that pulls off the sensitive task of leading us into the complex narrative of Kashmir. Mirza Waheed's remarkably confident debut is certainly that seed for the years to come.'

—Sanjay Kak in *Biblio*

'*The Collaborator* is that rare thing, a virutally flawless novel.'

—Eunice D'Souza in *Mumbai Mirror*

'A harrowing tale of love in a time of conflict and change … The language in this book is lyrical, indeed at times it seems to be poetry masquerading as prose. *The Book of Gold Leaves* is the sort of book one can read and re-read—and then read again.'

—*News on Sunday*

'A haunting illustration of how, at the end of last century, normal life became impossible for many of those who call Kashmir home … Waheed's talent lies in the vivid, convincing detail he brings to descriptions of everyday lives. The careful meshing of domestic intimacy with political events is done deftly, with integrity. Like his great-grandfather's gold painting, Waheed's work will undoubtedly endure.'

—*Financial Times*

'Poetic and political with a warm sensuousness, *The Book of Gold Leaves* is the year's best book. As beautifully written as the paintings on papier mache that one of its central characters executes, this fine examination of the Kashmiri condition through a Sunni-Shia love story leaves the reader both wretched and transformed, and brings us to a greater understanding of the fragility of love in a harsh climate.'

—*Hindustan Times*, 'Books of the Year'

'Waheed's work comes at a time when we have pushed the bar lower and lower about what we can say and do with impunity. [*Tell her Everything*] is a simple yet powerful book in itself, but the rudderlessness of these times makes it resonate with an even deeper urgency.'

—*The Hindu Literary Review*

'The triumph of *Tell Her Everything* is that it slithers away from neat categories. It is a love story. But it is not just that. It is a thriller. But the big reveal is a series of smaller disclosures. It is a political novel. But it doesn't deal with politics. It is a monologue. But it is also a conversation. It could be a memoir. But it is more of a confession.'

—*Open*

Maryam & Son

MIRZA WAHEED

Published by Context, an imprint of Westland Books, a division of Nasadiya Technologies Private Limited, in 2026

No. 269/2B, First Floor, 'Irai Arul', Vimalraj Street, Nethaji Nagar, Alapakkam Main Road, Maduravoyal, Chennai 600095

Westland, the Westland logo, Context and the Context logo are the trademarks of Nasadiya Technologies Private Limited, or its affiliates.

ISBN: 9789371977104

10 9 8 7 6 5 4 3 2 1

This is a work of fiction. Names, characters, organisations, places, events and incidents are either products of the author's imagination or used fictitiously.

Typeset by Jojy Philip

Printed at Parksons Graphics Pvt. Ltd

For
Mehdi Ali Mirza & Abrar Khawaja

Why wait at all?
Hope springs alive,
Good may befall
I yet may thrive.

It is because I can't make up my mind
If God is good, impotent or unkind.

'The Reason', Stevie Smith

PART I

ONE

Maryam Ali found her son missing on a Monday morning in early February, his bed empty, the duvet folded at the edge, two pairs of trainers tidy against the wall. Some of his clothes, a red Nike T-shirt, a grey tracksuit hoodie and track bottoms, and his brown leather satchel hung from the door hooks. She breathed in sharply, to smell his smell, his breath, the lingering remnants of his deodorant, somehow reaching for and feeling his presence. She knew he had been in the room just hours ago.

Outside, it was an overcast day, the persistent drizzle making the daylight dim and unfriendly. The air still bore the piercing sting of winter. The cold hush that descended on Homecroft Street, on the outer edges of Walthamstow, didn't lift all day. Maryam's flat was one of eight in a pale brick block built in the 1990s; the morning's gauzy mist hadn't cleared yet, leaving blue folds pinned to the thresholds and doors of the ground-floor flats. At the lower end of the street, Maryam's oldest friend and neighbourhood shopkeeper, Tony, was absently running a ragged mop up and down his glass front with one hand, the other clutching his first rollie of the day.

Closing her eyes as she stood in Dil's doorway, Maryam went back over the weekend, searching for anything unusual or untoward. Had she missed anything out of the ordinary? It had been a normal, uneventful weekend, like most they had. He had spent much of the day in his room on the computer, working or playing, she presumed, while she'd gone grocery shopping, cooked two dishes, watched some TV and done the laundry. As usual, she had waited for him to emerge in the evening so they could eat together—her only wish and demand of him. She had long given up asking him to get out more, spend fewer hours in front of the machine—a part of her secretly relieved he was home much of the time. She didn't have to wait for him to get home safe at night from trips out in the city with the boys. It had been soporific, predictable, like most weekends.

She reported him missing two days later, her younger sisters, Zarrine and Saffina, insisting they must go to the police. At first, Maryam tried to ignore the suggestion. What is wrong with the two of you? He's done something silly, fought with his girlfriend and is embarrassed about it. That's all. I told him I don't ever want to see his face again if he's rude to her. Maryam knew she wasn't making much sense but said it nonetheless to keep her sisters, or herself, from contemplating other questions.

'Baji, it's alright, we get it, we understand, but we can't keep it a secret, can we? When was the last time Dilly spent two full nights out? Night-spend with that smelly Andy doesn't count, innit? There's no one left to call now, I even rang Aunt Kulsum's, not that Dil's ever going to be found in the same postcode as tangy Taz ...' Zarrine said in one breath.

'We've got to go down to the station, Baji. I spoke with Uncle Sharief too, and he said the same thing. I know it sounds scary, but it's the right thing to do. We have no way of finding him without their help, do we? I know you don't like the coppers much, nor do

I, God knows what they'll think … but we must go,' Saffina, one year older than Zarrine, said.

'We have nothing to worry about, yeah? Dilly doesn't fit the profile—' Zarrine cut in and then quickly made a solemn face as her older sister's eyebrows rose.

Saffina came forward and put an arm around Maryam. 'You know what Zee means, Baji, come on, let's just get it over with. You, I mean we, need help. Dilly needs help … How about this? We're doing it for him, for silly Dilly … Wonder where he's fucked off to, careless twit!'

Love, solidarity, bottled-up anxiety hung in the air.

It was another cloudy day, the air cold and the light muted and pale. February had made London quieter, sadder, but also clearer somehow; one saw more of its bare form, its vast skeleton of endless terraces, housing estates, tower blocks, train stations, motorways, and its old streets and town centres. By this time, many a New Year resolution had crumbled and unravelled, as unavoidable cares of the world—jobs and credit card debts, mortgages and rents, long overdue GP appointments and electricity bills, or, in the case of the three sisters, puzzling, nerve-wracking thoughts about a disappeared boy—had started to weigh heavy on the city's people and weaken their resolve. Saffina was one such Londoner; she had just this week, the night of her older sister's frantic, worrying call, gone back to her late-night G&T habit, helping her sleep for some hours.

Maryam looked at her sisters one by one, as if to seek confirmation they were going to stand with her, by her side.

'I am doing this for you, mind you. Once I go in, you know there's no going back? His name will be in the records.'

'But that's assuming the impossible, innit,' Zarrine said, nodding to Saffina.

'I know, I know what you mean, hun. There's no way on earth Dil's going to have anything to do with them lot, is he!'

'Exactly, Baji, exactly. It's just very strange that he hasn't come home for three days now. He's like home all the time, playing games and all, innit? What the fuck!' Zarrine said, pushing aside her wayward fringe.

'Two and a half days. I feel like slapping him.'

'Yeah, you do that when he gets back. We must go and tell the police. They'll haul his ass back in no time. You just wait and watch. Please, let's just go!'

—

Maryam grabbed a few photos from her bedroom. She saw one in which he's in the middle of an escalator at The Mall in Wood Green, the squiggly red signs of Burger King glinting in the background. She put it back; he has a thick stubble in it. She took the one from the polytechnic where he's standing behind a lectern pretending to be a tutor, and another in which he has his arm wrapped over the balustrades of the staircase at Britech Solutions, the computer hardware and networking firm where he worked on freelance jobs now and then.

'Pick job, finish job, ta-ta bye-bye, that's how I like it, Mums. Hate sitting in the office, you know. Cubicle, open plan, posh office, they all smell of cleaning liquid, innit, gives me a headache,' he'd said last summer when she had, in the roundabout manner she'd adopted with him since he grew tall, suggested it might be better for him to start looking for a proper, grown-up job.

'Mum, those days are over, innit, one doesn't need to go to an office anymore! Your time was different, and you're, like, actually needed at school. But I can make enough dough sitting right here in my track bottoms. You've got to trust me on this, Mums. I'll show you.'

'Alright, alright ... just don't become an odd-job man, Dilly, that's all I'm saying. I just don't like the idea. When people ask, what am I going to tell them? That my son goes on calls, helping old people put floppy disks in their computers?'

'Ha-ha ... you're very funny, Mother, I've never seen a floppy disk, like never ever in my life. Before I googled it, I thought it was some kinda hat, hehe.'

'Don't make fun of old people. God bless Stevie, he used to keep all our records on disks when I started at Mortimer, you know. He showed me a stack once. Man for every job, that Steve, bless him. I thought I was on Dr Who!'

'Alright, alright, I won't make fun of you all, *floppy disks* on Dr Who. Sick!'

--

The police station was opposite a Greggs store and a new place called the Gastrologica where Zarrine had been meaning to try the inaugural two-for-one lunch offer. As they walked towards the station, she looked at it with longing and disappointment. Crumpled McDonald's boxes, drinking straws that rolled annoyingly back and forth on the ground, a stained community-policing poster and many cigarette butts greeted them as they reached the dour, grey station building. Maryam felt like smoking after a long time and thought of asking Saffina for a cigarette, but changed her mind at the last moment. As she went up the concrete stairs to the entrance, with Saffina and Zarrine either side of her, she tried to convince herself she hadn't really called Dil an odd-job man, but a tinge of regret remained.

It was a tedious and sigh-filled afternoon at the station. The young PC they met appeared baffled after the first few questions, went inside for a short while, then showed them to an office with a frosted glass door. A tall, lean, silver-haired man with wide shoulders, probably in his mid-fifties, stood up to meet them. 'Hello, I am Richard,' he said. 'I'm the duty officer ... What can I do for you, ladies?'

He asked them to fill in two forms, one of them twice, as Zarrine made a few errors, her mind elsewhere, thinking about her nephew, where he might be, why he'd left home … Maryam sat in the chair the duty officer had nudged towards her and watched him check things on his computer, his large hand clicking lazily on a mouse after long, strangely suspenseful gaps. She noticed it was a Dell computer. Dilawar had brought home a large monitor of the same brand last year and said it was better suited to game play.

The officer said they needed a photo they could release department-wide. Maryam glanced at Saffina, who reached for her bag. The officer looked at the 6x4 print and said it would do. She remembered watching it slide out of the self-service kiosk at Asda as Dil printed photos.

'Have you thought about putting out posters in the neighbourhood, darling? Fliers too, maybe. It's your choice, goes without saying, but sometimes it helps to have people on the lookout, you know,' he said.

Still Maryam didn't say anything. She had a lot to say, probably too much, but didn't know where to begin, whether to begin at all. Dil had folded his quilt at the foot of the bed—he never did that. Why had he done that, she wondered, as the police officer waited for her to answer. Or had she done it herself and didn't remember now?

'Yes, we've thought of it too. I've seen missing posters myself in the café, Zarrine. We will do it, defo … We came here first, so you guys know he's missing,' Saffina answered in place of her older sister.

'Of course, of course, I can imagine how worried you all must be, goes without saying … In my experience, they usually come back after a couple of days of partying, a bit of fun with friends, boys, eh, some beers, a few spliffs, clubbing in town … you know. Do you reckon he has a group of close friends; they all have a group at this age, own gang, etcetera? We will need their contacts asap. If you have names and numbers now, that would be grand, if not, you can send them later. On this number here, can you do that for me, darling? And this is the email address, if you prefer …'

Maryam wanted to give them Andy's number; he was kind and protective of Dil, he was bound to say good things about his friend, but she didn't have the number.

Saffina leaned forward. 'Yes, we can send an email, yes …'

'Thanks. And if you happen to know who he was with before he went missing? Was it someone he met often, someone you know? That would be grand. The more you tell us, the easier it is to start a search, darling. Would you like some water, a cup of tea maybe?'

'No, thanks, we'll leave you to it …' Saffina said. 'Please just find him, will you? He's not a bad boy, just a bit moody sometimes, you know, but which young man isn't … Alright then, we're going to go now.'

Maryam sat silent through all this. The officer walked across the hallway to another room, talked to his colleagues for a short while and came back. As Maryam turned to follow his movement, she noticed last year's Christmas cards tacked to the inside of the glass door. On the wall behind him were three framed photos, each with a football team posing with trophies and medals. Maryam found herself trying to identify the officer in them, then gave up quickly, shaking her head.

He cleared his throat. 'Ahem, ma'am, Mrs Maryam Ali, I assume? I have to ask, did he, please don't mind my asking, alright … He wasn't into any drugs and the like, you know, pills and stuff some young people take these days … was he?'

'Naah, never pills and the like, not Dilly. His mum would kill him!' Zarrine answered this time.

'Okay, thanks, that's it for now then. Anything comes up, you give us a ring, alright? And do send that email with the names and numbers today.'

'Yes, sir.'

'Someone will ring if anything comes up. Try not to worry. I know it's hard, what with some boys going off elsewhere these days, you know ...' he looked at Maryam, eyebrows raised for a fraction, 'but likely, yours isn't the sort. You've got to be strong, ma'am, not lose hope, alright? Remember, the more you tell us about him, the sooner we can find him ... Alright then, I'll let you go now.'

'Thank you,' Maryam said at last and stood up, her hand clasping the bag tightly.

--

'Don't even think about it. I'm not putting Dil's poster on the park gate or the café.'

'It's a small thing, Baji, might help, you know. Every little helps ... Okay, okay, how about we do it? Zarro and I will do it. You can stay home if you like.'

'Not a chance, Saffo, I'm not going to turn my son into a missing puppy or ... cat. I see those photos on the electricity poles, what do you call them, pylons ... all the time. It's only been two days, he'll come back anytime. What if he sees his poster on a wall or lying about on the street? His face on it! He'll flip. What am I going to tell him then?'

'What's there to tell, Baji,' Zarrine interrupted, 'just the truth, innit, you went AWOL, Dilly darling, you had us fucking worried, so we went a bit crazy looking for you. Simples.'

'Language! I'm still here, you know.'

'Come on, Baji, slips out sometimes, yeah, you do it all the time. Innit, Saffs?'

'You can't use eff words in front of him.'

'Erm ...'

'Anyway, I'm not making posters of Dilly, he's not a cat, he's not a puppy. That's my decision. The police have his photos, that man at the station seemed nice, they'll bring him home in a day or two if he doesn't turn up before then! Idiot, fucking idiot!'

Later that evening, as she sat down on the edge of his bed, gazing at the clothes hanging by the door, she suddenly felt deflated. The visit to the police station somehow felt unsatisfactory, not special enough. The officer had been matter of fact about it all, she thought, it ought to have felt momentous, more urgent and pressing. They should've shown more interest and keenness, it wasn't every day that her son disappeared, and although the officer—what was his name?—was courteous, he had gone about the whole thing as if it happened every day. But maybe it does, she paused to think, maybe it does, London is such a huge city, after all, people must go missing all the time, Dil just one of them. This was the thought that deflated her, but soon after, it also brought a sudden sense of hope. If people go missing all the time, they must be found all the time. What else!

TWO

The next morning, the doorbell rang three times in quick succession, someone not accustomed to closed doors, someone impatient to get in. Maryam knew it was Ama, and she dreaded what her mother might say—even at such a time as this—and what she might say in response. She took a deep breath, picked up her teacup and went to the door. Outside, a hazy, copper-tinted sun was struggling to break through the clouds, revealing parts of a broken disc now and then.

Ama was carrying her walking stick, she was wearing her stained blue Skechers under a checked shalwar kameez and a thick black cardigan, her hair tied into a fierce silver ponytail. She was short of breath.

'You're going to catch a cold like this, Ama, where's your hat, what's this!'

'Where has Dil gone, Maryam, what the hell did you say to him? Where is he?'

'I didn't say a word, Ama, why do you always assume—forget it, I'm just so worried and stressed and scared, and you … what the—forget it!' She checked herself, swallowing her fury. 'The policeman said not to worry, they're on the … *case*, but how can I not worry?'

As Maryam closed the door, Ama rushed in, threw her stick against the wall and embraced Maryam, squeezing her shoulders, rubbing her back in the way she used to when Maryam was little. Mother and daughter then moved slowly towards the kitchen, arms entangled, Ama bent with anxiety and bafflement, Maryam's shoulders sunken in an unknown terror.

As Maryam made fresh tea for them, Ama put her fists on the kitchen table, looked at the chair where Dil sat when she came for dinner and said, 'Did something happen, Maryam? Did he, Allah khair kare, get into some kind of trouble? Did you have a fight? You can tell me …'

'Oho, Ama, you don't have to pick on me, I don't know what happened,' Maryam shouted, then paused, looking at her mother with perplexity and appeal. 'I don't know anything, Ama, I swear …' She sighed.

Ama rubbed her hands, swallowed and said, 'Allah will protect us … He's such a good boy, maybe he's just hiding somewhere?'

Something in Ama's tone told Maryam that she didn't believe her own words, and she looked at her mother's old yet firm face, the wrinkles on it set and glowing, as if they had always been part of her look.

Sensing Maryam was examining her face, Ama hastily added, 'It's just my bad kismet … what can I say. They had better find him. Allah protect him!' She sighed, turning her face away.

At night, Maryam was filled with an inchoate sense of foreboding as her mind raced, trying to figure out why Dil had left home. She looked for reasons—whether she had said something or done something to upset him—and considered where he might be, to keep the fears at bay. There also came a sense of disbelief that it was real, a state of mind in which she wondered if she could hold everything still, find a lever or sentence that could be pulled back and unmade, so it would all be reversed in no time. Perhaps it was just a prank—idiot, she thought, taking it too far, that's what it is, it's not like he's really missing, you know what I mean.

Then, remembering something suddenly: oh, the news from the city, from the south of the city, no, it happens here too, in north London, doesn't it? She gasped, thinking what if Dil had been stabbed and was lying somewhere! There were so many stabbings nowadays, young boys' lives ended with the slash of a blade, she thought, trying hard not to but unable to keep herself from imagining Dil's body being cut, stabbed with a knife over and over. My God, she thought, they have these scary long knives these days, machetes and the like! Why, why? She gasped for breath, panicked, upset and teary-eyed. Why had Dilly done this! She missed her husband with a pang, missed Ash's calm, nodding ahems and hmms, his long bendy arms on her shoulders, drawing her in. 'Let's not jump the gun, Em, it's the way of the world, bringing up boys isn't easy, heck, bringing up children isn't easy, they will give us grief no matter ... So let's just calm down and let the police do their job, darling.' Yeah, that's what Ashoo would say, wish he was here, though. She steeled herself, hardening her back, straightening her spine. 'I must do as Ash says, wait for the police to do their job and find Dilly.'

—

Maryam went to the police station twice again: the week after they filed the missing person report, and the following week. Once with both Saffina and Zarrine, the next time with just Zarrine. On both occasions, they met the same officer. He spoke to Maryam calmly, explaining in a stepwise manner—as if she were a student and he her teacher—what they were doing about her missing son. He said the case was a top priority, a part of their daily briefings and bulletins.

'We've sent it across to the neighbouring boroughs and will be going city-wide too. The phone records didn't reveal much, to be honest, just a few calls to his friends a week before he disappeared. The computer analysis will take longer,' he said apologetically, as if he'd been personally slow in the matter. But she ought to rest assured they were doing everything to find him.

Then she stopped going to the station, suddenly exhausted. The short walk to the building filled her with increasing dread as she grew more and more frightened that Dil hadn't been found yet. She also couldn't shake off the notion that one of these days they'd tell her he had been stabbed. But still, hope pulsed somewhere in her heart. If she closed her eyes long enough, then opened them, she might find none of it had happened.

During her last visit to the station, the police officer, he was called Richard B., Zarrine reminded her, was polite but firm. 'Mrs Ali, you really don't need to come here in person, we'll call you the moment we find anything. We're doing what we can. Please have patience.'

They did not call or visit, and the three times Saffina and Zarrine inquired on the phone, they were told the same thing. Please have patience. Please wait.

Maryam did not agree to the posters.

THREE

At night, this part of outer Walthamstow became unexpectedly quiet given the busy daytime traffic from the motorway to the north (A 4 or a 6, darling? she used to joke with Ash) and the din of the service lanes closer to her home. The silence was broken only by the worried squeals of London ambulances now and then. As the trees were few and sparse in Maryam's immediate neighbourhood, the night sky over the houses often turned a diffused pale under the light from the high streetlights. They towered over the roads, casting a speckled golden halo over all the nooks and corners, reflecting like tiny moons in the shiny pebbles of the worn asphalt of Homecroft Street.

It was going to be a month since Dilawar's disappearance, and Maryam had, much to her surprise and unease, started to become used to having the flat to herself. She had the full measure of its space, its breadth and silence and aloneness. She missed his presence behind the door, the awareness of his body in the room, and was sometimes startled, wounded by the sound of her own footsteps as she went back and forth between her bedroom, the living room, the kitchen, and Dil's bedroom, where his clothes still smelled of him.

The police had found no trace of Dil so far. They were still hopeful, they said, though they hadn't made much progress. He was officially a Missing Persons case now. If there was a development in the case, they said to her, to her quiet heartbreak, they would send for her 'without delay'. Officer Richard B. came to see her once—to reassure her, to check on her, he said. 'Don't lose your heart, Mrs Ali,' he said. He also took Dilawar's toothbrush with him, sealing it in a ziplock bag. 'It's just procedure, Mrs Ali. Have to follow the rules, it's for DNA purposes if needed. Chances are we won't, so don't worry.'

--

She started to spend long hours in the garden, walking from one wall to another, going round and round at intervals. Sometimes she sat down if the sun was out, and sometimes she stood next to her balcony, gazing at the flower beds, the little plants, their sullen branches, their struggling leaves. She considered her options and felt she didn't have any—if she had even the faintest idea where Dil was hiding, she'd run this very moment to bring him back. But there was nothing she could do to find him, though she found some solace in the fact that the police hadn't turned up at her door to say they had found his body, discovered in the woods, fished from a canal, with stab wounds ... She must banish the stabbing fears, she told herself again.

Dil disappeared on Saturday, the sixth of February, she recalled, as she strolled in the garden. Since he hasn't turned up dead, it means he's been somewhere all these days, living, eating, sleeping. Living. 'Suppose that's good, isn't it,' she muttered, then remembered she had said the same thing to herself yesterday and the day before. She had said the same thing to Zarrine and Saffina when they came to see her. They brought news of their families and the rest of the clan. They brought gossip about the bua brigade—Aunt Kulsum, Bua Sayeeda, Aunt Sugra, the Finchley cousins, and the rest of them. She knew they gossiped to distract her, and she let them.

She spent much of February like this, in a state of waiting and not knowing. Saffina and Zarrine came every weekend, called every day. Ama was forbidden to come over owing to her weak left leg, although it didn't stop her from dropping in suddenly now and then with old ice-cream boxes filled with food.

March came and brought with it a resignation to the state of not knowing. If there was no news, it at least meant there was no bad news. He's somewhere, my baby, she told herself at night, tidying up his room for the hundredth time.

--

Four weeks after Dilawar went missing, Richard B. called on Saffina's phone as she was clearing the dishwasher at her home.

He said he was 'calling about Mrs Ali's report, there's been a development—'.

'This is not my sister's phone,' Saffina blurted out, instantly nervous and frightened, not knowing how to respond.

'I know, miss, I know. I wanted to talk to you first. The thing is, we need to speak with Mrs Ali soonest, it's important we do, so how about we come to the house? If you or any other family members are there, that would help … You, your other sister, perhaps a male member of the family? Whatever suits,' he said.

Saffina kicked the dishwasher door shut and hopped over to the kitchen table, her breath shaky. She sat down. It was early evening, and the stars hung low over the narrow, long garden of her Leytonstone semi. In the slanting light from the loft conversions opposite her house, she saw that the grass in her garden was overgrown but looked pretty. A dewy wash made the tufts look artistic, as if part of a landscape painting.

'Erm, what? What is it about, though,' she said, struggling to find the right words. 'Is it about Dilly? Do you have any news?'

She paused, moving the phone away momentarily, swallowing, and brought it back to her ear slowly as if to prepare for impact. 'Has something happened to him? Is it bad news? How bad? You can tell me … whatever it is,' she said in a single breath, one hand digging into her bag for her cigarette pack.

'The thing is … I can't say much on the phone. I'm not authorised, to be honest, but we want to come down to see you soonest. I will be there too.'

'What the hell, what the f—' Saffina began to shout, but checked herself immediately, glimpsing a faint split reflection of her face in the bifold doors as she shifted in her chair. 'It's about my nephew, sir, about our son! How can you say you can't tell me? What am I supposed to tell my sister?'

'You know it's a police matter, darling, can't do anything about it.'

'Oh, okay, alright, alright, phew!' She took a deep breath. 'How about I come over to the station, then, and you tell me? That way, we can spare Baji, I mean my sister, if there's anything … Is Dilly alright? He's not dead, is he?' She found her Silks and fiddled with the lid to extract a cigarette with one hand, saying 'fuck it, fuck it' under her breath.

'I'm afraid it's got to be done through proper channels, darling. It says next of kin is Mrs Ali here. You wrote it yourselves …'

'Alright, alright … come to the house then, if that's what you want! God. Let me know when, though, so we can all be there. I've got to be with Baji, you know, I've got to be with her.'

'Of course, of course, goes without saying. The thing is … it's got to be done first thing, to be honest … Tomorrow, as a matter of fact. So if you can be there, and anyone else you want, not too many, mind you. It's a sensitive matter, with your nephew involved and all. We don't want the whole neighbourhood there, now, do we … We will see you tomorrow morning then, alright.'

Saffina sat with the phone in one hand and the dying cigarette in another, trying to imagine what she'd say to Maryam. She looked at the garden outside; the grass had changed colour as the night grew. She ignored bedtime demands from her daughter upstairs, hoping her husband would come down from the loft room where he watched the Premier League in the evenings.

FOUR

Maryam and Saffina watched from the kitchen window as the cars turned into the parking lot behind the block of flats. To get to Maryam's door, they would need to walk back to the front of the building and past the first three flats. Maryam's was the last flat on the ground floor, with direct access to the communal garden. She noticed these were not the usual police cars, the kind you saw hooting a siren, but regular, nicer looking vehicles. She took a deep breath, put a hand to her chest. They hadn't told Ama.

Last night, Saffina had driven to Maryam's flat smoking all the way, flicking ash from her window as she whizzed along the North Circular, rehearsing how she was going to talk to Maryam, what she was going to tell her. In the end, she told her everything that the police officer had said, word for word, leaving out nothing. Baji is a grown, strong girl, she had thought, best to tell her the truth.

And Maryam had listened quietly, swallowing a few times, sipping water a few times, a steely, gritty look on her face, as she imagined scenarios in her head, all of which concluded, to her relief, that Dilawar was alive. It was Saffina who shed the tears.

'We have to let the police do their job, hun, isn't it? You said so yourself, didn't you? It's been a month, but they finally have news of Dilly!' Maryam said, hiding her trembling hands behind her.

Saffina held her hand and pulled her away from the window. Maryam craned her neck, trying to catch a glimpse of the group of people on their way to her door. 'We must look normal and see them in the living room, Baji, have to face it.' Saffina wished she had said something better. She also wished she had time for another cigarette, but it was too late. Maryam understood her sister's craving and nodded to her. Zarrine had come soon after dropping her son Zak at school, but was uncharacteristically quiet, pacing non-stop in the living room, stopping to hug her older sister every few minutes. Her husband Aziz had said he'd take the day off to be with them, but he hadn't arrived yet. 'He's always late, isn't he,' Maryam mumbled.

She stopped Saffina, who had started for the hallway, and pointed to the sofa, expecting her sister to understand and obey. 'I'll go myself.'

Maryam walked upright, straightening the green cardigan she wore over her black trousers. She had washed her hair the night before; she ran a hand through some strands down her side. She looked alright, composed, not distraught. Something had told her she mustn't come across as a helpless, distraught woman. She wanted to appear more or less together: upright, firm, not bent.

She opened the door before they rang the bell, before anyone knocked, and stood in silence in front of the arrived party. She recognised the officer from the station and noticed there was a young woman with him.

The light outside was brighter than she had thought it would be, a fresh, breezy chill in the air, but it wasn't too cold.

Standing behind Richard B. were two white men. One exceedingly well-dressed in a bluish suit and mac, tall, with elegant glasses on a lean, tan face, and cropped greying hair; the other, a considerably younger man, with a full, reddish face as if cold-blushed, wore a dark brown jacket over blue jeans and deep red or maroon brogues. At the back were two men in uniform, one bearded and thickset, his Met Police jacket tight on him, the other boyish and clean-shaven with a precise moustache.

'May we come in, Mrs Ali,' Richard said, having waited for a long moment for Maryam to ask them in.

'Oh, yes, come in, come in,' Maryam said, reminding herself to be composed, to stay firm, not cower.

Maryam's living room was large, rectangular, its walls painted a pale, sun-baked blue, a glass-and-wood cupboard affixed to the wall near the TV cabinet. A black BT phone with a blue LCD screen rested on a crochet-covered round table in the corner. A glazed wood frame on the wall had her parents Ama and Aba in it, the photo sepia-tinted with age. A smaller frame had a black-and-white photo of her father when he was young, freshly arrived in England in the late sixties, in a park somewhere, a little Maryam wearing a furry hat in his arms.

She gestured for them to sit, her hand pointing to the sofa.

The two officials sat down quietly. Richard dragged a chair over and sat next to them, the young woman took the armchair in the corner, the two men in uniform stood on either side of the sofa. Neither Maryam nor Saffina registered how they had so neatly arranged themselves in the living room.

—

The middle-aged man with the salt-and-pepper hair, who Maryam assumed to be the senior of the two officials, leaned forward with a straight back, locking his fingers in front of him, and said, 'Mrs Ali, my name is David, and this is my colleague, Julian. You've already met Richard and Hannah, I believe.' She hadn't met the woman, though she felt she had seen her somewhere. She didn't feel the need to correct this man.

'Now, Mrs Ali, I believe Richard here has already given you some information, spoken to you about our visit. I'm sorry to have to say this …' He took a moment. 'I'm afraid we don't have great news, ma'am … It's not terribly bad, but it's not great. A government department which deals with this sort of thing may have found the whereabouts of your son … That's the reason we are here, and I wanted to speak with you in person. Hannah's here to help us, help you, and answer any questions you may have. She will stay for a bit,' he said, acknowledging the young woman with a quick nod. 'Now, the good news is your son is alive …' He paused, letting the statement settle in the room, knowing he'd had the desired effect. The only word that Maryam heard was 'alive'. Dilly was alive! He hadn't been stabbed.

'The department believes that he may have left the country sometime last month—he's alive, please don't worry, but he's not in the UK, and I'm afraid he may have fallen in with some very dangerous people, if you know what I mean …'

Maryam felt a surge of emotion heave somewhere, heat rising to her face and ears, a long-suppressed cry stirring, reaching into her throat, but she stared ahead, gazing at the framed inscriptions of Allah and Muhammad in the glass-and-wood cupboard. Saffina drew closer and squeezed her hand, tears brimming on her eyelids. Zarrine stared at the visitors.

'I'm sorry I have difficult news … There's no other way to put this.' He turned to Saffina, then back to Maryam. 'A video has emerged from somewhere in Iraq. We are still ascertaining its specific origins, but the department believes that the person in the video may be your son, Dilawar Ali.' He paused, waiting for the sentence to work its way around the room, settle down in the house somewhere, take root. This wasn't the first time he had said this sort of thing to a parent, at a home, among relatives of the disappeared or the fled.

Maryam flinched, her face crumpling into countless crinkles, and she felt a sound escape her lips which she thought only she heard. Her stomach felt icy, her chest heavy, as if a wet rag was lodged in her throat. She struggled to speak but couldn't form the words, the cry lurking closer.

'It will no doubt come as a shock to you, I understand … However, this is a matter of national security and a high priority case for us … As you probably know,' David quickly glanced up at Saffina and Zarrine, 'associating or affiliating with groups such as ISIS in any manner or form is a criminal offence. There will, of course, be a thorough investigation, and due process will be followed …' He spoke in a clean, precise and serious manner, as if each word and phrase had been weighed before being chosen. Saffina watched her older sister's face and started rubbing her sternum with the side of her thumb, as if trying to distract her rampant heartbeat.

Maryam felt her breath stutter, she knew she wouldn't be able to hold her poise any longer. The words rushed out, floundering. 'What are you saying? What have you heard, mister? I don't understand … You said Dil is alive! So you know where he is, then? Has something happened to him and you aren't telling me? Hai Allah, why can't you tell me? What are you saying!' She turned to Richard B., leaning in towards him. 'I came to you at the station, sir, didn't I? You said not to worry—so tell me, please. Is Dilly alright? Where is he? Has he done something?'

Everybody in the room was looking at her, drawn to her flushed face, and now they turned towards Richard, the oldest person in the group, who nodded to acknowledge Maryam's appeal. Even David gave the impression that he wanted to hear from the senior man in uniform.

Richard B. cleared his throat, brought his hands together, turned to David for a fraction as if to seek approval, and said, 'I am sorry, Mrs Ali, I already told your good sister here,' his eyes turned to Saffina for help, 'the matter is not in our hands anymore. We did what we could, to be honest, and I'm sorry we weren't able to trace him sooner but, as explained, a different department is dealing with this matter now. They will take it on from here. I'm, of course, just down the road—goes without saying … So anything you need, please call. But as regards your son, it is these gentlemen who will deal with you from now on. They will require your full cooperation, I've assured them that these are good people, a nice family …' He looked at Saffina and Zarrine again.

It struck Maryam that they had referred to her son as 'a matter to be dealt with' a few times. A matter, the matter, this matter.

David took over quickly from his local police liaison. 'My colleagues will need to spend some time at your house, ma'am, I'm afraid,' he gestured towards one of the two uniformed men standing next to him, then at Richard. 'Just to look at some of your son's belongings and any other materials that may be of significance, and anything else you can show us …' he said in a calm, authoritative voice, unlocking his fingers, leaning back.

She was counting in her head: Dilawar had been missing for twenty-nine days, how come these people had only turned up now? She was convinced they had made a big mistake. A blunder—she liked the sound of the word.

The younger man, Julian, clearing his throat, spoke for the first time. 'Mrs Maryam, I understand the position you are in. I do … It's possible there may have been a misunderstanding, that's why it is all the more necessary to help us, tell us everything. Where Dilawar might have been going before … who he had been in touch with lately …' He spoke in a gentle, low voice, his hands folded in his lap.

'Help you with what exactly? It doesn't make any sense, does it? It's so terrible, so horrible, so … removed from me, from *us* … that I can only laugh …' she said, turning to Saffina as she felt her voice quiver. Then she fell silent. As if suddenly drained of all speech, the words dying before they could reach her lips.

Julian noticed the mild tremor, the faint jittering in her ankles, and the movement she made to hide it. He knew she was scared.

'This is a highly sensitive matter, Mrs Ali, we would, therefore, like you to keep it to yourself for now—I'm sure you don't want this to be public,' David said, looking at Maryam with an expression that suggested he knew she understood, that she had better understand. There was a sort of condescension and judgment in that look, Maryam sensed.

'Until we know more and get to the bottom of this awful situation, two of my colleagues will be visiting during the day. It's only for a few days … We want to make sure you feel safe, Mrs Ali.'

Maryam started to say something, but before she could get the words out of her mouth, David raised his hand. It reminded Maryam of her head teacher, Mrs Price.

'This must come as a shock, we understand, and it's no doubt a difficult time for you, so if there's anything we can do, do let us know. My good colleague here,' he turned to Julian, 'will be your main point of contact. He will check in with you regularly. You have any questions, you want to tell us anything, please feel free to speak with him. He's very good at what he does, you won't be without help, I'd like to assure you.'

Maryam looked at Saffina with melting eyes: this isn't, this cannot be true, she said without speaking. Saffina threw her hands up and rolled her eyes at the officials on the sofa. She didn't care how it appeared to the men.

'Mrs Ali, as I said to your good sister here,' Richard spoke again, 'if you need more of your family here, we can organise it …'

'You are scaring us,' Saffina said, raising her voice, a hand wagging in the air. 'Why won't you tell us what's happened? We don't know anything about a video—what video? Dil doesn't post videos, as far as I know. He fixes computers! What the hell are you sayin'!'

As Saffina spoke, everyone shifted in their seats. Hannah stood up and walked towards Maryam, followed tentatively by Julian.

Maryam's veneer of patience had broken. She couldn't pretend to be strong and stoic anymore. She felt she might get sick. What were these people trying to say? What had happened to her boy? Tears started streaming down her face unbidden, she sniffled and sighed, trying not to sob. She feared the worst fears. She cupped her face in her hands and wept. Zarrine held her shoulder, rubbing it softly.

Julian whispered something to David and went closer to Maryam. 'Mrs Maryam, I'm so sorry you had to find out this way, I'm sorry for the trouble we've caused you. That was not our intention, but it was necessary for you to know,' he said in a soft, low voice, like a caring friend. 'We have a duty of care to the families … I'm here to help. I will leave my personal number here so you can call me anytime you want. When you're ready, of course …' He looked at Maryam's face and saw a stark sadness, like that of a small girl who's used to crying herself to sleep. Then he turned to Zarrine, who was standing next to Maryam, and said, 'We're going to leave now, I'm sure you want to be with your sister without all of us here … I think we've intruded enough for today.'

'You think?' Zarrine shot back.

'We have some more formalities to go over, but I'm sure they can wait a day or two,' Julian said, and with that, they started to leave.

Maryam wanted to go after them, to see them off at the door, to walk with them to the parking lot. She feared letting them go like this meant they were walking away with her son's story, taking Dil with them in some way. She wanted to have the last word: it can't be Dilawar, you're wrong, it's not him! But Zarrine's hands on her shoulder kept her still, and Saffina in front of her kept her seated where she was, her face in her hands.

FIVE

It was the third item on the evening news. Maryam had closed the windows in the living room, peeping out briefly from a corner to check if anyone was in the garden. Outside, it was pitch dark, aside from the occasional flutters of light escaping from the houses on the other side of the garden. The news presenter with short bushy hair and a square jaw returned to the screen after the previous story and began, 'And now to the allied campaign in Iraq. The militant group ISIS has released a video in which it claims to have twelve Western hostages in its captivity. The video shows two of the hostages: an aid worker from an Australian charity group and the other a US soldier whose identity we cannot reveal. Both the hostages, as you can see in the clip, are masked. A partially masked man, allegedly an ISIS operative, can be seen with a sword. Sources say this man is believed to be British and is from London. Investigations are ongoing. We will bring you further details as the story develops.'

'No way on mother earth that's Dilly! How's that even fucking possible!' Zarrine was the first to speak. They were seated around the TV, Saffina deep in thought, worried for her nephew, worried for her sister, for her own children. She hadn't been sleeping well and had gone to her GP for pills.

Maryam sighed endlessly, a cold hollow growing in her chest, saying the same thing over and over, 'My boy, my little baby, it's not true, it can't be Dil.' Her sisters and her mother, one after the other repeating, 'Of course not, it's not Dilly, how can it be', like a backing chorus from a tragedy.

It was two days after the officials' visit, and this was the third news bulletin they had watched, every channel running the same clip, of the same duration. A ticker ran over and over, spinning in Maryam's eyes, making her vision blurry. 'Swordsman in ISIS video believed to be British man from London.'

'He's not a man, he's my boy,' she said to her mother for the third time that evening.

'Yes, he's a little boy, Maree, haathon se pala hai, ho hi nahi sakta!' Ama replied, shaking her head, caressing Maryam's shoulder, forcing a broken smile on her face.

Earlier that day, Ama had threatened to stop eating if she wasn't brought to Maryam's, so Zarrine had made a detour to Blackhorse Road and picked her up. Ama brought food with her: chicken pulao, potato curry and sweetened yogurt.

'You are not going to do any "I can't eat" nonsense, are you,' she said to Maryam as she stood up to open the bags.

'Ama! You literally threatened to stop eating two hours ago!' Zarrine said, her hand cutting the air.

'Threatened, yes … but who's brought the food, you or your Ama, hain? Now go and get some plates, you always talk too much.'

'Ama, Dil's been missing for more than a month, I can't not eat that long, can I? The food tastes like socks, but I eat,' Maryam said, sniffing.

Saffina was waiting for dinner to be over, when Ama would go into Maryam's bedroom for her evening namaz, and she could smoke freely by the front door.

Maryam ate some of the food Ama put on her plate, lingering over small, slow morsels, wondering why her mother had cooked pulao this day of all days, then deciding she must've raided her freezer and dug out one of her double-bagged Tupperware boxes. She swallowed a few spoons of the sweet curd, then sat back, sighing deeply, tears welling up in her eyes. Ama watched her as she ate her own dinner. Then she went to the sink and washed her hands, accidentally splashing some water on the window over the sink. As she wiped the glass, she thought she saw some shadows outside in the driveway that led to the parking lot but ignored it; better not tell Maryam, she told herself. When she came back, she saw Maryam leaning back in the chair, her wet cheeks glistening in the pale light of the kitchen lamps. 'I'm sure Dil's alright wherever he is, Maree, he's safe, I know it in my heart, and he's eating ...' She did not ask Maryam to stop crying.

Later, in the car, Ama sighed deeply, shed some tears, wiping them off with her chadar, cursing her kismet. Zarrine waited for her to calm down and then started driving. Ama talked all the way home. Zarrine judged it was best to let her go on. 'It doesn't make sense, Zarro, how can it be? Who would've thought we'd see this day, who would've thought. Allah raham kare! It just doesn't make any sense, and I don't trust a word those white afsar folk said. Dil nahi maanta!'

'Would we believe it if the officers looked like us, Ama,' Zarrine couldn't resist asking.

'I know, I know, but I just don't believe it. Dil is such a homebody, jaan, woh toh Naani ke ghar nahi aata without you or Maree driving him. How did he get to Iraq!'

'Getting a ticket there isn't the issue, Ama, don't you get it? You do know what happens over there, don't you? You know who all go to Iraq, Syria?'

'I'm not an idiot, Zarro, I don't see the news much, but I know what's happening in the world, can't escape it! Since when did you become a journalist, hain?'

'Let's not, alright, let's just not. Dilly is missing, Ama ...'

'It is not possible. Dil can't be one of those fundoos. Allah toba. Impossible hai.'

Ama wanted Zarrine to stay the night, but she knew it would be too much to ask; Zarro needed to go back to little Zak. She decided she would recite from the Quran at night, one full Siparah, and pray for her grandson's safety. She was sure he'd come back home soon.

SIX

The next day, a little after ten, the cars drove into Maryam's parking lot again in an orderly fashion, smooth and decisive. Soon, Richard was standing outside her door with the two officers, David and Julian, their small team behind him. Richard had called Saffina earlier in the morning to say they were on their way.

Maryam was wearing a blue-black kurta with a thin, embroidered magenta border on its neck and sleeves. She quickly fixed her hair and checked herself in the mirror. She didn't want to look dishevelled in front of the government people. It was a chilly, crisp, bright morning, the sunlight pouring in through every window in the kitchen, long white sheets unfurling through to the living room.

When she walked into the living room, she saw that the men were seated in the same arrangement as the last time. David appeared more relaxed today, with an arm spread over the sofa, commanding it, his head thrown back. He was wearing a blue-and-white combination again: white shirt, blue tie, blue jacket, dark blue mac and off-white socks. She noticed that Julian, dressed in a dark brown blazer and blue jeans, was standing with his hands clasped at his back and looking at the photos on the wall and in the cabinet.

The photos on the wall were from an older time, some bearing the feeble discolouration characteristic of Polaroid prints. Maryam's parents with their three girls, a lean teenaged Maryam flanked by ponytailed Zarrine and Saffina. Other pictures showed various uncles and aunts, the men in wide-collared three-piece suits and the ladies in floral shalwar kameezes of the 1970s fashion—the shirts short and the trousers wide and expansive, a stylish riff on bell bottoms in vogue at the time. The families looked into the camera from home lunches and dinners or from picnics in parks in London and Birmingham.

She followed Julian's gaze as it lingered on photos of her and Ashfaq, both so young and striking in their poses, she thought, her smile uninhibited and wide, beaming into the camera.

Julian hurried back to the sofa when he noticed her watching.

——

As she heard David issuing instructions to the two men in uniform in an assured, business-like manner, Maryam felt less and less in control of her space, as though she'd lost possession of her own surroundings, of her home. The man who'd suddenly appeared in her life and read the rule book to her sounded a bit too important and officious. She overheard the phrases 'check around' and 'collect everything', and, although she tried to ignore it, she sensed a sudden anger rising, her breath turning shallow. She felt a flush of indignation washing up the sides of her face, bringing an unexpected sense of humiliation, an embarrassment born from a feeling of being put in her place, of having to obey this man in front of his cohorts. She wanted to object to everything that had been said, and that which was happening in front of her eyes. How can these people order me around in my own home?

'Where do you think you're going,' she said, surprised at her own abruptness, staring at the men in uniform. 'Don't you think you need to ask my permission before you walk into my bedroom? This is my home! I am not letting you touch anything without my permission, do you understand!' Flustered, she tried to bring her voice down.

She saw that the men, one of them a boy really, and the woman called Hannah, remained standing in the doorway, staring at her. There was a moment of quiet tension in the room. Julian put his head down. He became aware of the folder in his hand and a part of him wished it had been with someone else, David probably.

'Mrs Maryam, you do know you are legally required to hand over your son's belongings,' David said coldly. 'We do have the paperwork, if you want to—'

'I'm not letting anyone change a thing in Dil's room! He will be back any day. This is my house, I will decide … who comes in here,' she said, staring back at David.

David pursed his lips and said, 'We believe it's in your interest to let us look at everything, ma'am, given the circumstances, given what's happened … It's temporary, of course, I must add. But you must let us check everything.'

Maryam knew he'd been impeccably well-mannered with her since the moment he'd walked in, saying 'ma'am' and 'kindly' after every sentence, and it was perhaps this discordant gap between speech and action that grated on her mind and added to her indignation and anger.

'I will not let anyone touch Dilly's things. How can I? He's my son! I don't believe any of this … strange nonsense. There's no way he would do … such a thing! How on earth can he! Only Allah knows the truth …' She trailed off, tears brimming in her large eyes.

Julian stood up and walked slowly towards her, and said in a soft, pleading voice, 'Mrs Maryam, please, this is standard procedure, we're simply following the rules. It is necessary for us to investigate, find out … Don't you want to know? How can we help if you won't let us do our job? Please …' He remained standing in front of her, slightly bent, his hands folded. He had left the case folder on the table.

'On one condition ...' Maryam started, trying to keep her lips from quivering, steadying her breath. 'They will not disturb anything in his room and leave his clothes exactly as they are. I can decide what happens in my own home, can't I,' she said, unsure of what else to say, as she sensed David's eyes on her. But in the younger man she noticed a moment of openness, even tenderness perhaps, so she drew her gaze to him.

'If they make a mess, or upset me in any way, I swear I will pack up and run away,' she continued in an aggrieved, complaining tone. 'Then you will never have his things. I want to check everything, look at everything, read every word before I give it to you people. If not, I swear on Allah I will make a scene here. All my friends and neighbours are here. Tony, Gemma, Pat and Sheila, yes, shrieky Sheila, will throw you out of here in no time. And I know the internet, I know how it works,' Maryam said, her voice shaking now, as she kept a storm locked inside. She didn't want to cry in front of these men again.

Deep down she knew it was pointless, her against the government people, but even so, she felt impelled, and she was trying hard to put on a brave face. She felt she must make a stand; she couldn't simply give in.

'My only son's gone missing,' she said. 'I am yet to understand, let alone accept my loss, and it's my loss alone. I am yet to cry properly, I am yet to scream and howl and beat my chest ... and you come into my house, my home, and order a search? A fucking search of my cupboards and drawers. I thought you had dropped in to give me support, as you said, didn't you? Do I not deserve it? For a moment I wondered, what biscuits shall I bring out with the tea? Do I even have any good ones left? For a moment I thought, of course it's possible for government folk to be human like the rest of us. But no, you are all the same, heartless, soulless drones in three-piece suits.'

Zarrine froze at this outburst; she wasn't unfamiliar with Baji's occasional flare-ups, but this was something different. She didn't want to intervene, certainly not now. Saffina stared at Maryam, trying to hide her embarrassment.

David chose to stay quiet at first, then he tried to reassure her, 'No, Mrs Ali, perhaps you misunderstand ... As Julian said, we're simply doing our job so that you, too, can move on—'

At this, Maryam stood up, patted down the creases in her kurta, and said, 'Move on? Really? How do I move on from this? If you think your job is to rifle through my cupboards ... look at my private things, if you think your job is to order me around in my own home, you and your minions can just fuck off. If you had really been doing your job, you wouldn't be searching through my cupboards and undergarments, mister! You people think you can harass me in my own house because I am a lonely woman, because my son is not here? You, your minister, that two-faced behenchod who talks bullshit on TV, and his boss, you can keep all the paperwork you think you can scare me with, and fuck off right this moment ...'

'And do you know what ...' she said as an afterthought, raising her finger, 'I'm going to ask Uncle Sharief to go to the court, tell the judge I'm being harassed, bullied even! Let's see what you have to say about that. Now please take these people with you and leave my house.' Maryam felt her hands shake, so she closed her fists, the nails on the verge of piercing the skin on her palms.

Nobody moved. When she saw that David remained sitting there on the sofa, his legs spread, with a knowing expression that seemed smug to her, something snapped inside her. She stood up, walked down the hallway, pushed open her front door, and started shouting, 'Tony, where are you? Tony? Sheila, are you there, Sheila?'

Alarmed by the outburst, David turned to Julian, signalling with his eyes and hands. The younger man rushed towards Maryam and pleaded with her, hands folded like a namaste, the expression on his face begging her not to make a spectacle—not to make a spectacle of herself. Maryam was out of breath, short of words, exasperated. She found herself alone at her doorstep, on the verge of crying. Turning in, she was distracted by Julian's pleading hands. She was panting, her hands trembling, but she relented and walked back.

On their way in, Julian saw a battered Gray-Nicolls bat in the umbrella basket and found himself wondering what kind of batsman her son had been, what number he had batted at.

As Maryam walked back into the living room, she felt relieved she hadn't run into the street like a mad woman. She felt embarrassed at this realisation. So undignified, so unseemly!

Inwardly relieved, observing Maryam every moment, David concluded that this small woman from the city's suburbs, who they were meant to keep a close eye on, was rather different from the type he'd encountered before. He felt something sharp, a quick sensation in his body at the close proximity with her, seeing her properly, how her face had an openness, as if drawing him in. He looked away. He pursed his lips, nodding to himself. After speaking quietly with Hannah near the doorway, he slipped out with a pronounced nod towards his junior colleague.

Cursing her kismet and her son, Maryam sat down in the chair next to Zarrine. Saffina gave her the glass of water she'd kept ready. Julian sat on the edge of the sofa, next to Maryam's chair. Matt, Lucas and Hannah slipped out and went into Dilawar's room.

--

Julian stayed behind after David left with Richard, explaining to Maryam in a sympathetic tone that it was all a matter of procedure, reassuring her and her sisters that he was there to help them at this difficult time. Yes, it was a lot to take in, but she had to let them examine her son's possessions.

Zarrine eyed him suspiciously, while Saffina remained silent, resigned to a chain of events set into motion by things beyond their control. She wondered for a moment, what if her nephew really had fled to the Middle East—but she felt it would be unwise to air her suspicions. She went out to the garden frequently to smoke, Zarrine giving her company.

——

As the afternoon wore on, Maryam felt restless after sitting quietly for some time, looking at her sisters, the young officer. There were people inside her son's room, doing God knows what with his things.

She stood up and went to the bathroom. There, she sat still for a long time, her mind aching, conflicted. She felt embarrassed at the way she had shouted and behaved in front of these people, in front of the man who was trying to be kind and helpful.

Next, she went to the kitchen and poured a glass of orange juice, arranged some brownies and flapjacks tidily on a round steel tray, and walked back to the sitting room. Julian was surprised at this. The woman who had been distraught a short while ago appeared much calmer now, a change of mood as swift as her movements when she'd opened her door and started to shout.

She looked slimmer to him than the last time he had seen her, somehow trimmed down, her straight hair loose, resting down the shoulders. It struck him again that she was considerably younger than he'd imagined. He felt an inward blush at this.

Maryam was of medium or slight build, average height, her bright face full-ish, with sharp features, a pinhead-sized mole just above her jaw line on the right. Faint lines creased her eyes and mouth ever so slightly. Her upper lip curved up slightly to the left. She had the habit of flicking her hair away with the back of her fingers, and moved about quickly, decisively. Her large eyes were striking, and he remembered the fat tears that had dropped off them, how she'd covered her face.

'Best way to re-up, Dil says,' she leaned in and said, pointing to the drink and the snacks. 'I'm sorry about earlier, I may have been a bit too loud … I don't usually do that. Haven't been myself lately, you see …' She sighed. 'I don't believe anything you say about my son, you know, not a word, and yet my life has changed more now than it did when his dad passed away.'

Julian stopped drinking the squash and started to say something, then stopped, feeling he had already wronged this woman.

Maryam looked at him. 'You still haven't told me your full name?'

'My name is Julian Chapman, I'm the family liaison at the Joint Section, the human face …' He tried to affect a hesitant smile.

In between sips of the juice and bites of a flapjack—he didn't touch the brownies because they looked dry to him; Maryam nudged the tray forward a couple of times but then gave up—it struck him that he was going to see her often in the next few months, certainly until the mystery of her son was solved, maybe even after.

SEVEN

In the leaden, dismal days that followed, Maryam let them have Dil's things, a few at a time. She was determined to take her time with the 'belongings'. She knew her world was broken, so she wanted to hold on to the pieces, gazing at and feeling the T-shirts, the jumpers, the notebooks, the photos, headphones, scarves, even the coins she found in the corners of his drawers …

She also suspected that, although they had checked everything—her home, her belongings—what they were perhaps really after was something else: a beep, a ping, a whisper, a trace, as if she was … She went through bouts of flushed anger and crushing doubt and confusion. She ached for one word from Dilawar but dreaded it at the same time, fearing it might prove what they said about him was true.

The uniformed men, Matt and Lucas, came every morning for three intense days, depositing their bags and man-grunts in the lobby, their presence a stifling reminder of her new reality. She felt a tinge of sympathy for them for some reason, then resentment too. How long were they going to do this! 'I should ask them to pay the fucking bills, Zarro,' she said to Zarrine on the phone. 'The electric bill has gone through the roof!' Still, she wanted to keep a distance, as if accepting their presence would amount to acknowledging what the officials had said about her son.

'I'm not sure they understand how a woman thinks,' she said. 'Why would I want to see shadows hover outside as I sit down to pee? How can I not sense the presence of men outside my bathroom window?'

Lucas, the younger of the two, hardly looked at her, keeping his face down all the time. She could see his long, girl-like eyelashes drooping over his eyes. He's just a boy, she thought, probably doesn't even know it's rude. Later, when she found out he was Cypriot, she thought maybe he meant no disrespect, maybe he'd been taught to keep his head down as an elder spoke. 'Yeah, ma'am, just my nana and grandfather … he died the year before last, they came from Cyprus a long time ago. But I'm from Southgate, ma'am. Yeah, it's not far from here … I take the Victoria Line to Finsbury Park, then Piccadilly. It's like door-to-door in forty.'

She knew they came between nine and nine-thirty, catalogued and photographed things in Dil's room, went away for long lunch breaks, stayed until early evening, and left together. When not searching Dil's room or checking things around the house, they hovered outside, in the parking lot, at times strolling in the garden.

It wasn't their fault, she knew, but she marked the corners furthest from their movements. She felt suspicious of everything, walked barefoot in the flat, and she resented them for it. She had to remind herself not to lash out at them. 'They're just doing their job, Maryam, you mustn't get angry,' she said to herself. To reassure herself—to provide proof for herself—she offered them tea and McVitie's Chocolate Digestives biscuits. They refused at first, but she persisted, until Matt said, 'Since you insist, ma'am, we'll have it here by the door, if that's alright with you, ma'am, if you don't mind …'

During this time, Julian called her twice to ask if she needed anything, if there was anything he could do for her. He reassured her again that the men examining her son's room were going to be done soon and that he would see her soon. 'You can call me anytime you want,' he said. She remembered his face and his gentle manner.

As promised, Julian came to see her a few days later, a Thursday afternoon, when Matt and Lucas were packing up, their bags and folders in the lobby, fresh red seals taped on top of the packs. Maryam saw Julian's car pull into the parking lot, a mix of anxiety and relief coming over her as she recalled the last time he'd been at the flat, spent time with her, bringing a kind of sudden relief to her after the cold pronouncements of his boss, who had been such an unfriendly presence, filling her with a sense of dread, as though she knew he wouldn't do well by her. But the man walking towards her door now, he seemed unlike the others, more open somehow ... someone she could talk to without fear or stress.

Julian knocked on her door with a soft tread, his tall frame filling the doorway. When Maryam opened the door, glancing askance at the men in uniform, he seemed different from the last time, less formal, his hair just the normal kind of unruly, as if he'd been messing with it.

'Good afternoon, Mrs Maryam,' he said, 'I hope you've been alright? I just wanted to check in, see how you're doing ...'

She stepped aside, letting him into the flat, walking in front of him, her scarf trailing behind her. What did they expect to hear—how did he think she was doing? But she chose not to say this to him.

'I'm trying ... trying to understand ...' she said, as she sat down, her voice tight. 'It's ... not easy ...' she added, nodding towards the lobby.

'I can understand,' he said, running his eyes over the framed photographs on the wall, the faces of her family, her parents, her late husband, her son.

'I can't imagine what you must feel, but I know what you're going through. It's the hardest thing …'

As she turned to look at him, she saw a flicker of genuine concern in his eyes, and the unexpected kindness surprised her. She felt strangely relieved she'd been right in her assessment of him. He was different, wasn't he, or maybe he was meant to be, but irrespective, he didn't fill her with the dread and despondency that his boss evoked.

They sat across each other in the living room, the silence accentuated by sporadic sounds from the neighbourhood, a car trudging along, the TV running too loudly in Sheila's flat above her, someone's plumbing groaning faintly … Julian asked her about her parents, about Ama, about her school, his attempt to understand her life before Dilawar's disappearance quite conspicuous, though his questions were as gentle as they were probing. She remained cautious, her guard still up, the memory of her near meltdown a bitter, corrosive taste in her mouth, but his interest seemed honest, and she felt an unexpected ease with him, recalling how he had, with folded hands, pleaded with her not to make a spectacle of herself.

At one point in the afternoon, he went to speak with his colleagues for about five minutes. She heard the outer door shut, and when he came back, he smiled at her broadly and gave her a single nod.

Later, as he was leaving, he paused at the door. 'Mrs Maryam,' he said, his voice soft, 'I understand this is a difficult time, I do. As I said on the phone, I want you to know I'm here for anything you might need, anything at all, really. If you hear anything, or anything bothers you, please call me anytime.' He looked at her with clear, thoughtful eyes, closing them as he finished talking.

She nodded in response, her chest pressing in. A part of her wanted him to stay longer, but she banished the thought.

Often, she stood at her favourite spot in the flat, the niche between her bedroom wardrobe and the window, gazing at the garden she shared with the other flats. Used to share. Now she rarely went there, wary as she was of the neighbours' eyes on her. From her window, the garden still looked gorgeous, still inviting in its manicured beauty—its shapely evergreen hedges, its spiral flower beds—and the shaded wilderness of the larger plants, the overgrown wisteria, and the tall young oaks that lined the two walls of the high maroon fence.

EIGHT

The Joint Section office hummed with the buzz from the server towers behind the woodcarving screen, its orange chakra motifs like cartoon suns. Grown lemon trees stood on either side of this decorative partition. The open-plan work area, where some of David's staff sat in front of large screens, was at the opposite end. The sofa square in the middle was demarcated by bean bags and diagonally positioned green-velvet chaise lounges. Some nights, this sitting area was busier, especially if files from the D Wing, the other half of the Joint Section, arrived late London time.

Julian's cabin was to the right of David's glass-and-wood office, which gave David a direct view of the open-plan area and the sofa island. A dimly lit hallway that led to the bathrooms separated the two offices. Two biodomes, a Swiss cheese plant, a weeping fig, moth orchids and cacti in glass lined the wall between David's office and the hallway. Julian sometimes watched his boss's upper half float above the house plants, dipping and rising as he walked and talked on the phone, and thought he looked like a character from a silent film.

To the left of David's office was another office, longer, larger than Julian's, where the head of digital forensics, Faroukh

Ispahani, and senior analyst and house whiz, Alexei, sat side by side. Their expansive twin desks were the nerve centre where all the digital files—field reports, intercepts and intelligence from 'other sources'—came for analysis and allocation. It was Alexei who ran the images through face-rec on the custom-designed system and called in Julian or David to take a look when the matches exceeded 60 per cent. That was the agreed bottom line, more or less, give or take, depending on …

All that Hannah had scanned at Maryam's house had found its way here. Everything that David's CIA partners sent also came here. It was all stored in a shared server between this office and the D Wing building somewhere near Washington DC.

As information funnelled into its core from near and far, a live, pulsing charge seemed to thrum around the machine, its proclamations clear-cut and inescapable for its operators. Julian had been shown the machine and its workings a few times since joining the Joint Section. Its mother console—which helped create and collate target lists in Iraq and Syria, Alexei had whispered to him—sat on the fifth floor of the US part of the Joint Section.

Nobody walked into the by-lane where the entrance to the Joint Section office was, because the pigeon-shit-speckled, imitation-antique busts at the front dissuaded people from traipsing through. There was nothing here. To onlookers, it was a perfectly ordinary, mid-sized London office building. An architecture and design firm on the first two floors and a company that specialised in electronic sunshields, shutters and blinds on the next two, made it mildly interesting but nothing more than that.

Around three weeks ago, David's hopes were raised when a CIA field office in Iraq sent a dispatch to Washington that they'd traced the origin of the Swordsman video to Mosul, somewhere in the neighbourhood of the regional university. A scan through the on-site face recognition program had yielded five hits, one of which partially matched three photos from Maryam's albums.

David's team had nothing on the Swordsman until Ispahani's algorithm hooked into case photos tagged 'Missper' in a Metropolitan Police dataset. It was Alexei who picked up the match one evening as he ran a scan against the photo frames that the Americans had put together from the video files. He had high-fived Ispahani, who obliged promptly but pointed to the 70 per cent green pie in one of the grids on screen. Secretly, though, Ispahani had felt smug, proud of the software genie he had invented. It could pick every bit of visual information from a photograph or set of photographs and create what he believed was the characteristic 'photo smell' of a face. The program could then trawl any database or the internet to fish for the closest match. No one except Alexei knew he had named it The Gecko.

David's liaison at the CIA and the head of the D Wing, Oskar, had held two encrypted meetings with David in the last month. Julian was aware David didn't fill him in on everything, and he felt left out now and then. For David, though, it was simply a matter of procedure: a strictly need-to-know policy. There had also been one or two occasions when David had wondered whether Julian fed anything back to the Chief Special Advisor on whose recommendation he had been given this role.

--

'Yes, Julian, they've had multiple matches, I know. The Wing are onto something,' David said, leaning back in his tall chair. They were sitting in David's soundproof office, the grainy photo printouts from the video spread on the table. 'I'm told it's a large group. Mosul corridor from the looks of it, I had a quick look at the imagery. It's clear something interesting is going on over there, we can certainly ask to rerun the face-rec for Dilawar Ali, but I say a 72 per cent match isn't bad for now.'

'I agree, David. I asked Alexei to look at the port files again, just in case, not that I have much hope. They've been parsed frame by frame a few times.'

'I wouldn't spend any more time on how he travelled, how he got out, it was like a carnival last year … and the year before last, remember? Mind you, everyone doesn't show their face on CCTV. In any case, it seems we are past all that now. How is it going with the mother?'

'She's talking. I'm seeing her again this Friday, I get the feeling she wants to tell me stuff, you know. I sit with her, and listen to her … but the thing is, we've got to be patient.'

'It's likely to be him, Julian, but I wouldn't be shocked if it turns out to be someone else,' David said as he saw Julian raise his 'I have a question' hand. It annoyed him sometimes, this public-school sanctimony and fixation with classroom manners.

'I agree, we need a couple of solid, conclusive hits, but I'm sure our friends will turn up with something sooner or later,' Julian said with the air of someone familiar with high-level intelligence sharing between American and British agencies.

Julian recalled David sometimes curled his eyebrow at praise of their US partners. It was an equal exchange, quid pro quo, David had let it be known. 'We bring proper intel to the table, JC, as good as some of their key partners in the region, if not better. What do the Arabs send, chit chat off phone intercepts or torture confessions that we have to action on? My translation budget could buy us a small island nation somewhere.'

Julian bristled at the mention of torture, a retort on the tip of his tongue about confessions that the Americans extracted in dark sites across the region, but he thought better of it.

—

As David and Julian talked, their heads visible from outside, Alexei sighed and dipped into the shared drive. Ispahani leaned back in his chair, hands crossed behind his neck, watching his colleague.

'What do we have in the dump today,' he said.

'They've chucked in some fresh footage from Mosul, a group parade or something. I bet it's grainy as cow dung and I'll get cataracts going through it all. But yeah, that's what we have, and I can bet the mummy minders have uploaded some massive files from the house search. Boy has picnic with mum, boy's side profile from dinner with best buds at Nando's. Boring,' Alexei said.

'Boring,' Ispahani agreed.

'At least we've got some lives in the Mosul files, there's also that night vid of some IS guys moving between locations. I could set up a body-motion analysis, lay it over the stills, you know.'

'It's a show of strength, Alexei, they're telling the locals to stay put. I doubt they'll take our boy along to this. And what good would a Body-Mo do, he's not moving in the video, is he, just staring like a psycho ... You don't have a frame of reference.'

'I almost wish it was a proper beheading video, you know, with movement and all, with him ... you know what I mean.'

'Come on, that would mean somebody's head getting chopped off, mate.'

'I know, I'm just saying ... I still think it could be him ... I get the feeling there's more to Dilly Ali than the sword thing, you know. The Americans aren't going to put a tech team on him just because he appears in a weird vid, are they?'

'Could be someone who looks like him,' Ispahani answered, raising his eyebrows. 'Let's just stick to what we—'

Cautious not to reveal his suspicions that D Wing had hidden some Swordsman files from them, Alexei said, 'By the way, Hani, I was thinking ... What if we tweaked the code a tiny bit, jacked it up, you know, I'm just saying, to ... 89 per cent, 91 per cent, and be done with it for fuck's sake.'

'But that would be wrong.'

'Of course that would be wrong, pious prick. I'm just saying.'

'Boring.'

--

In the last two or three years, the number of British boys and girls, men and women, travelling to areas under the Islamic State in Iraq and Syria had risen steeply. It was like a festival in the desert, David thought, and it had become challenging to keep tabs on all those who had fled the country. But it was all the more important to track them: to know where they were now, what they were up to, and where they were headed if they came back home.

All the data from people with 'roots in the community', from property searches and extensive interviews with mothers, fathers and siblings, intel from undercover officers in mosques and community centres, from eager volunteers with morsels of information from inside prisons, all the data from the web of cameras spread far and wide, from travel records and ATM appearances, chatroom transcripts, social media journeys and dark web footprints, phone intercepts and hacks … all of it had helped the Joint Section trace IS recruits to training camps, refugee centres on porous borders, diffuse battlefronts in Iraq and Syria, or on sour journeys of disillusionment back to the homeland.

They appeared as flashing, moving or static dots on screens in top-secret facilities in the country and across the ocean, in David's ultra-high-tech facility and its partner station near DC. The boys and girls who'd left their homes to join a new kind of nation were being tracked this way and that, their traces picked up by man and machine—except a shadowy, elusive few, except the boy from Walthamstow and two others from outside London.

--

The missing report that Maryam and her sisters had filed at their police station had surfaced in the form of notifications on the system that Alexei monitored in person during the day and via alerts on his home laptop at night. The high-spec system was capable of hearing, watching and capturing just about everything associated with a set of pre-programmed tags, from almost every landline, cell phone, internet connection and game console in the country.

The preset parameters in Ispahani's program—age, ethnic background, religion, socio-economic strata, education profile—had flagged the police report from outer London as interesting. When the usual protocols (digital footprints, chatter scans, a clone of the mother's phone) didn't yield any leads after a week of analysis, David had been intrigued. 'Got to crack this one,' he'd said as he left work one Friday in late February.

When Alexei broadcast an alert about a possible match the following week, it was Julian who had read the police file. It was he who had then rushed to David and said, 'I think we should perhaps start with the boy from Walthamstow. He could be our man, David. We may need to go on a home visit soon.'

David had skimmed through Alexei's briefing notes and said, 'He lives with his mother a few miles from here, for god's sake! What is wrong with this country! Don't you live close by, Julian, same area, roughly, would you say?'

'No, David, not at all, I am in Muswell Hill, next to Ally Pally.'

'What's that?'

'Alexandra Palace, it's next to Muswell Hill. Our house is next to the park—'

'Of course I know Alexandra Palace,' David had said. 'Anyhow, I would like you to take the lead on this. We don't have much on this Dilawar Ali, no priors, no socials, never been on any chatter. Missper came up with zero. Anyhow, the mother is supposed to be on the edge, a school chef or something like it, shouldn't be too hard …'

J-Sec had been founded with one objective: to follow ISIS-affiliated Britons wherever they went, whatever it took, in particular if they were headed back home, but David was increasingly bothered by this new case from his city. He couldn't afford to take a chance—the Americans had been clear about that. 'You don't want to be sleeping the one time he makes contact with his mom,' his partner had joked.

Whether the ISIS boys of Britain were in camps, in weapons factories or in recruitment units online, many had been accounted for, or deemed missing—until the dead-end with the Swordsman who, the Americans said, was of enormous interest to them.

In the much-viewed video, the Swordsman just stands there, looking straight, unmoving eyes focused on something up front, with an ornate scabbard hanging off his waist. The sword has a dark red handle that glints. 'These are staged videos,' Alexei had written in his memo. 'Carefully framed and put together for the web.' The Swordsman doesn't touch the sword or gesture towards it.

NINE

At night, Maryam dreaded hearing sounds from Dil's bedroom; even the tiniest, faintest hiss or tinkle could be unsettling. She had never believed in ghosts and spirits—but still ... It's his things. It's his things.

The evening after the officials' last visit, she'd locked the room with a padlock and knots of nylon string. She recalled how David had spoken to her in a stern tone, telling her she was *legally* required to let his team do their job, as Julian looked at her with an expression of empathy. Although a part of her knew her defiance was in vain, she had derived some satisfaction from speaking her mind, from answering back.

'In this house, under this roof, these people will follow my rules. I know you've got all these papers from the government, but here, in my home, I make the rules. So I will hand over everything after I've looked at everything,' she'd said. 'One more thing. These people call me "The Mother". I've heard it said a few times and I'm not happy about it. I have a name. Maryam Ali, Mrs Maryam, Maryam is fine too, but not Mary, because that's not my name either. I have a name that I have answered to for forty-six years! The Mother, for god's sake, I'm not their mother! I haven't said anything to them yet, but I can't promise I'll remain quiet for long,' she'd added, staring at David.

—

Considering what he had seen of her, what he had heard her say, David had come to the sobering conclusion that too much pressure wasn't going to be of use with this woman. More crucially, they did not have concrete proof yet. There was no CCTV footage, no record of Dilawar Ali slipping away, leaving the country. Word from his counterparts in the US, too, was to observe and monitor, to 'not upset the applecart'.

The fragments of Dilawar Ali's life left at his home were, therefore, all he wanted. 'It's enough to pass on to the stakeholders at the moment,' he'd said to Julian as they were driving back from Maryam's. 'Our friends want something from her son, and I want to know what he's up to.'

Julian had quietly nodded in agreement. He believed it was wiser to wait for the parents to open up slowly. And he certainly didn't mind coming to Maryam Ali's flat, spending time with her. He felt he had established a rapport with her somehow, a connection.

'Do we really need to have those two at the house,' he'd asked.

'I'm sure you've seen the news, Julian. What if someone digs up her address? It's for her safety, while we gather what we need—we must check every corner, mustn't we? Also, when you have them removed, someone will see it as a favour.' He had looked at his junior meaningfully.

—

Terrified though she was by what David and Julian had said about him, Maryam felt close to Dil as she went through his things, touching them, remembering where and when … It kept her threaded to the one person she loved the most in the world, even if he was still a missing person, or, as David had put it, a person 'of enormous interest'.

'I can't just stand by and watch these men unmake and rip apart my life; it's my home, my life …' she said to her reflection in the bedroom mirror.

Slowly, day after sorrowful day, she went through Dilawar's old books. While tidying up after Matt and Lucas, she found *The Faraway Tree* tucked behind a heap of textbooks on top of his cupboard. She used to read it to him often when he was little—she herself had never tired of reading about the Saucepan Man, who she thought was such a desi figure. She also found notebooks from his secondary school and the polytech, going over his scribbles several times, feeling the writing with her fingertips. She came across lines written on the margins of textbooks and mock test papers, sentimental ruminations on love and friendship. She felt she must preserve these, so she asked Hannah if she could have the pages scanned for her. 'Can you do that for me, please? Dilly said if you turn old documents and such into images on the phone or computer, they can remain forever. Do you understand, darling,' she said, smiling.

'Yes, ma'am, I understand.'

Hannah Lewis, Hackney born and bred, had taken a liking to Maryam from the very first day. A mutual recognition of their north London inflections made her smile sometimes. Maryam saw it too, and felt comfortable in her company. 'You wear nice belts,' she said to her, admiring the wide, pale leather belt Hannah wore on her dark blue jeans.

In one note, Dil had written about the loneliness of friends without girlfriends, about Aiden who was incapable of speaking with girls and was, therefore, the only one in the group without 'a girl'. 'Adi spends all evening by himself in the house, we go Vue and Nando's. Feel for Adi, they're loaded but he's kinda lonely. P doesn't want him along.'

Maryam thought of Dil's girlfriend Piya, daughter of a Leytonstone pharmacist couple, whose existence he had kept secret, but she'd always known and thought they made a nice couple, even though she thought it was too early for them to be playing couple. But she'd decided to let him be—and now, upon reading his thoughts, she was pleased she had let things be—even as she'd kept a close eye on his movements, timing and manner. She'd rehearsed her speech should she find condoms and other such things in his pockets, she recalled. Although what other things, she wondered.

God knows where that girl is now, wish I could speak with her, ask if she is alright, ask about Dilly, she thought, but knew she couldn't call her, that the girl wouldn't pick up. 'Piya, Mum, P-I-Y-A, not Priya, they are different names, innit,' he would say every time Maryam used the more common Priya, sometimes deliberately, just to hear him shriek in protest.

'Piya.' As she spoke the name again, that overwhelming desire to howl—to ask him where he was and why he had left her: 'what the hell did I do to deserve this, what wrong did I do, Dilly?'—resurfaced, but she calmed herself, breathing in and out slowly, hands on her knees, eyes fixed on the framed inscriptions of Allah and Muhammad in the glass cabinet. In the days after she'd broken down in front of David and his posse, she had trained herself to deal with panic attacks by trying to take her mind off what had happened, shifting her attention to something else, then something else. She'd taught herself distraction and deflection. Hurriedly, she rolled out her prayer mat and started reciting the Surah Fateha.

Bismillah ir Rahman ir Rahim, Alhamdulillah ir Rabiul Alameen …

It didn't matter that it wasn't prayer time, it didn't matter the Azan hadn't echoed from the mosque in Aunt Sugra's neighbourhood, or that she had already prayed …

She started folding the washing while she still had the rolled-up velvet mat in the crook of her right arm. Next, she called her bank—customer service—to check for the second time in a month what might happen if she withdrew money from her ISA, and once again heard the breakdown of charges should she decide to 'expire the ISA'. 'No, I'll just wait, hun,' she said to Tomalin, who, Maryam thought, had to be Irish. Her bank had informed her via several glossy letters that all customer calls were answered in the UK, by which it was meant they were not dealt with from call centres somewhere in the country of Maryam's ancestors. Maryam added a 'fuck it' under her breath as she hung up.

--

Even as she played these little games of distraction and deflection, at night she felt an aching pull towards the photo albums, as if drawn by a magnetic force inside the covers, and in her heart, she knew she wouldn't stay away for long. It made her chest heavy, as if wet, with anticipation and sadness. Comforting herself with his photos would be sad and pathetic, she thought, and yet she desperately wanted to.

She would've liked to make a kettle of tea, take the box out into the garden, and recollect cherished moments while looking at Dil's photos. In her mind, she had often derived a kind of solace from it, because each image, every frozen moment of life, was incorruptible, safe from the heart-shrinking callousness of the present. Surely the memory of it, she thought, the looking back at the time and place of the picture was inviolate, despite her current state, despite the growing whispers in the extended family, despite the image and name with which her son and she would forever be associated.

This last thing, this unceasing burn in the pit of her stomach, was her main quarrel with the world, and with herself too. No, I will not be the mother of the Swordsman. You cannot blot my name and replace it with something from the news or from your code-word world. And, in any case, it's not him in the video, I can tell, it's definitely not him, it's not my Dil! It cannot be.

After putting it off many times, after changing her mind as to where and when, after some deliberation, some torment, she decided to look at the pictures in her bedroom, in the safety of her niche. She made sets of photos that were loose or had come unstuck and thought she'd look at those first. She knew David's team had seen all the photos. Though she wasn't entirely sure of this, it gave her a certain satisfaction, nonetheless, that Julian had made an effort to keep her happy. But it also made her sad that looking at her son's baby pictures was no longer a private, solitary affair. Anyhow, she understood sorrow, and it was part and parcel of who she had become, of who her son had turned her into.

But she needed to hold on to these little, feeble consolations; they were precious, not to be given up, no matter what the officials said. They wouldn't understand. A flick of the index finger on the face, a palm wiping off the thin sheen of invisible dust, even opening the sticky cover of the album where an entire childhood lay—no one could take that away from her. There was a scent to the photographs that belonged to the good before, to when life was in her hands.

TEN

There he is, three years old, glorious, showing off his shining fat belly in the paddling pool she'd bought second-hand from South Woodford. In this very garden, outside this very window, just the other day. It was sunny, it was hot, and he'd had three glasses of Robinson's Lemon (I want more yumon!) and refused to eat the chicken goujons she had made for lunch. Later, she'd given him a few spoonfuls of the mince and rice and ketchup concoction she'd made for herself but knew he loved it because of the 'chupchup'—a word he'd invented when he was two as he couldn't say ketchup.

Zarrine had mocked her 'degenerate taste' in food and 'rotting cooking skills'. 'What's next, Baji, ketchup korma or chicken karahi with mayonnaise?' The younger sisters had come to spend the day with Maryam and Ash on Dilawar's third birthday, food and drinks in the garden, fags under the oaks.

'Go to takeaway hell, Zarro. When you have kids of your own, I'd love to see how you feed them,' Maryam had said, smiling.

Saffina and Zarrine had both trained as stylists (for the entertainment industry, Baji), and since they'd wanted to set up their own studio, they had moved to Tooting to be near the big desi parlours, breaking their teenage oath that they'd never be more than a few streets away from their big sister. To realise their dream, they spent four years working six days a week in South London as 'hair and nail plumbers', as Maryam used to call them in those days. It was clear to everyone in the extended family, as well as to some in Maryam's neighbourhood, that the two worshipped their older sister, not least because Maryam always watched out for them, defended them, and supplied foolproof alibis for their personal and professional escapades, which often came under strict scrutiny from the 'bua brigade' and 'aunty mafia'. The sisters remembered in particular how some of the elders had not merely disapproved of their choice of career, but were keen to deploy it as added justification for quick weddings to the first or second matches that could be found in the clan, which extended from Barcelona to Birmingham to Northeast London and from Amritsar in India to Sargodha in Pakistan and Thessaloniki in Greece. They had rushed to Maryam's as soon as they got wind of cross-continental marriage proposals discussed loudly on long-distance calls.

'Who shall we kill, Baji, ourselves or Bua Durdana, that old hog, she looks like eyes and mouth on shrivelled old bark? She's the one who's been calling Ama—they think we don't know what's going on. Why not get her fat boy grandson Taz married, yeah … Leave us the fuck alone, man,' Zarrine said at her sister's doorstep.

'Who's going to marry that large lamb doner, Zee, always smells of kebabs, innit,' Saffina said, trying to slip past her younger sister into the flat.

'Be kind, girls, Taz is your first cousin, after all.'

'Baji, remember that one time Ama dragged us to lunch there? India–Pak match, yeah? Cousin Taz was, like, sprawled on that smelly leather sofa, doormat-size doner kebab and a 1.5 litre bottle of Sprite on the table. Total weed-pusher bruv vibes, innit. I didn't say nothin', just looked at the set, yeah, and he says, "The Sprite kills the fat, Zee, it's not all that unhealthy, you know, you can 'ave some if you like, come on, dig in, mate." He had a potbelly even then, Baji, he was like, what, seventeen?'

Amid laughter, Maryam had pushed them in, fed them cream chicken with naan and settled down on the couch with a pot of green tea. Saffina later said that Maryam had talked so much that night that neither of the sisters remembered who fell asleep first, but the next morning they had a plan and some money to set up shop.

Maryam had called Ama the next evening, the phone trilling for a long time in the carpeted hallway of the old house near Blackhorse Road Station. 'If we pile on all this pressure, they will run away, Ama, what will all the aunts say then? Let's be smart about it, alright, time for us to bring them back to the neighbourhood, not push them further away. Let them have their own little salon, it's just a shop with a fancy name, that's all. All the buas can get their hair dyed too, jet black or purple or blonde even, whatever they want ... A few years of that and then we get them married.'

'Oh, of course they came running to you, Mother India! Everyone should calm down, Allah vaste, no one's getting married this Friday, alright? I still make decisions around here. Are they still there? So spoilt, I swear ...'

'That Saffo thinks puffing away on the streets makes her modern and whatnot ... Bewaqoof! Money makes you strong, your own income. Are they with you?'

'But first you promise—'

'Oh-ho, so you also assumed I'm going to pack them off like rubber dolls, hain? Well done, Maryam, well done! Have you forgotten your time? You think you wed Ashfaq all by yourself, is that it? Brave independent woman and all that. I still remember the digs about mixture babies, you may have forgotten but I haven't ...'

'Oh, Ama, come on, don't go there, there's no need to bring all that in, I didn't mean to ... I was just worried Zarrine might stab Bua Durdana in the face—'

'Yes, Zarro has threatened to take the meat cleaver to Finchley a few times. But don't worry, Maryam, these things have to be dealt with calmly, without noise and shouting matches. I can't yell at all the aunts and uncles, can I? Have some pity on me. They watch reruns of those Indian and Pakistani soaps during the day, Kumkum, Kasauti Zindagi, Humsafar, Ghar Ghar Ki whatever … they're like never-ending weddings, and then they try to arrange marriages in the evening. They have nothing else to do, trust me, I know.'

'So, just to be sure, they can have a go at the salon thing then, yeah?'

'Yes, yes, my mother, now stop harassing me. Give Dil a hug, bring him along on the weekend, will you?'

'Will do, Ama, will do. You be good, yeah. Allah Hafiz.'

—

These days, Saffina and Zarrine were only allowed a weekly visit. Their sister had decreed that one of them, or both together, could see her once a week, 'or maybe once in ten days'. That was that, and there was going to be no further discussion on the matter. This was because, Maryam said to her reflection, she needed clarity and calm, not the stress and hurt that remembering Dil together inevitably brought on.

Yes, they were brilliant and incredible when Dilly was born, when he was one, when he was two, toddler, eh, and three and four … Yes, there was all that, and they were there for that third birthday party. Truth be told, they were the ones who had carried the paddling pool all the way from that charity shop. Cheeky devils, always looking for an excuse to have some fun … they thought they were being clever mixing gin in their lime soda, as if she was stupid, as if she'd never been young and single.

—

Some more photos from when he was two and three popped out; he's in onesies in some, the pale green pair Ash had bought from GAP. They made her look away. Then, with delicate hands, as if she was handling family heirlooms or antique jewels entrusted to her care, she nudged them back in, wondering if it was all worth it, holding on to everything. Would it not be better if she just gave up and ran off somewhere, far away from everyone, away from this house, away from the cartons and shoe boxes, the photos and the papers, from the knick-knack museums of childhood and youth? What for, Maryam Ali, what for? He has abandoned you! Would it not be simpler if she disappeared rather than be a difficult, stubborn woman? Would it not be better for everyone, herself and Saffo and Zarro, particularly for the sisters and their families, if she gave up and left the country, and went to … hmm … Mussoorie and stayed with Aunt Noorie and her husband? Their bungalow on the hill was a perfect hideaway, wasn't it? Would they even have her, though? Wouldn't it be better if she vanished from these parts and reappeared on a totally different side of the world? Where no one knew her or her son?

She stopped after the first few pictures. Once again, she debated, going back and forth, yes and no, of course I must, but what is the point of it all, Maryam, no, you must fight, find Dil, why can't I live the rest of my life in peace, what's the point of fighting—they're government people, after all—but I can't let them push me around, I'm not going to let them turn me into this person and always be known as the Swordsman's mother.

ELEVEN

In this way, Maryam remained both steadfast and fragile, relenting only when she felt her actions might be construed to echo something from the world of her son, or the world into which they said he had thrown himself. She was unsure of this sometimes, not knowing what might raise eyebrows, and it made her feel sadness and rage.

In the old world, she was more than happy to not know much about technology, email-she-mail (please don't say that, Mum!) and certainly didn't care about Dil spending whole days in front of the computer. In the old life, as long as he was home, as long as he didn't mix with the lager louts, as long as she knew where he was, who he was with—mostly Aiden, Andy and Rezlan—she was happy. And they did eat meals together on the weekends, even if he didn't say much, even if he seemed distracted, with that old elsewhere look on his face, but then, he never did talk much, did he? Or was it after Ash died that he'd started saying less and less?

Four jobs in two years had seemed alright then, kind of normal for kids these days … A young, upcoming IT professional—or was it 'consultant' he said?—was surely free to hop jobs if he wasn't happy, and he was very good at what he did, he'd said, network admin, Microsoft certified. How else would he get a new job within a week or so of leaving one?

—

Her income had been sufficient for a few years after Ash's death but as Dilawar grew older, as his needs grew, she saw that he felt embarrassed having to ask for money for everything, and so when after his GCSEs he mentioned the IT diploma—that he'd prefer to do an apprenticeship rather than spend years at uni and still have no guarantee of a job—Maryam had simply said, 'Do what you think is good for you, Dilly.' She wasn't worried at the time because she knew she would be able to take care of them both if things didn't go to plan, if, Allah forbid, he was unable to have a stable job and income for some time. She told herself that if he didn't turn out to be a 'successful man', as defined by the unwritten tenets of the clan, she would have enough to leave something behind for him. Hope for the best, prepare for the worst, wasn't such a bad motto after all.

There was the salary from her school job of twenty-three years, plus the pension she continued to receive after Ash's passing. That small pot from Ash's job—she called it pocket money from the grave—had been quite useful. At 147.50 pounds a month, she preferred to withdraw it annually and spend the money on the flat: having the carpets deep cleaned, the vents in the double glazing fixed yet again, the radiators bled, the boiler serviced even if it didn't need servicing (she had from a young age been terrified of not having hot water or heating in the house), bathroom fittings and plumbing checked, fixed and rechecked. And if any cash was left, she'd buy clothes for herself and have a night out at the bingo with Saffina and Zarrine who, despite Maryam's assurances that it was all on her, sometimes brought their own gin in the bag so that Baji didn't have to spend too much. 'You only buy the first drinks, Baji, then maybe juice a couple of times, innit.'

In the old life, Maryam had, bit by bit, made sure that, after Ash, they were still on course for relatively hassle-free sailing.

--

Ash led a very good life, didn't he?

Spent a lot of his time with us.

It's God's will, we shouldn't be ungrateful, and we should celebrate his life … rather than … mother and son had agreed, despite the daily desolation.

Can't wallow in self-pity and misery, can't let grief take over, define life for us, isn't it? He wouldn't want that, Dilly, the mother said day and night, and the son nodded in agreement, his head bent over a bowl of flakes and fruit.

'It was unfair, cruel of Allah to take Dad, I don't think I can ever get over it, Mum, but we can't do anything about it now—now that he's gone. I still can't believe it though, I still can't. But I guess we'll be alright, Mum, don't worry, it takes time …' Dilawar had said at last, many days after the burial, curling his long bendy arms around her.

There was no drama, no flailing of arms, no loose hair. No one heard Maryam say 'my life is over' because Maryam knew it wasn't. She didn't want it to be over, she couldn't afford for it to be over.

There certainly was no encouraging of pity towards her wise and 'mature beyond his years' son because Maryam would not have it. She believed she was not an object of pity because life had been alright until then, the three of them together and cosy in their own centrally heated flat with access to a maintained garden. Of course, some in the extended family, especially the Finchley aunts and cousins who they met Eid to Eid, were alarmed Maryam hadn't looked sufficiently distraught, hadn't even waited for the fortieth day to start working again. Allah toba!

When Zarrine reported the shortest possible version of what had been said at the funeral lunch at Ama's house, Maryam had responded in two ways. First, she'd sighed a deliberate, long sigh, held her sister's hand and said, 'Can't afford not to work, hun, you know, with Ash gone …' Then she'd stood up, hand resting on the sofa, and enumerated the various small slights her father's youngest sister, Aunt Kulsum of Finchley, had sent their way over the years. 'I mean, which sensible woman, brown, black or white, wears thick flannel tights in the summer? No wonder Bua Kulsum smells like stale beans sometimes. Finchley this and Finchley that! Just because some rich fat Arab auntie says Assalamualaikum to her at Waitrose, she thinks she can sit in judgement on everyone in the whole family. We are more Golder's Green than Finchley, huh! Did you know she still plays the namaz on her iPhone so she can repeat after it?

'And guess what she said when Obama became the president of America? You remember how it was, right, everyone cheering? But do you know what our lovely lady Kulsum says? Go on, take a guess … She said, "Oh, but he is black, poor man." But he is black! Poor Ashoo, I had dragged him all the way to Finchley to look at their accounts so her carpet-king husband Showki could save some tax. Who knew!'

Later at home, Maryam had prayed in her room, looked at Ashfaq's face in the wooden photo frame, kissed it and said, 'Go well, darling, you gave us everything.' When she left the room to be with Dilawar, she thought she saw a fleeting glimpse of his legs in the hallway.

TWELVE

When Ash died, Dil was thirteen—going on fourteen, some relatives said. That was Maryam's main worry then, whether he would cope alright, if he'd miss his dad too much and lose years of his boyhood, his youth, to grief and self-pity and fury over fatherlessness. After the burial, he'd been silent mostly, head down too often, receiving condolences and hugs from mournful relatives with a certain poise, a stoicism that had surprised her—he never once let his guard down. She had kept an eye on him and assigned Saffina to watch him closely during the funeral rites. 'Be with him all the time, alright, and do everything he asks, okay?'

'Of course, Baji … You didn't need to ask.'

'And please don't come to me for every small thing, alright, only if it's absolutely necessary, alright? I've got a thousand things to do!'

There was no drama.

Maryam saw that he cried properly only after the funeral, after they had come back home, when no one was around. Sitting on the sofa where Ash used to sit, mindlessly fiddling with the remote, as Ash used to do, bringing on the TV too loudly, he broke down and buried his face in her shoulder, making her kurta wet and sticky. As his breath stuttered, she wept too, and the two of them then had a long cry together, their sobs and gasps mingling, muffled echoes ringing faintly in the long-curtained living room. Then they quietened down to a heavy calm during which mother looked at the son and the son at the mother, and this way, she thought, they told one another a lot more than they had done by way of words. She knew they only had each other from then on. It was alright to let him stay in that state for as long as it took, she said to herself in the mirror. She'd never done this before, speaking to her reflection in the bedroom mirror.

—

On the evening of the Soyem, three days after Ashfaq's burial, Saffina and Zarrine had come with their husbands and mothers-in-law, bringing food that would last more than a month. During dinner Dilawar didn't leave Maryam's side, she noticed, right until the moment she stood up to wash her hands.

When she returned from the bathroom, he stood up to get some air, to spend a couple of minutes by himself, she thought.

She watched him closely, to see how he carried himself, to look for signs that might tell her he wasn't coping well, so that she could call a special session with the sisters later, without worrying Ama. But he seemed to be coping alright, a bit more hurried than usual, a tiny bit restless, but of course, who wouldn't be with so many eyes watching, and perhaps a bit weakened in his body, a bit shrunk maybe—or was that because he kept his head down?—but overall, he appeared to be alright, and she felt … she felt proud of him, and of Ash for having instilled a certain strength of character in him. Maryam had, of course, always been the primary parent, chosen to be so, but at the time, all she saw in her son was the husband she had lost.

In the four or five minutes he took to be with himself in the bathroom, Maryam calculated income, expenses and savings, and arrived at failsafe sums per month, per year, that she would need to keep their lives more or less as they'd been until a few days ago when Ashfaq died suddenly. 'You unreliable bastard, Ash, you could've waited at least until he became a man,' she mumbled, then brought her attention back to more practical matters. She knew which expenses could be cut down without Dil noticing much change in his day-to-day life. In that interregnum, when they'd briefly detached themselves from one another, she rolled some broad calculations in her head and felt they were going to be alright—he was going to be alright. Ash had been on a part-timer's income anyway since the estate had shut down.

When Dil came back, she put her hands on his shoulders and drew him to her. He leaned against her shoulder, but then, glancing around at the others, straightened up at once. His face had turned stiff, Maryam felt.

During all this time, Saffina had kept an eye on him, following every word he spoke, watching every gesture he made.

'He's going to be alright, Baji, don't worry, alright,' she said to Maryam later, as the sisters smoked in the garden after a long time. Saffina smoked, and Maryam and Zarrine took drags from her cigarette.

'Yeah, but give him time to grieve, alright, boys miss their dads a lot more, you know, but they don't want to show it,' Zarrine said, cutting Saffina short.

'Oh, yeah, we must listen to her majesty's chief grief counsellor, isn't it ...'

'I was just saying, man, don't bite my head off!'

Maryam exhaled from the side of her mouth and looked at her siblings one by one without speaking.

Saffina lit up another Benson & Hedges and offered it to Zarrine, who gave it to Maryam after two quick puffs. There was dew on the grass that night, which reminded Maryam of the green, pink and yellow glass beads she used to weave into bracelets for

Saffina and Zarrine when they were little. She longed to lie down and roll on the grass. Just a few times, she thought.

--

The next morning, Maryam did heaps of laundry, washing almost all of her and his clothes, turning the garden into a vast laundry park. She spread the clothes everywhere; she tied lines from tree to tree, tree to hedge, hedge to balcony; she filled all the spaces where she believed the sun might shine. She spread jumpers, pullovers and hoodies on the grass. She arranged socks around the clothes in formations that looked like totems from an ancient burial site. She formed a zigzag line with Ash's office shirts, arranging them in a daisy chain of collars and hems and sleeves.

The neighbours in the other flats watched her as she bent and rose, hopped and lunged, mainly out of concern but out of love too, just to check whether Maryam Ali was alright after terrible misfortune had struck her. They didn't say a word about the occupation of the garden by the scores of trousers, T-shirts, kurtas, shalwars, scarves, bras, night suits, and dozens and dozens of socks, neither then, nor later.

Dil watched her too, although only briefly, as he searched for his most comfortable tracksuit in his room. He favoured the Adidas over his other clothes, especially when he sat down to play Grand Theft Auto on the PC, which he had wished to do that day after a hiatus, even as he'd been torn about it—what if Mum thinks it's not right to be gaming so soon after the funeral, what if it really isn't good, he'd asked Saffina earlier. Is gaming appropriate after your dad dies? He gave up on the idea as soon as he saw his track bottoms resting next to Mum's underwear, something that made him look away.

Maryam knew her son sometimes flinched on seeing her underclothes drying on radiators in the house but had decided not to do anything about it, because the boy had to grow up at some point, but that day, as she noticed his shadow behind the glass panes, she turned her back towards the flat, fiddled with this and that, put her small clothes in the laundry tub, and came back in. It was time for lunch, she thought, a chance to inspect the towers of Tupperware that the sisters had brought. At the thought of Saffina and Zarrine and the food they'd cooked for them, for the first time in days, she felt they were going to be alright.

THIRTEEN

That was Maryam's world then, and there had been a world before then, with a chatty, affable Ash in it, with the three of them in it, behind the solid wood burgundy door.

Then there were two of them, as thick as ... as thick as mother and son in shared, echoed grief could be, as tight as Maryam and Dil could be, which was close, too close perhaps, but neither had reason to complain, she felt, because once inside their world of two double bedrooms, a spacious living room, a sit-in kitchen, a utility area and the buffer of the visitors' lounge by the door, they were in an impregnable cocoon of double-glazing and heating and Ash's Yale locks, with the world of violence and war, resentment and suspicion firmly shut out.

As grief began to withdraw its dark, tense coils from the air in the house, they began to see each other more clearly. Maryam started to throw open all the windows at once, letting the sunlight, the air and the smells of the neighbourhood breeze through, something she seldom did before Ash's passing.

--

Maryam looked at her son and wondered where he might be in ten, fifteen, twenty years. He would probably be a father by then, bringing his children to her on weekends, for a night's stay maybe, she thought, or leaving them with her for a couple of nights if he needed to travel. They might even go on holiday together; a beach holiday probably; it was certainly in the realm of the possible but she shouldn't think too much of such things or else she'd jinx it. In her mind, Dil in the future was an independent man who'd be able to look after himself well, should her time, too, come suddenly.

She chose not to dwell too much on chapter three—in which she'd look after her grandchildren, feed them and babysit them—for another reason. She'd always wanted to live life on her own terms as she grew older, which, she'd promised herself, would include travel (Haj certainly, but not only Haj, as she wanted to go on holidays with her sisters), a bit of bingo but not too much, and that long overdue trip to India where she had been only twice. Once as a little girl when Ama and Aba had taken her to be with her grandmother Dadi Ama, and the second time she went to 'the grandmother-land' was when she was fifteen. She hadn't wanted to go; in fact, she had been quite upset about the whole affair because it was the summer holidays and she'd wished to go on a school camping trip to Lake Windermere with her friends, but in the end, she had gone along to Indore instead, because she worried her intransigence might lead to shouty quarrels between her parents.

Wouldn't it be great, Maryam said to the sisters, to go on a tour of the land of the ancestors, as she laid out her plans before them one day. 'The antiques roadshow land,' Saffo said. 'The three bus-keteers, waah, Baji,' Zarro replied. This was around the time Dil had finished secondary school and got into the City Polytechnic to study computer science. They were in the garden outside Maryam's, seated on a picnic mat in the mild October sun with tea and biscuits.

'Don't be a dumbass, Zee, I'm not travelling hundreds of thousands of miles just to get sores on my backside, why Baji,' Saffina said.

'Oho, stop it, you two. I swear on Allah, sometimes you make me forget you are fully grown women with babies of your own. And for god's sake, Saffo, it's not hundreds of thousands of miles to India, your geography still sucks.'

As grief receded into the distance, the younger sisters often spoke of their admiration for their older sister, with one another and among others in the extended family.

'Oh, how brave she's been, like an iron lady,' Saffina said.

'True, babes, but you know who else is called iron lady? Maggie Thatcher, that's who! Some piece of work that woman, but yeah, we're lucky to have her, she's fucking unbreakable, Baji Hulk, innit! If something ever happens to me, make sure she's the first to know.'

'Defo! And you do the same if anything happens to me or to my kids, yeah? She's like a second, more durable Ama, ha-ha ...'

'Sure babes, but you know how she feels about all that.'

'I-am-not-your-frigging-mother. Thanks-but-no-thanks, I-am-your-big-sister. And I am only ten years older than you two, please grow the fuck up!'

'Even though it's twelve years, actually.'

'Ha, ha.'

'Oh, come on, Baji, I was only joking, yeah. Do you want a ciggie al fresco? I can keep him distracted if you like,' Saffina said, taking out a cigarette from a new pack.

'You're going to get me into trouble someday,' Maryam mumbled, glancing towards the flat and lazily advancing her hand to receive the lit cigarette.

--

As the run of days and nights and seasons took over, as she worked extra hours and Saturdays in another school kitchen, in big, noisy Ilford, Dilawar, too, settled down, or was sucked into the intoxicating rhythms and chaos of youth. As she watched her purse strings and ran a tight but full household, he transitioned from secondary school to polytech, busy with his friends and his computer games. Sometimes at night, he spent hours digitising the micro-VHS tapes that Ash had made of him and her, of all of them together, of long Sunday lunches in the garden, of waterside picnics in Epping Forest and Alexandra Palace further away, of Eid dinners with Ama and the aunts, of that extravagant wedding at the Finchleys' where father and son had gone in matching three-piece suits. Maryam knew about the tapes and was moved as she watched him play the videos on his computer. At first, she had been in two minds about it, excited at the process but anxious about his state of mind, but then, upon seeing him pleased with his work, she banished her worries. The son watching the father's record of their lives, the son rewinding and forwarding his father's film of him, to catch that word or sound, to hear what he'd said at a certain point during the picnic, to see how 'cool' they looked in those suits at the wedding. 'What's Dad sayin', Mum?'

Ash on the pedal boat in the lake at Ally Pally, 'looking like a puffed-up orange penguin' in his life jacket—she had said, teasingly—smiling at the swans near the tree-lined island. 'Top scene, Mum, come on!' Dil had played that clip over and over for some reason.

When Dil relaxed, Maryam relaxed and began to worry less and less about how her son was coping, whether he was coping.

--

As she felt more relaxed, reassured that they were going to be alright, it occurred to her that it had taken her more than three years to let her shoulders relax. At the big funeral dinner, she couldn't have foreseen how hard and delicate it would be to watch him day and night, his manner, the way he walked and spoke, to check if he wasn't too sad, to find out if he wasn't too lonely, or turning into, *becoming*, something else. But now she'd calmed down. Dil was a clever young man who didn't moan all the time like some other boys did, although he did spend far too much time cooped up inside, on that damn computer of his, but she supposed it was better than having him out all the time. At least this way I know where he is.

As a part of her post-Ash life adjustments, Maryam had stopped going to the Saturday bingo altogether, even after she'd saved a bit of cash from the lunches she cooked or supervised on summer fete days in school kitchens out of town, in Hertfordshire and St Albans. But that long summer day during the holidays, nearly four years after Ash's death, when Dil seemed to have settled in well at the polytechnic, she felt she had earned a break, so she phoned the sisters and made plans for a night out.

'You stay in, Dilly, order takeaway, yeah ... whatever you like, Pizza Hut, Chinese, burger, whatever, okay?' She gave him some cash and a hug. He didn't always like it when she came close to wrap an arm around him, to flick a hand through his hair, or to touch his face and peer at his eyes to see if they were alright, but he rarely let his impatience become too apparent.

'I'll ring twice when I come back, just so you know it's me—okay?—but don't get up, darling, alright. I have the keys. Alright then, I'm off.'

'Have fun, Mum.'

'I will. You have fun too but not too much, alright? And please don't spend all your time in front of the computer. You have to look after your eyes, baby.'

—

Maryam splurged at the bingo, insisting on paying for everything. She had wanted to do it for such a long time. 'They act like I'm their mother but it's me who's got two extra mothers, isn't it,' she'd said to Dilawar earlier in the day. More than ever, she saw that her life after Ash had remained intact thanks in large part to Saffina and Zarrine, in the way they had stood by her, like pillars on either side, firm and unshakeable. She couldn't imagine how she might have coped if they hadn't been around.

'Baji, come on, we can take care of it,' Saffina said, flashing her debit card, but Maryam simply wouldn't let them pay for anything, apart from one round of soft drinks when she went to the toilet. Maryam didn't drink in any case. She had quit her occasional G&T evenings at the Lordship the day she found out she was pregnant with Dil and had never gone back.

She let them hop from game to game, from win to loss, then loss to loss, and was pleased at their shrieks of triumph and tragedy. When, around midnight, she somehow made one of the slot machines sing at last—a cascade of shining change falling by their feet—Saffina and Zarrine jumped and screamed and hugged her. Zarrine, stuttering and swaying, knelt down to grab the coins with her hands but ended up sending some into the air and some clanking and ringing around the other patrons' feet. The front desk manager, who had recognised Maryam earlier, saw this and asked two of his staff to help the 'old birds collect their coins'.

Zarrine heard him, and before Maryam could pull her back, she swung towards the front desk and started yelling, 'Oye, oye, you bean-counting wanker, who the fuck did you call old? Do I look like your mum or your nan? Did they not teach you how to talk to women? How old do I look, man? Fiff-fiff-fifty, er … fifty-five? Rude fucking tosser! Go back to your wife and tell her she's old, yeah.'

Maryam came up to Zarrine and put her hands on her shoulders, pulling her back gently. She gestured an apology to the manager and the young women near him who were too terrified to come out to gather the escapee coins.

'How dare that greasy prick call me old, Baji? You know how old I am, don't you? You should've let me sort him out, he needed to know what this bird's foot can do to his balls … Why did you save that mannerless wanker?'

'Zarro baby, you're wearing one shoe, there's ketchup on your hips and shoulders—how on earth did you manage that, haan?—and you've got some of my treasure in your boobs, so why don't you sit down, drink some water and we sort him out another time? How about that, haan? He's a good chap, that Andrew … Now sit down, darling, come here, let me get those 50p coins out of your bra.'

Saffina, who'd had two less mixers, gave Maryam a smile and put her arms around Zarrine, who readily gave in but not before raising a finger towards the manager's desk. 'You feel like a heavy doll, Zee, massive, can you stop wagging your finger, please?'

--

Maryam dropped them home one by one in a cab and reached home after midnight. It was a cool and pleasant summer night in London, filling her with unexpected happiness. She looked at the clear, star-filled sky with gratitude and a sense of fulfilment that she hadn't felt in years.

Dilawar was fast asleep when she went to his room to switch off the fluorescent night lamp he often left on. A dusty glow persisted in the room for a short time as she looked at his quiet face. His nostrils flared gently as he breathed and the short hairs on his face appeared golden. A thread of saliva had left a trail down the corner of his mouth. Before the room went dark, she saw the new posters above his desk and marvelled at how swiftly time had flown, how quick and sweeping the march of days, weeks and years can be—how true it was what people said about time being a great healer, etcetera. The tall, lanky young man on the bed was proof she'd done alright after Ash. They had both done alright, by each other and in the world.

He was seventeen then, bigger, taller and stronger, she thought. Ash would be proud, chuffed at the sight of the near-six-foot young man who had taken the place of the hunched, gangly teen he had left in her care.

She closed the door, washed, and crashed in her bed after a quick prayer, thanking God 'for everything despite everything'. As she lay down, she touched Ash's place in her bed and fell asleep with an arm curled around the double pillow he had insisted they fit into the cover despite her protests that it might all get misshapen.

PART II

FOURTEEN

As he stepped out of Walthamstow station, the first thing Julian noticed was the size of the bus depot on the other side. It was enormous, busy, disgorging bus after red bus, sending swirls of pungent blue mist across the road.

He had meant to book an Uber but decided against it so as not to come across as spoilt or entitled—he wasn't sure which—in front of Maryam. He turned right at the crossing on the opposite side of which stood the Goose pub. A series of tinted windows with flowerpots hanging off iron chains on either side like banished cats advertised pale ale and real IPA in flaked gold lettering. Soon, he was walking down a long street with restaurants, off-licences, and fried chicken and pizza outlets on every block. He saw glistening red chickens revolving languidly on rotisserie grills behind sweaty glass cases and wondered what they tasted like. As he walked past another restaurant, he noticed long steel trays of karahi and korma and chicken biryani lined up one after the other. Oil piping glistened at the borders of each stainless-steel vessel. There was a Paddy Power betting shop next to a tailoring boutique; the latter had stationed four tall mannequins in bridal wear outside. The gold-and-lace chunri of one of the brides waved in the breeze and brushed against his shoulder. He paused to look. Her bare pink feet were covered in dust and a cigarette butt was wedged between the toes of the left foot. Someone had drawn a heart with pink marker on her right breast. The street stretched far, a long staccato caravan of cars, vans and buses, so he checked Google Maps again and learnt it would take him thirty-seven minutes to walk to 22 Homecroft St. He turned back, remembering he'd seen a minicab office near the station.

The woman behind the black grilled window wore a silver nose ring and had painted her eye lashes purple. She had an impeccable fringe. 'You're gonna have to wait five minutes, love. It will be sixteen pounds, cash only, love.'

'Yeah, yeah, that's fine,' Julian said, trying to sound casual and easy, as if he were local.

The woman looked him up and down and smiled. Julian avoided eye contact and looked inside the office. The wall at the back had rock album posters plastered from the ceiling to the floor, thin red, yellow and black paper tongues dangling off the plaster in some places. Led Zeppelin dominated. Electric Magic Featuring Led Zeppelin, Wembley, Stairway to Heaven, Mothership, Kashmir ... he read.

'Just wait round the corner, mate, he'll be with you in a minute,' she said and answered the phone.

The large Ford Mondeo smelled of Febreze lemon, damp leather and airports. On the dashboard was a plastic replica of a temple, the golden statue and its pearl garland shining under bright white LED lights. The cab driver dialled down the volume on Sunrise Radio and pressed his foot on the accelerator.

'Where to?'

'Homecroft Street, I gave her the postcode. Didn't she ...?'

'Yes, but I always check to avoid confusion, you know. Some customers, you know ...'

'That's okay, how long will it take?'

'Fifteen to twenty minutes, depends on the traffic, though.'

Julian looked out at the street and noted the frequent appearance of women wearing headscarves, hijabs or full-length black abayas. He didn't see that many in Muswell Hill. Pakistani women, or could be Indian, and black girls, probably Somali, he thought, and some sari-clad older ladies too, Tesco shopping bags swinging from plump, dimpled arms. Amid phone and IT repair shops, he saw a few hair salons, expansive places behind full-length glass doors, women standing behind other women, some boys in body-hugging T-shirts and low-rise jeans. Adele's Here, Karachi Qurls and Bollywood Bangs stood out. And there were many men at the shopfronts, outside breakfast cafés and hookah joints, black, brown and white faces passing in a film-reel parade. 'London, innit,' he said. The cab driver stared at him from the mirror.

As they approached the town centre, the look of the street began to change. A bit of Islington and Crouch End and his own high street began to pop up here and there. He had never been here. Why, he wondered. He recognised an 'artisan café' when he saw one, and if there was any doubt left, it appeared in cursive on a few blackboards and glass panes. Soon, they gave way to the usual franchise names. A Pret here and a Costa there, and, of course, a large Starbucks near a busy crossing where buses from the left and the right seemed to merge to form the pulsing red artery that was the main street. This is where his cab took a sharp left; it was his turn to stare at the driver in the mirror.

From there, he thought he remembered the way to Maryam's neighbourhood, but he wasn't entirely sure. The first few times he'd been here, he'd come in official vehicles, a black BMW in which David and he sat, and the grey Jaguar for the cavalry when they visited that first time. Hannah had made a face on being asked to sit with the boys in the Jag, but had complied quietly.

The streets narrowed, the shops disappeared, wheelie bins and weathered old hedges sprang up at neat intervals between greying, rain-pecked wooden pylons, and now and then a corner shop or off-licence appeared, bright neon lights shining inside. The impression he had was of quiet, warm domesticity, a sleepy neighbourhood of middle-aged couples or pensioners, severed long ago from the pulsating life of the city. He saw rows and rows of Edwardian terraces, some brick-faced, some plastered and painted over, and some bearing the marks of recent refurbishment, boxy dormer lofts sitting precariously at the top, an extra bedroom with ensuite for a newly married son or a lodger. They kept driving east. They had yet to drive by a defunct industrial estate, he remembered. The block of flats where Maryam lived was past it.

'Be there soon, got to drive slow here, you know, with them speed breakers,' the driver said, navigating another turn. At the corner ahead, there was a large pub, the Lordship, but it didn't seem open. It was pretty, the size of a detached house; perhaps it was closed or it only opened in the evenings. They went past a tall oak and what seemed like a church building, then a grocer's and Royal Mail store called Tony's.

When Julian handed him a twenty-pound note for a fare of sixteen and said, 'That's alright, mate, thank you', the driver looked at him in surprise. Then he shrugged, said thank you and sped away.

As Julian walked towards Maryam's block, he felt some nervousness, but it was overtaken by an anticipation he hadn't felt in years.

--

Maryam opened the door, stepping aside to let him in. She was wearing a pale pink shalwar kameez, a floral chadar draped over her shoulders. Her hair was combed back and tied into a knot. Her face glowed. He was conscious not to stare but he couldn't help looking at her eyes—big, bright, puffed-up eyes. She'd applied some make-up, he thought, and she smelled nice. Did she cry when she was alone and fix her face when someone came to visit, or was it perhaps because she knew he was coming?

He started to look at the photos on the walls in the living room again. This time, he spotted two of Maryam's late husband Ash, and one of the three of them together. He thought he recognised where it had been taken and was pleased he had. Dilawar is small in the picture, probably eight or nine; they must've gone boating in the lake behind Alexandra Palace. Small world. In the cupboard with the blue doors there was some chinaware and two metallic frames with Allah and Muhammad written in silver Arabic calligraphy. A young Maryam and Ash, arms entangled, looked out of a wooden photo frame at the opposite end. She is wearing a long collar shirt and has a dark red bag on her free arm.

Maryam sat down on the sofa and spread her arm on the backrest; she always did, he remembered. He saw her reflection in the glass doors of the cupboard, and other fuzzy reflections in the photo frames. Many Maryams in the room.

'I'm relieved you don't come here with that man. I can't lie,' Maryam said.

'David is occupied elsewhere; he's got a lot on his plate. It's a … sensitive time … But that's not why I wanted to see you, Maryam. I wanted to make sure you're alright, if you need anything.'

Glancing at her reflection in the cupboard, Maryam rearranged her scarf and cleared her throat. She looked towards the window, momentarily worried she might not have closed the curtains. But she had. 'Would you like some water?' she said, standing up, thinking she'd have until she came back from the kitchen to rehearse what she wanted to say to him. She'd thought about it the previous night, the night before last, and the days before then. But still.

'Yes, please. I hope the guys weren't too much of a bother. Sorry about it, I promise they won't bother you again … Hannah is good company, though, isn't she?'

'Yes, she's alright. She comes once in a while or calls,' Maryam said, wondering whether he knew that already.

She came back and put a hand to her chadar as she bent down to put the glass of water and the coaster on the coffee table. She glanced at him fleetingly.

'So do you have any news …' she said in a soft voice.

'Mrs Maryam,' Julian began, putting his glass down, 'I'm afraid there's no new information. We think he's still in Iraq. These days a lot of boys go to Syria, but we are almost certain he is in Iraq.'

'Almost?'

'Our analysts … who look at video footage, etcetera, they're sure it's from Iraq.'

'Oh, that. But it's not him in the video. I thought you had something new to tell me.'

'Maryam, I didn't come to—'

'It's not him. It's not him.'

'I came to ask if there's anything I can help with?'

He glanced at the photo of her with her husband and guessed it was probably taken when they were recently married. She looks glamorous in the checked shirt and the wide sunglasses.

'Our first anniversary. I wasn't one for anniversaries, but Ash was keen on these things, birthdays too.'

'Such a lovely photo.'

'Do you know what, if Ash was here, we'd be visiting you every day for Dil's news. But I just don't like going to police stations and offices, you know. Don't get me wrong, I don't mind you dropping in, but I don't want to visit and then wait for hours for you to tell me something, like one of those sad mums waiting outside police stations in Bollywood films. I'm not one of those.'

'That's perfectly fine, Maryam. As I said, it's part of my job to make sure you are alright.'

She looked at him, his tall form in the chair, his clothes, his light-coloured hair. 'Come with me, Julian, come …' she said, straightening her shirt front, and stood up quickly. Julian followed quietly. He looked at her back, saw the elegant patterns on the cotton shirt around her waist, noted the swish of the fabric against her body. For a moment, his eyes caught the outline of her bra strap visible underneath the shirt—was it purple? He lowered his gaze then, colouring a bit, his throat dry. Maryam turned into the hallway and pushed open the last door on the right. He had been to this room before, during their first visit, he remembered. It had been a raid, a quietly managed one but a raid nonetheless. They had wanted to take over the Swordsman's house quickly and efficiently, without creating a scene, without noise, without a media scrum. But there had been no need for them to force their way into the flat. Maryam had let them in.

The next time he'd come to see her was with David again, but they'd remained in the living room throughout—David reading the riot act to Maryam in the stern tone Julian hadn't heard before. 'Look, Mrs Ali. I've been patient because we have a duty of care towards the families. Your son could be a member of ISIS, which is a criminal offence, in case you didn't know. So, I'd say it's in your best interests to do as we say. It's an ongoing investigation and we're looking into everything. But until we know more, we'd like you to behave well, please.' He had stayed with her for a long time after David had left, watching her become calmer, having noticed the flush of suppressed humiliation on her face earlier.

He had come to see her again three weeks later, sat with her, telling her that though there hadn't been any progress, it wasn't bad news. She had listened to him, nodding.

Maryam entered Dil's bedroom and sat on a corner of the bed. There was a folded quilt at the foot of the bed. Julian saw the desk chair and sat in it. He knew who it belonged to. That it was a lived-in room was clear, but it was the orderliness of the objects that struck him as peculiar. Everything seemed to have been arranged with a purpose. The grey tracksuit upper hung neatly on top of the trousers; the red T-shirt with the black and silver Nike mark across its front hung next to it; the brown leather satchel hung from the third hook on the door—they all presented a picture that had been cared for, put together by design.

In one corner of the room were two pairs of trainers, newish-looking black Air Jordans and a scuffed Adidas pair. The desk bore a symmetrical stack of books at the back: Java, C++, Advanced Networking 3.0, Dragon, Cisco Manual VII, Correll's Guide to Encryption, read the spines. He looked at the desktop PC, which they'd combed through circuit by circuit, kilobyte by kilobyte. The Dell Inspiron stickers glinted in the white light of the side lamp. The HP Inkjet slept under the table. On the cupboard to his left, the two gaming posters were still there: Call of Duty Black Ops III and FIFA 16.

Maryam shifted her weight on the bed; it creaked mildly. Julian's eyes caught a glimpse of the house slippers under the bed. Camper, they said in blue ink. He shifted his attention to the desk again and noticed the Uniball roller pens. He recognised them by their caps; he had preferred them over the Pilot rollers through his university years. Slowly, so as not to startle her, he rotated his chair, making sure it didn't make any noise. It was then that he saw the laminated Arabic inscription nailed to the wall above the door. It was Ayat-al-Kursi, he would find out later, the verses from the Quran meant to endow protection and sanctuary. A source of calm and succour for the faithful in times of distress.

'All this will be over the day he's back. It's not too much to ask, is it?' Maryam said suddenly, leaning on her elbow, her body curved on the bed, her voice echoing in the room. She was looking up at the group photo of Dilawar and his friends—Aiden, Rezlan and Andy—pinned to the felt board above his desk.

'They're all home … Only Aiden must've left, his dad wanted to send him to America, Dil said. Wasted a year waiting, isn't it … I don't understand why people want to send their children all the way to America … What's wrong with here? I'm sure he will come back to see his family in the holidays, though.'

Julian looked at Dilawar in the photo and saw the striking resemblance to his father, whose open, smiling face he'd seen inside the glass cabinet in the living room. It occurred to him that until then he hadn't really *seen* Dilawar—what he looked like, what kind of face he had. He had a lean, long face, the colour neither white nor brown but that of someone from … he searched his mind … from somewhere like Algeria or Morocco, like one of those footballers in the French team. Large, round, clear eyes with prominent eyelashes. That was Maryam, he thought, unmistakably his mother's eyes, but he didn't look like her.

'Handsome, isn't he?'

'Oh, yes, Mrs Maryam …' He wanted to say the correct thing without adding anything more. 'Yes, he's a good-looking boy.' He wanted to get out of Dilawar Ali's bedroom now.

'Takes after his dad, mashallah, got his height too … I'm not very tall, you see.' She stood up with the same abruptness with which she'd left the living room. A part of her chadar slid off her shoulder and she caught it on her right arm, furtively turning to look at Julian who, she noticed, looked down.

As he walked behind her, he caught her smell again and knew she'd showered earlier. That was the fragrance, the pleasant, fresh, flowery scent he'd been thinking of and which he'd started to associate with her. A scent of soap or cream or lotion—he wondered what she might use. He found himself breathing it in.

He turned to look once more at the group photo on the soft board and couldn't help wondering whether Dilawar could pass for an Arab, for someone Middle Eastern …

'I will be back in a minute,' Maryam said, as they started walking back to the living room, 'I wanted to show you his certificates, remember I mentioned it on the phone? I could get them now; I'd asked Hannah if she wanted them but she said it was alright … But maybe you should see them, alright? It won't take too long, I've put them in one of Ash's file folders, you won't believe how many he has, used to get them all the time from work. Said Mr Whiteley orders the best quality ones.'

'Of course, Maryam, sure.'

--

On his way home, Julian sensed there was something else he had felt that day. A certain allure or charm, a disarming and sometimes distracting appeal about the forty-something Indian woman whose son had supposedly run off to Iraq. The school chef from Walthamstow, whose case he was meant to manage, held his attention in a way that wasn't meant to be. He noticed her movements, her conversation, her manner as she walked, and a grace he had not come across before. He was startled to realise he was pleased at the idea of meeting her again, meeting her regularly.

FIFTEEN

Maryam watched from the door as Julian left. He walked with a straight, upright gait, his strides swift and brisk. He was wearing faded grey jeans, a navy-blue jacket over his shirt and deep brown shoes that glinted in the slanting evening light. The soles of his shoes were thick. She kept watching him until he reached the turning past Tony's store at the end of the street.

He had shapely, long legs, she thought, as he disappeared around the corner. She wondered whether she could've been with a man like Julian when she was younger. Would she have met such a man, though? She hadn't been with any man since Ash died, she thought next, then admonished herself for letting such a thought occur to her, but the harder she tried to banish the thought, the more vividly it came back. She felt a flush across her face and sighed deeply. She knew she liked him, but also knew who he was, so she promised herself she'd never get too close, Allah toba! Although, although, if they somehow became closer, who knows, who knows—

She shook her head forcefully to free herself from these thoughts. Allah toba, what's got into you, Maryam!

—

Ruminative, still at her doorstep, watching the evening London haze gather over the neighbourhood, she glanced across the street, turning her gaze left and right, up and down. She had promised herself she wouldn't care if she spotted any of her neighbours spying on her, but she couldn't resist checking. She thought she saw a curtain shift in one of the tall, three-storey townhouses across the road. Tony appeared outside his store and waved to her, fag in hand. She nodded back, unsure whether he noticed. When he made further indecipherable gestures and started to walk towards her, Maryam raised her hand, making a stop gesture with her palm, like she used to when she helped with the juniors at playtime. She missed school.

Poor Tony, she mumbled, and went back inside.

At the end of the hallway, she stopped to look at the discoloured paint on Dilawar's door where his palm had pushed it in. She pressed at the same spot, her fingers feeling the surface; the door swung open and she went in. She looked at the chair where Julian had been sitting a short while ago, she gazed at the posters on the wall, she saw the slippers she'd slid under the bed. She sat down in the chair and considered the computer on the desk; she pushed it gently, making the monitor swerve. She ran her fingers across the spines of the books she had stacked up. Then she stood up and struck her hand hard against the pile, scattering the books across the table and onto the floor. She pushed at the monitor, making it tilt all the way to the wall with a scraping sound. She then flung Dilawar's clothes off the door hooks, the sweatshirt landing on the bed. She kicked at the trainers, flinging them away from the wall. She tried again when she saw one of the Nikes hadn't moved much. Next, she attacked the felt board on the wall above Dilawar's desk, tearing off old A4 sheets, printouts of network diagrams, a Papa John's flyer and some course brochures. Two photos of Dil and his friends came unstuck too; one landed on her lap and the other on the floor, face down.

She picked a hanger and slid the track bottoms onto it, then put the sweatshirt on top, and hung the outfit from a hook. She bent down and crawled under the bed, pulling out the long stick from behind the camper slippers under the bed—she and Ash used it to shake the dust from durries at springtime. She was relieved Julian hadn't seen it. Now she weighed it in her hand and swung hard at the sweatshirt, at the trousers, the door echoing the whack from under the fabric. She swung the stick again. 'You've brought shame on me, on your father, on your aunts, on all of us, Dilawar!

'I never laid a finger on you, not even raised my voice after Ash left, do you not remember—Mums counting to ten, again and again, so I wouldn't shout at you? I wish I had smacked you, a hard one every now and then, so you knew your limits … I should've kept you under control, but what does Maryam Ali do? Give you all the freedom in the world, do as you please, Dilly, and this is what you do with your freedom! You ungrateful scoundrel, you've brought disgrace to the whole family. You have any idea of the shame you've brought me!

'How dare you ask why you deserve this! I will tell you. You've humiliated me, Dil, you've hurt your father's soul. You've driven a spear through my heart. You better come back and tell everybody what they're saying is not true. It's all a lie …' She paused. 'Please come back and I will fight with them all, I can take on the fucking world then, do you hear me, you heartless, loveless idiot.'

She bent down and picked up one of the photos from the floor. It was Dil's solo photo from the polytech: he's at the lectern in a classroom, pretending to teach. She threw it on the bed, slumped back in the chair. 'I hate you, Dilly, I hate you.' She wondered whether it was possible for mothers to hate their children, their sons and daughters. And what if she'd had a daughter instead of a son?

There was a man in your room, Dilly, a well-educated, well-behaved man, he comes here to check on me. They think I know what you're up to, huh. Why did you have to do this, why the hell did you have to do this to me? I was crushed when your dad left, but I made my peace with it, because he died, you know. But what the hell is wrong with you?

She put her head in her hands and remained silent for a long while. Then she heard the doorbell ring, but she decided to ignore it, at least until she was done tidying up her son's room. She picked up the clothes from the floor and hung them back on the door. This time, she thought she would put the red T-shirt on top and the track bottoms and the sweatshirt could go under it. He did wear a T-shirt over long-sleeved shirts once in a while, didn't he? Then she picked up the books one by one, wiped them with her chadar and stacked them on top of each other, exactly like before. She nudged a few this way and that until it was a perfect tower. Next, she gathered the flyers and posters and pinned them back on the board. She kept the photos for the last, polishing them delicately with her sleeve. She realised she hadn't touched the printer, so it didn't need to be rearranged. Maybe just a little bit, so she pushed it back under the desk a few inches.

She arranged the trainers against the wall next to the door and left the room. 'I'm sorry, Dilly, I just get tired sometimes, you know,' she said, and shut the door.

SIXTEEN

It was a beautiful, calm Sunday morning. Julian wanted to stay home all day, make tea, catch up on TV on the BBC iPlayer and read in the conservatory. He looked forward to reading *The Sense of an Ending,* a present from his father from a few years ago.

He was fond of the light in the conservatory, the pale green paint of the framework blending with the shaded light of the garden outside; it brought a sense of peace and calm. The rockery that he and his mother, Anne-Marie, had put together when he was in Year 10 attracted birds all day, thanks to the seven little pools, named after the seven continents. He made sure there was always enough water in them and enough grain sprinkled around. He'd meant to buy the *Collins Bird Guide* but hadn't done it so far in the vague hope that something better might come.

It was also the perfect light for his sketching, although he didn't do much these days. The Faber-Castell pencil set and the drawing pads sat on the glass and wicker table next to his mother's expansive armchair that he sat in when she was away. And she was away more often than not, sometimes for months on end in Europe and the US where she lectured as distinguished professor of twentieth-century European history. Anne-Marie's popularity as a speaker had not waned in the fourteen years since arriving on the lecture circuit with her third book, *From the Abyss*, which traced the history of West European regeneration after the war.

Being by himself in the house on the weekends had become a particularly precious time of leisure for him in the three years since he'd started working at the Joint Section. He had never really minded being alone in the house; in fact, he had, with time, become so used to the solitude that it took him time to readjust when Anne-Marie came back home and stayed for long periods. He'd done this for years growing up anyway, being by himself, particularly after he turned sixteen, when Anne-Marie and Sebastian Chapman had amiably agreed that they couldn't live under the same roof anymore. When his father, sought-after management consultant and professor of international business studies, had recognised he had no choice but to move to the flat they owned off Tottenham Court Road. 'We can have a massive scene in the house, in a courtroom, or both if you prefer, Seb, but I say having the flat to yourself and visiting Jules, or having him over when you want isn't such a bad deal given the circumstances … Just don't expect any hugs from me. Can't tell when you'll stop smelling of central Asian whores.' Anne's words echoed in his head.

--

He poured himself another cup of tea, remembering Maryam's tea, and went out into the garden, strolling purposefully. In the near distance, the crowns of the oaks and poplars in Alexandra Park gave the impression of a soft green shield that separated the house from the city.

'Close your eyes, take a few long breaths, be still and ask yourself whether you're being perfectly honest with yourself. In the heart of your hearts, in that deep unperturbed corner, you will always know if you're being even a tiny bit untrue.' Anne circling round the kitchen island.

He put his tea aside and, facing the shrubs and the rockery at the back, closed his eyes, breathing slower and slower. When he opened his eyes, he saw some birds perched on the rockery and suspected they'd been looking at him all this time. They looked familiar, he thought.

It didn't take him long to grasp and separate the loops of thought in his head. He wanted to get Maryam to open up more, to talk to him and him alone, so the Section could have more background on her son. Sometimes, when he met her, he had the impression she knew more than she let on, but he wasn't sure of this, and he sensed a tinge of guilt at being suspicious of her. He knew he was taken in by her, her manner and talk, her looks and her … personality. He knew he would be happy if they became friends without the case being in the middle—the thought often brought a smile to his face.

He gazed at the rockery which formed a semicircle at the back of the garden. When it rained, the small pools of water overflowed, creating waterfalls at the brim. Sometimes birds tried to drink from these, and he found the sight hypnotic. Once, he had spent the whole day in the conservatory and finished reading *The Subtle Knife*. He remembered the day well because the birds had kept coming all day, and he had kept reading, looking up now and then to watch a bird dip its beak in the water trough.

Was he spending too much time with her? Would it raise suspicions in the Section, in the neighbourhood—among Tony and others—among her family? But he was meant to, wasn't he, to find out more and be her friend. A woman whose son could, at that precise time, be plotting an attack, or, for heaven's sake, already have massacred people in Iraq or Syria or wherever the hell he was! But most likely she really didn't know anything—how Dilawar had gone, with whom, and why he had gone. Maybe David had got it all wrong, maybe the Americans had fucked up—wouldn't be the first time—and here they were, wasting time and resources on a perfectly fine woman, even if a little bit unpredictable at times, though he couldn't deny how much he enjoyed her company. In all her protestations and objections, in her fighting tones, there lay an elegiac plea, a lamentation for what she had lost, and he found it moving in a way he wasn't prepared for. His heart went out to her, though he wouldn't put it in those words.

SEVENTEEN

Tony slipped in the paper on an early June morning, soon after his first tea of the day. Looking at the front page on top of the bundle, he paused for a moment, unsure whether Maryam should see it. Maybe he could hide the whole stack, he thought, so that no one would take it to her, but in the end, he felt she was going to find out one way or another; he might as well take it to her.

She has to know, he told himself again as he walked away from her door. He had some idea of how she was going to react, so it was best not to be in firing range, even though he knew she was fond of him. Fucking unbelievable, he mumbled, and kicked away a few empty Walkers bags by his shopfront as he went back in.

It was an unusually wet morning, the rain falling in incessant, slanting threads, encouraging people to stay indoors, apart from those who, like Tony, had to leave their beds to lift shutters or catch buses into the city to start their shifts in hospital wards and in train stations, in the tunnels of the London Underground, in basement kitchens and butchers' backrooms, or on crane shafts crawling up spiderlike on the glass fronts of Canary Wharf. Birds hung around in corners and under gabled roofs, looking vacant-eyed at the people out and about at this early hour.

Maryam heard the metal thwack of the letter plate from her bedroom and waited a short while before putting on her gown. She switched on the light in the hallway and at once saw the lurid colours of the newspaper. She took a deep breath.

She brought the paper to the kitchen table, spread it out and stared at the front page, her teeth digging slowly into her lower lip. Outside, the morning's light struggled under the busy drizzle. She made her tea and picked up the phone.

'Hello, Julian … What is this? Who the hell did this?'

'Good morning, Maryam. Is everything okay, are you alright? I was just getting some breakfast—'

'Was it your boss? Was it Hannah? I like her, you know, I didn't think she would be such a … bitch. Or was it someone else? I know it wasn't you …'

'Maryam … I'm really sorry, I don't understand. What's happened? I … don't know what we're talking about. Is everything alright, is anyone bothering you?'

'Have you not seen the paper? Do you really want me to believe that?'

'I'll go and check, please give me a minute … which paper?'

'The filthy paper, what else?'

'I'm afraid I don't read it, Maryam—'

'Oh, yes, I forgot, you're the *Guardian* type!'

Julian was amused to hear this description of himself but before he could think of something to say, she went on.

'What I want to know is, who the hell leaked this photo? What is wrong with the lot of you!'

'What photo, Maryam, I really don't—'

'Of course they had to use this one! Maryam Ali in a headscarf works—perfect, isn't it? It's a Friday prayer photo, for God's sake, we had all gone to Ilford Centre after, you know, Dil, Ama and my sisters. He used to love that cheap merry-go-round at the mall when he was little, and Zarrine found a gaming arcade nearby when he was older. We went to eat at that Fatima restaurant later … That's where Zarrine took the photo.

'Have you seen the headline? No, of course you haven't—because you only read the *Guardian*! Let me read it to you, Julian:

'"Radical Mum Refuses to Cooperate: Security Services". "Abject Failure to Trace the Swordsman Leaves Our Streets Unsafe."

'I'm sure David and his daddy must be delighted. What a great shot! They have an extra-large photo of me under the black headline, Julian. Tony must've slipped in the paper through the door. I look big in it, you know, because Zarrine took the photo sitting down, silly cow! I look like a sad, fat woman in a swimming cap, and you've put me on a national fucking paper. Well done, guys, well done.'

'I'm so sorry, Maryam … I had no idea, this is completely unacceptable, of course. But I have no idea how this happened…'

'Of course you don't, you must've been busy with the weekend supplements … Someone from your work sold this photo to the paper, Julian Chapman, what else! It's obvious. They *wanted* to show this photo. We all wear a headscarf at prayer time, cover our hair for namaz, don't you all know anything? That's how I ended up looking like a jacket potato, but I don't mind it, you know, it's the rule, and it's not as if I wear the headscarf all the time, it's only when … But hang on, hang on a minute … What am I even saying, even if I did, Julian, so what, so fucking what!'

'I do apologise, Maryam, I'm so sorry,' Julian said.

'They even did a close-up, I can see dark circles under my eyes, I used to wake up very early in those days, the bastards … Scary-looking mother works fine, isn't it? The behenchods!'

'I'm very sorry you had to see that …'

'It's not about what I am seeing, Julian, is it? Someone from your office sent this photo to the paper or someone at the paper selected it from the lot your friends sent. Either way, it's how these people ... I don't know, Julian, I don't know anymore ... it's how these people think about me.'

'I understand, Maryam, I really do ... Different people have different ... erm, different ways of thinking, but please trust me, we mean the best for you.' Julian was lost for words, embarrassed, feeling caught out.

'How Julian? How?'

'Hmm ... It's just that we happen to know what's going on, Maryam. There's probably no better way of saying this, but we're all grown-ups, so I'll just say it. Dilawar has fallen in with dangerous people, men who organise and commit acts of large-scale violence. You know what that means, killing innocent people, many, many innocent people, even here at home, in my country—' He immediately regretted saying that but knew it was too late.

'My country? Really, Julian? That's what you want to say because we're grown-ups—your country? Allah toba!'

'I didn't mean it that way, I'm sorry, Maryam, you misunderstand—'

'No, I understand perfectly what you're trying to say. You probably think soon after I send my boy to school, soon after a walk in the park, I go home, check the latest beheading video and start clapping? Draw the curtains and do a quick Muslim dance? Habibi, Habibi! You think Ami, my buas and khalas shut their double-glazing and celebrate the latest video from Iraq or Syria over kebabs and biryani. Is that what you think, Julian Chapman?'

'Maryam, that's not what I—'

'Please, Julian, please listen ... Your boss, what's his name, David, David ... thinks I have to answer for the actions of a random behenchod who decided to be my caliph ... in fucking Iraq? Trust me, I wasn't asked. We don't even have caliphs anymore, for God's sake! I don't know this pretend bastard, he's very far away, so maybe I should be excused for not keeping tabs on what they're up to over there. You think all the muzzie uncles and aunties must know, let's go grab 'em. Let's go talk to muzzie mum Maryam!'

'I really don't think you have reason to think like—'

'Oh, I have every reason to think whatever the fuck I want.'

As Maryam paused, Julian heard her hurried breathing through the phone, each breath sharper. He knew he shouldn't have interrupted her, shouldn't have said anything to upset her. He wanted to tell her he'd never thought of her like that—that she wasn't just another case. He imagined her pacing in her living room. He remembered how he stole looks at her in the glass cabinet. He shook his head and sighed.

'Do you know what it means to have a missing son, Julian? Can you understand what it means to be told my child has become ISIS and whatnot? Do you know how it feels to listen to what you all say about him, what they say on the TV … I have a son who's been missing for four months. Not days, not weeks, four months! I don't know where he is, what he's up to, whether he is alive. He hasn't come home for such a long time. Do you know what a knock on the door does to me?'

She took a deep breath, feeling pressed in, a cold, heavy weight on her chest that refused to shift. She wanted to think with clarity, speak her mind freely. She wished the tension that ran through her mind day and night would dissolve and she could find a sturdy rope to hold on to. She needed something to hold on to. If Julian was in a position to find her son, maybe she ought to be friendlier with him, not fight with him. Do as they say, Maryam … But she was, wasn't she! Or maybe she should just keep them busy somehow, spend time with Julian. Dil might come back in that time and then there would be no problem!

'What if it is him in that video …' she said, her voice resigned. 'Do you know how that makes me feel—to have my boy turned into the Swordsman or affiliate or whatever David says Dil's turned into. God save my Dilly. What if it really is him? Why is he standing there like a statue in a museum? You can't know how I feel, Julian.' Julian heard her breath stutter.

'I am so sorry, Maryam, I am. I honestly didn't mean to upset you. I was trying to explain—'

'If my idiotic son hadn't gone off like this and I didn't depend on you all for news about him, I would've asked Uncle Sharief to file a massive court case against all of you for printing this fucking photo. Jehadi Mum! How dare they! I'm sure it's that David's doing, is it not, tell me! Ask him, how would he feel if it was his mother's photo on the front page of the fucking *Sun*? Proud, hain? Tell him Maryam Ali is very, very pissed off.'

Julian wanted to tell her it was unlikely that David had seen the paper, he might not even know about the existence of the photo, and that he didn't care much about what appeared in the press, but he chose not to. It was best to let her have her say. Surely he could do that for her.

Maryam looked at the front page again, holding the phone away from her ear, thought of Dilawar, remembering the first grainy photo Julian had shown her. She saw Dil as he was, as she remembered him, a boy in a hurry to get back to his room, not as the person behind the black mask that the Swordsman wore. She raised her left foot, held it in the air for a fraction and stomped on the newspaper with some force. The pressure from her heel tore the photo from the chin down.

'Bastards,' she said and put the receiver down.

EIGHTEEN

In the early days, when Alexei found the match with the Swordsman files, Julian had thought of Maryam as a sensitive, high-profile case, but, essentially, a case. There were so many across the country; at least he'd been given an interesting, intriguing one. As family liaison, he'd met quite a few ISIS parents: the stunned and silent ones, the non-cooperative, secretive types, the suspicious and disbelieving kind, and the utterly devastated, grief-stricken ones. He had learnt how to deal with them: be kind, be firm, stay patient, absorb information.

Though he was well practised in helping the families cope with and understand what had happened to their children, something about Maryam's dignity and defiance had unsettled him. She seemed to be holding onto something he couldn't quite grasp; she existed outside his normal 'frameworks'. There was certainly more to her than the despondent parent figure he'd often come across; her refusal to be submissive in front of David had made him stand up in surprise and awe. He often found himself thinking of her, both at work and home, remembering her face and speech and sudden shifts in mood and tone.

A few months into the new assignment, therefore, every time he set out for a home visit, he felt his professional mode, his practical turn of mind, deserting him. He was mindful of the guidelines, acutely so, and probably even self-conscious because of them, but if he was honest with himself, if he looked himself in the eye, it was hard to escape the notion that he was attracted to Maryam Ali. In a few weeks of this troubling, thrilling sensation—the tightening in the back of his throat as he approached her door—the distance between the everyday reality of work and his own inner truth began to blur.

He must listen and remain patient, he reminded himself, as he approached 22 Homecroft Street. A few times during the short walk to Maryam's flat—he preferred to get off his Uber on the main street outside—he'd seen the close-shaven, grey, curly-haired shopkeeper with caterpillar eyebrows smoking outside his store, eyeing him through wisps of blue smoke. It was her friend, Tony, he knew. Was Tony envious or merely protective of his neighbour? He hurried on as the latter exhaled in his direction. Tony had man boobs and a large belly under his scruffy charcoal-grey jumper.

As Maryam opened the door, he saw that she was wearing a fitted sweatshirt and track pants and had tied her hair back. In that moment, she appeared closer to him in age and he felt … he felt the distance between them suddenly shortened. He wished the situation that had brought them together would vanish so he could just be with her, know more about her, have a coffee with her like people do, without the weight of his role hovering in the air around them.

'Would you like some tea, Mr Chapman? Proper tea, not the ginger-coloured thing you get from Tesco. I mean chai,' Maryam said as he settled in the armchair. He was wearing light-brown khakis and an ink blue jumper over his white shirt. His shoes were spotless.

He noticed the way the light caught some loose strands of her hair as she stood opposite him, how her hands moved when she talked. 'Oh, sure, I'd love to … Why the switch to mister, Maryam, you really don't need to. Julian is just fine …'

'If I don't call you that now and then, I might forget you're from the government. You might be nice, or pretending to be nice, who knows? But you're still the man from that department …'

'But Mrs Maryam—' He checked himself.

She left him there with his unfinished sentence and went to the kitchen where she took out a small sieve pouch into which she put three green cardamoms, a few slivers of ginger, a little cinnamon stick. In the saucepan half filled with water, she threw four teaspoons of premixed Taj Mahal and Lipton Tea, which spread out like a flock of starlings, scattering in expanding loops. Into this pool of black mesh she dropped the pouch and covered the pan.

'So … Julian … I was thinking … Actually, Saffo was talking about it the other day, we wanted to go on a picnic before the weather turns, you know. Staying home like this is doing my head in, I think … Someone from your office could come along—let me finish—what if your boss wants to keep an eye on me, huh? You don't have to worry, though, it's just Saffo and Zarro. You could … if you want to … What do you think?'

Julian looked at her, uncertain how to respond. He had been concerned about her state of mind since the appearance of the photo, and suspected Matt or Lucas had leaked it to the newspaper. Though he was appalled by it, he knew the Section wouldn't do much about it—there was a full-scale campaign underway in Iraq, these things were minor.

'Well, Maryam, you're of course free to go where you want, we just want you to be cautious, that's all. After the photo … Anyhow, I'll quickly run this by the office, just in case—' Then, against the voice of wisdom in his head, he found himself saying, 'I'm sure it's fine, David doesn't need to know …'

'Yes, a bit of fresh air for Maryam Ali, that's all. A bit of the sun if we're lucky.'

'Of course, of course … Do you not go for walks in the neighbourhood? I'm sure there are parks around here …' he said, looking out of the window.

'The park is for women with menopause or dogs, I have neither at the moment. I'm joking, of course … But I am allowed to say that. I've walked all my life, Julian, I like sitting down on a picnic mat with a cup of tea.'

'Please let me know when you want to go,' he said, meeting her eyes.

'Let me check on the tea …'

Maryam stood in the kitchen, about to pour tea into the thermos kettle, pensive. She took in the steam from the pan a few times, holding her breath, then breathing out with an extended aah. Ash used to call it 'Maryam's lung massage, a homemade cold defence shield'. He would join in sometimes and had one day tried to persuade Dilawar to try it.

'If someone sees us, they'll think I run some kind of steam cult in my kitchen, Allah toba,' she had said before Dilawar could say yes or no.

'Would you like to come along, though … ' she said, as she put down the tray and started pouring the tea. 'Be nice to my sisters, alright? They will chew your head off if they think you're being less than a gentleman.'

'But why would they think—yes, of course, I'll be nice …'

'Here's your tea,' she said and found herself watching his hands as he held the cup, surprised how much she wanted him to enjoy it.

At first, Julian felt as if he was drinking a hot broth. After a few sips he knew he'd not tasted anything like this. For him, tea had almost always meant one bag of Twinings Breakfast dipped in hot water for two minutes, topped with a splash of semi-skimmed milk.

'You wouldn't mind giving me the recipe for this, would you,' he said hesitantly, tasting the ginger and cinnamon in his mouth.

'There's no recipe for chai! You just bring it to a boil, but please don't use a kettle, that's all.'

'I mean, what are the ingredients, how much do you put in?'

'Oh, did you go to a private school? I'm sure you did. How about you just watch the next time I "cook" chai.'

Julian smiled. 'That's very kind of you, Maryam, thank you ...'

'You could record it with your phone ... as long as you don't put it on YouTube. I will kill you if you do,' she said, half-joking, half-teasing.

'I won't,' Julian said, still smiling, taking another sip from his mug, also rehearsing—uncertainly—in his head what he had come to say.

'Erm, Maryam, I wanted to remind you about the press conference ... I'd mentioned it on the phone ... People at the office think it might help. It'll only be a few words, trust me, but they might persuade Dilawar to come back—'

'I haven't changed my mind, Julian, and I don't think I'm going to. What is it about you all, always trying to change minds? You just say it and I flick a switch, hain? Basically, you want me to ask Dilly to hand himself in, don't you? But that would mean I accept it's him in the video! So, no, sir, I'm not going to go on TV and make a statement to the nation! Who exactly does your boss think I am? Nigel fucking Farage? Chief Jihadi Mum? Dilawar Ali's mother breaks her silence, bah!'

Julian looked into his empty cup, recalling her outburst on the phone. He noticed she'd rolled up her sleeves, revealing slim, smooth wrists, a thin bangle on each forearm.

'I'm being flippant, I know ... Would you like another cup of tea,' she said, conflicted and nervous at the thought of appearing on TV, talking about her son. 'I know you're probably passing on instructions from your boss and may have a different view of all this ... Or may not, what do I know?' She gave him a friendly, though questioning look, suddenly alert to an urge to touch his hand.

She fell silent then and watched him. His tall body made the chair appear smaller than it was. He had sturdy shoulders, his hands were on his knees, he was staring at the floor. She looked at his face and wondered why this man was sitting here. He had a gentle way about him. He carried himself well, conducted himself well, gave her all the time. He was maybe twelve or thirteen years younger than her, she thought.

Julian's mind was at the last weekly briefing at the office, about plots and cells 'brewing here and there in the country, in Birmingham and Manchester and very much here in Zone 3 or 4!' David speaking.

Ispahani's interactive map—with red, green and black pinheads denoting active, solved and unresolved cases—sprouted elliptical curves linking places, organisations and people across Britain, the US, Syria, Iraq, Turkey and the internet. This mapped data, Ispahani said, showed how a majority of current or aspiring British affiliates, 'ISIS bros and brides', were mostly homegrown and directly or indirectly linked to influencers in the UK, the Middle East and the US. David had stood up, leaned on the back of his chair, and said it was gratifying to see the digital intel back up the groundwork of the last couple of years. He said he felt reassured knowing men like Alexei and Ispahani were working 24/7 to thwart both the influencers and the influenced. 'Of course, it's profiling, JC,' he said, 'guilty as charged. How can we zero in on anything without it? If there's a plot being stitched together in a Muslim family, that's where we're going to look, aren't we? We can't pay much attention to the Saturday op-eds.' Julian had noticed Alexei and Ispahani making faces at each other.

--

He sat in front of Maryam now, observing her face. He saw the stress in her eyes, watched her shoulders rise as she breathed. She'd tied her hair up in a tight bun with a butterfly-shaped purple clip. For the first time, he saw with clarity how she was having to carry such an enormous weight on her shoulders. He realised he hadn't given this much thought until now. What must it be like to be her? He wished he could somehow reunite her with her son.

NINETEEN

It was late summer, and the sun described long arcs over the garden, ripening and crisping up the flowers in the beds and the thick, waxy leaves of the hedges at the fence. The oaks shone in the sharp light, their shadows moving in slow sweeps on the grass as the day turned. The flat felt hot and stuffy, its concrete giving off heat until late in the evening. Maryam kept the windows in the living room open all day, but the curtains closed. For weeks, she'd had an urge to go for a long walk, going on and on until she couldn't anymore. She had contemplated such a journey probably since the day the Joint Section people had arrived at her door.

She left the house early one morning in the middle of August and took the bus to Walthamstow Central Station. The driver was a grey-bearded man in a large blue floppy hat that touched his shoulders. On his pale sleeveless work jacket he wore various badges. As she touched her Oyster card on the reader, she smelled the cigarette he had just smoked and wondered if she should start smoking to beat the nerves, but by the time she looked out at the streets whizzing past her from the back seat, she felt it would be too much for her, the acrid taste in the mouth in the morning, the smell that seeped into the sofas and the curtains, and she hadn't smoked for years now, apart from the occasional drag or two from Saffina, so no, maybe she shouldn't. The bus smelt musty but also of cleaning liquid, it had new upholstery bearing the tidy red-and-blue Transport for London logo on every seat. She touched the fabric on the seat next to her. She had gone on numerous bus journeys with Dilawar when he was little, to Ama's, to the sisters', to birthday parties and soft-play areas as far as Hackney. It was easier than the car, you got on and you got off, and Dil loved having his own seat by the window on the top deck—how excited he would get when she opened her rucksack to take out the snacks she had brought along for the journey.

When she got off at the station, she prayed she wouldn't have to wait too long for the train to Clapton and was relieved to see it was due in five minutes. She immediately felt less anxious; she didn't want to stand too long on the platform and risk being seen. It was irrational, though, she told herself, breathing in a slow, controlled manner—why would anyone recognise her at the train station?

She got off at Clapton, took a right turn, and walked for a few minutes to Lea Bridge Road. There she waited for bus 56, which took her to the Riding Centre stop from where she walked at a fast pace straight to the Walthamstow marshes.

--

The sight of the water alongside the walking trail soothed her mind, the wavy reeds springing out of the greyish, mucky water gave the appearance of a pretty landscape in the early sunlight. At the back, there was a stand of willow trees, all swept at an angle, as if leaning in to hear the water. Some birds darted from this bank to the other, going crisscross or diving through the overhanging power cables, as if plunging into the water. The breeze carried with it a light scent of brackish waters and a tinge of exhaust fumes from the nearby motorways.

At one point, she paused and looked at her reflection in a stretch of the stream lit by sunlight. She stood still and considered her aspect in the water. She felt reassured about not having told anyone about the trip, about not phoning the sisters to ask if they'd come along, about not having to explain to Ama why she must go out all alone like this? Had she forgotten what had happened?

'Yes, Ama, I know the misery my son has brought upon us, you don't have to remind me all the time,' she had shouted the last time Ama had brought up the relatives' gossip about Dilawar.

'I'm just saying, Maree, I can't stop people from talking, can I ...' she had said.

'Alright then, let's forget all about Dilly and worry about what your sisters and cousins are saying, hain!' Maryam had retorted, unable to stay calm.

She was glad she hadn't spoken to Julian about this either. She needed to be away from everybody.

She stood up and resumed walking, picking a brisk pace, the warbling of the birds and the fizz and flutter of wetland insects accompanying her. On the other side of the canal, she saw a couple on bicycles ambling after each other in a straight line, their high-vis jackets shining like big bright limes. She kept walking and thinking, nodding to herself, sighing, shaking her head, remonstrating with herself, with real and imagined respondents. Her sisters, Julian, Ama, her dead husband, her missing son, the world. After fifteen minutes or so of brisk walking, she found a bench near some flower beds and decided to sit down for some time.

They want me to say it was ISIS who took Dil and turned him into that ... They want to put me to use ... But would she do it, she wondered, speak to the media, to TV people? How had it come to this! It was amazing, they can't do anything about finding Dil, their entire department, the whole lot of them, can't stop some bastards from taking my boy, and now they want to turn me into some broadcaster mum on the BBC. Is that why they printed that photo? *The Mother Breaks Her Silence. Mum's Heartfelt Message to Son and Other Jihadists.* That's what they want, isn't it? They don't really care about Dil …

She leaned back on the bench, her thoughts turning back to Julian. There was no one else she trusted really, and she was certain he knew where her son was, so maybe she should do it. He was from an important, well-connected family. Of course he was. If there was anybody who could get Dilly back, it was him.

If I do agree, I'll do it my way. If I must speak to the country—Allah save me!—to all the mothers and fathers and sons out there, I will do it in my words. I will talk and talk and record myself in my … bedroom. What the hell are you saying, Maryam? How is that even possible?

'We only want to draw him out. He has to go through the system like everyone else, Maryam. Before it's too late,' Julian had said, or something like that. What if it was true, though? What if Dilly really was over there and it was possible to *draw* him out? Oh Allah Mian, kis imtehan mein daal diya mujhe!

She remembered the times she would open his door slowly at dinnertime, so as not to disturb him, and how he would quickly shuffle, doing something swiftly to the screen, as if caught, as if he didn't want her to see, turning halfway towards her. 'What is it?'

'I was just checking if you're done, honey, dinner's ready.'

'Yeah, yeah, I'll be done in five minutes,' he would say and wait for her to leave and close the door behind her.

Kind of behaviour that seemed surreptitious to her now. Was he up to something then? Hadn't some doubt crawled into her head at the time?

She wished Ashfaq hadn't died and he was here with her, sitting by the water, talking to her, consoling her in his calm voice and reassuring her that Dil would be back, that he'd do everything to bring him back. She missed his voice, the way he said *daarling.* But Ashoo was long dead, there was no way any part of him could come back.

What if it's already too late, she wondered. Dilly hasn't come home in a long time and I don't know where he is. I have no clue and they have no clue either, or maybe they do and aren't telling me! I don't know what to do, I don't know how to grieve him. She gazed at the trees and thought she saw some gravestones in the grass behind them. Looking at the vegetation, the bramble and the moths and the baby butterflies flitting around, at the hum of life in this quiet forest patch, at the weathered gravestones in the foliage at the back, she wondered whether she would belong more—although what is more and what is less—if she'd been born in England. But she'd missed that boat by three years. What if Ama and Aba had come just before she was born?

—

'Please don't get me wrong, Maryam. I understand the position you're in … but we must think of others too, mustn't we? People who might lose their loved ones at the hands of the people who brainwashed Dilawar, possibly at his hands too,' Julian had said. The words bearing both pain and offence, an affront. How could he say that? And if true, how could her son do that!

A silence enveloped her, during which she became alert to the sounds of birds flapping in the sky. These were wrens, robins and magpies probably, she thought. She used to like watching them dart around the trees in her garden, emerging surprisingly from the hedges sometimes.

But they still won't tell me what Dilly has done. What do they want me to say to the mums and dads up and down the country? Is it going to be a written thing?

What should I say? Dear all, please forgive me in advance? You don't know who I am, oh no, you might have seen my photo in the paper. I'm sorry about my son. I don't know what he's done but I apologise in advance. Please forgive me for giving birth to him.

I didn't know he was going to turn out like this, if I had known, I would've …

Shall I visit some graveyards in advance? Or should I start composing letters of regret to future victims? Shall I write to other broken-hearted mothers? Or shall I just pray—pray hard and harass Allah Mian? Pray that Dilly never kills anyone, not that he's capable of harming even an insect. Hai Allah, please let it be that he hasn't hurt anybody.

How do they know it's him, though? Why should I believe them, why should I believe anything the government people say? Didn't that Tony Blair say Saddam Hussein was going to drop the atom bomb on Birmingham or someplace?

Her mind flew back in time, to the year of the protests in London. So many people everywhere, all saying the same thing. They went to bloody central too, but the government went ahead and dropped the bombs anyway. Behenchod Blair! Maybe all this wouldn't have happened, she thought, not for the first time. But I'm not allowed to say that, am I, going to be called jihadi aunty in no time!

She shook her head, trying to compose herself. Why am I even thinking like this, they don't know it's Dilly in that video. I could tell they weren't sure the moment David sat on my sofa. He sprawled. That cold, stone-hearted man didn't even try to disguise his suspicions, so little he must have thought of me. What does a school chef know about the world, eh … Especially one who hasn't a clue about what her child's been up to. They think I'm some silly desi woman who doesn't get it. Fact is they have doubts. If they had been sure, if they had proof, they'd have shown it on the TV. It would've been on the front pages! Someone would have had a press conference. That smug man, rather than being nice to me, rather than help me, just wanted me to give him everything pronto. But he gave it away, didn't he? They were never sure it's Dil, or were they? Is there something Julian hasn't told me?

The sun had risen higher, leaning in from the right, sheets of light pouring in through the treetops, a luminous, white parcel-box square on the path in front of her. A faint smell of damp and pond slime spread, mingling with the fresh breeze. She wished she had brought something to eat, she felt hungry. She swallowed, scratching the side of her chin, rubbing her eyes. The pang of hunger brought back memories of her school, her vast kitchen there, her turf of many years, her headteacher Mrs Price, and the last time she had gone to school.

It was the day she had decided to take early retirement.

She had gone to speak privately with her, to tell her what had happened, her son having gone missing, and that she would need leave until she knew more, until he was found. 'You have all our support, Maryam,' Mrs Price had said after listening to Maryam patiently, offering her water. 'Anything you need, please call me.'

It was later, as she left the office and was about to turn towards the kitchen area so she could exit from the back door, that a Year Six boy muttered 'ISIS Mum' behind her back. She shivered and froze on the spot. She knew the boy; his name was Luke. She had known him since the time he used to wet his pants. She knew his mum and dad, Emily and Rob, his little sister Sophie. She just looked at him, that little boy, and did not say anything. Then she walked straight back to Mrs Price's office.

Allah bless her, Maryam thought now, she had everything sorted without ever calling her back to school.

As she walked back home, her eyes stung, a bitter biting sensation at the corners. When she was near her neighbourhood, her legs felt a weakness and slowness that she had never felt before; she felt her gaze constrained in a way that was alien, she couldn't turn her head around, she didn't want to. She didn't want to see Tony, answer his polite Hello Maryams and Hmms … She didn't want to see anybody, not her neighbours, not her few remaining friends, and most definitely not Sheila who had said from her window upstairs, 'For your sake, *Maaryam,* I hope it's not true what they say about your boy, gaah, he's become one of those Islamic types too, God save us.'

She felt Sheila's eyes on her as she turned into the street, even though the block of flats was still further away. She had yet to reach Tony's store, so she decided to cross to the opposite side and walk quickly; she wished she could run but that would make him more curious. It was Tony who had helped her wipe off the blue 'Paki Traitors' graffiti from her front wall, they had done it the same night it had appeared, lest her sisters, Ama or anybody else saw it the next day, and yet, she didn't want to be seen by him.

TWENTY

After another night of sleeplessness and occasional episodes of passing into a state of half sleep, Maryam found herself on the sofa watching *Countdown* on Channel Four. As often, she noted that the man conducting the show wore a suit and tie and the woman a tight skirt. The man had to know all the words and remain seated in his tall chair as he dealt with the contestants, and the woman, well, she had to know all the words, have a shapely figure, and stand at perfect angles while she dealt with the man and the contestants. 'Allah toba, is this how they decide who gets the job,' she'd once said to Saffina.

She was determined not to open the photo albums this week. It was Thursday and she'd remained steadfast so far. Tempted, wavering and restless, but strong at the end of each night. Last weekend, she'd fallen asleep face down on Dilawar's bed with an album open on either side and had felt uneasy and fearful in the morning: I did it again, she'd said to herself.

In this, she had slipped into the routine of an addict, vowing not to smoke up the next day, then, just this night, just this night, then a break, then the same cycle of need, greed and self-censure. Then she swore she must take a break or, at the very least, make it a once-a-week affair. You will go nuts like this,

Maryam, she'd said to herself. It's not as if anyone's stopping you. But doing it every night would make you look like you're mad, and what's there to gain!

Since her walk in the marshes, she had been waiting for two things.

For Friday night when she would shut the door on the world and 'check on Dil' after five days. And the second thing she waited for was Julian. Even if he brought difficult questions with him, he helped pass the time. When he visited, the air in the house felt lighter, with a sense of anticipation that pleased her. Have to give him that, but where the hell was he?

Over the months, there had also been times when she felt she wanted to say everything to him, open up the wound all the way; she felt she could tell him everything because he was someone safe. But at other times she hesitated, prevaricated or adjusted her words because she was mindful of where he came from. As the days passed, she learned to find a place between these two states: she spoke when she felt she needed to speak and kept herself closed when she thought she was perhaps getting too close.

--

Last week, she'd stared at the photographs night after night, as if the images might reveal something new. As if staring at Dil's photo in silence might bring some news of him, some word. She'd given in to the impulse fully, abandoning the patience she'd cultivated in the previous weeks. She'd stretched full length on his bed, something she seldom did, rolling a little, sobbing a little, face pressing against his pillows. She'd felt a sharp anger rising in her afterwards. At what precisely, she couldn't tell. Then she had become even more agitated as she searched for the reasons.

'Mum, why do we always have white sheets and pillow covers,' Dil had asked her once, when he was about fourteen.

She'd been asking him to help with the laundry for some time and he had at last obliged by taking the folded sheets and pillow covers to the cupboard.

'Helps me put them in the machine on time, sweetheart. Do you mind?'

'Just sayin', Mum, just an observation.'

'Ah, good observation … Your dad always liked the pillows plain white so I thought I can't have mismatched bedsheets, could I …' she'd replied, piling the dried fabrics on his outstretched arms.

He had said nothing at this. Just the blank stare and absent-minded nod that unnerved her sometimes.

In those days, she had been suspicious that he sneaked into Ash's old estate to smoke. Tony had mentioned in passing that he might have seen Dilawar walking towards the lane that went to the closed-off estate. Soon as you turned into the lane there was a rain-beaten iron gate, behind which were scatters of rubble: cans of Red Bull, faded cartons of Pringles, packs of milk and Tropicana orange juice. A well-tended parking lot had stood here not too long ago, buffed maroon MGs and Jags waiting in front of the dark-glass offices of Whiteley's small-scale industrial estate.

A few months after Ash's funeral, Dil had found a carton of Marlboro Lights among the file folders in his father's cupboard, and asked Saffina, who'd seen him cradling the unopened white box, to promise she wouldn't tell.

Saffina kept the secret for years, but after his disappearance, she felt she must tell Maryam about it, shaking her head as she spoke. 'It means nothing probably, it was years ago … I'm sorry. He was being so sweet, Baji … I can't believe he's just vanished …'

'You don't even smoke, Dilly, but, yeah, I promise I won't tell Baji,' she'd said to him then.

Maryam took out a pack of chocolate-chip cookies from the kitchen cupboard and settled back on the sofa to watch *Countdown*. The new girl was doing alright, not bad at all, she thought, remembering Carol, who had quit the programme some years ago.

When Julian comes, I'll ask him why Carol left. Was it because they wanted to pay her less, or did she grow tired of swivelling like a peacock on her heels all these years? He ought to know because he must know the kind of people who run TV channels, important, high-flying people, she thought as the credits rolled. But where is he? Nearly the end of the week and he hasn't turned up. He's probably stuck with that smooth weasel.

What if I'd been a high-flying woman, she wondered? What if Ash and I had both been high-fliers, eh? Then Dil might have turned out like Julian, but would we have been happy to have a posh boy for a son? Come on, Julian isn't really like that, he's got a heart, he listens to you, spends time with you, and you like him. What more do you want!

Then again, Dil would be here now, wouldn't he? At home, not missing, not fled, not suspected to be …

TWENTY-ONE

Summer had started to yield to the sharpening colours of autumn; red, pale and burgundy leaves littered the garden outside, as if somebody had been spilling leaves from a basket. Maryam looked at the illuminated leaves and the pale, dried-up shoots of grass, and she felt she didn't want the gardener to hoover them up too soon. There was a violence to that green engine of his, making everything vanish in a moment.

It had been a long time since she'd seen Lucas and Matt. About two months ago, they had come to check on her unannounced, like distant relatives who may drop in if they happened to be in the neighbourhood. It occurred to her that maybe they came to see her because they were paid extra, maybe they needed the overtime. Matt was getting married, she had overheard him tell Lucas. She thought he looked leaner and fitter and felt strangely pleased. Hannah came on the odd weekend, asking her how she'd been, if she needed anything—as if going through a list of questions, as if she had a form in her bag that she filled in after leaving. Maryam offered her lunch one day, a dry chicken stew and aloo palak that she took out from the fridge.

Julian was going through Alexei's latest briefing notes that he'd brought home, marking lines here and there. He wanted to catch Alexei separately about some questions he had regarding the Swordsman case. Alexei had messaged he'd see him later in the week. He wasn't too bothered he had started keeping things from his boss, if not outrightly lying.

He'd also become alert to a nagging restlessness, even unhappiness, about not having seen Maryam in three weeks. He wanted to find reasons, and if he couldn't find them, then invent reasons, to spend time at Maryam's. The trek to the outer fringes of East London had turned into one of the more stimulating prospects of his life.

The conservatory was flooded with the morning sunlight—gleaming needles and shards all around him—and the garden outside looked as if it was a green-and-white carpet woven by toddlers. After a couple of attempts, he had made a half decent pot of chai. He was waiting for the weekend to be over so he could see Maryam. Something in her manner when he saw her last had suggested she needed him.

--

Maryam paced in the living room, her hands locked together. She was in a thick maroon kurta and black jeans, her hair loose on her shoulders. Julian had brought two forms for her to fill and sign, which were lying open on the coffee table. They were mostly about family antecedents, mother and father, date of birth, naturalisation details, and she had pored over them quickly but stopped at the mention of the 'Swordsman' and 'Next of kin' on the second form.

'Missing person, yes, an irresponsible son, betrayer of his mother, yes to that too, but a murderer, no, never. Never ever.

'Ash's son, my baby, cannot be that. It's not possible. My sweet and kind boy—how's that even conceivable? You think if you repeat it all the time, it will become a fact, and I will say, alright, I understand, thank you for opening my eyes, here's my denunciation? What time are the TV people coming? Hand yourself to the police, Dilly, it will all be alright.'

'Maryam, please ... You aren't the only parent we have been talking to,' Julian said plaintively. 'So many have gone over. We've been in touch with a few other families too, helping them out, but you know I can't give you the details.'

As he spoke, he had the dispiriting thought that she had gone back in time, wishing all that she'd been told wasn't true. He had seen her in this mood before, defiant, unmoving, but also teary eyed, on the brink. He'd started to recognise the red of her eyes. At the office briefing, Hannah had called it the 'dial back'. 'We've seen it happen with some parents, if not all. They seek comfort in their previous reality,' she'd said.

'What if I don't care about the others? I don't know anything about them, or their sons—didn't you say some girls went too? I care about my child. My one and only. Eklauta. Do you know what that means? That I have no one else. Can you understand that?'

'I do, Maryam, I do. I'm also—'

'In that case, your mother and father will understand.' She paused, her voice shaking. 'Look, Julian, I know Dilly better than anyone else. All I have is you and your boss telling me he's up to something terrible. But I am his mother, and I know in my heart he can't be what you say he is ... A would-be murderer? A killer of children, sons and daughters and ... He has two loving aunts, you know ... There's no way Dil would do that.'

'I understand how you feel, Maryam, and I listen to everything, don't I? But you must consider Dilawar may have actually gone there ... Of his own accord, it's got nothing to do with you.'

'It has everything to do with me! He came from me—I gave birth to him. You can't even begin to ... He's my body and limb, Julian, you won't be able to understand it. Please just take my word for it.'

'Alright, Maryam, alright, how about this? We have looked into two other men who may fit the profile—and at this stage, we cannot rule out anyone, but the closest match we have had is Dilawar. I must tell you the facts.'

'Men? Did you say men? He's just a boy. What if he's upset with me, what if he has one of his big sulks? Maybe he's gone travelling. How do you know he hasn't? You know, when he was eighteen, I didn't let him go backpacking with his friends, I thought it was no way to travel. And I said to him, listen Dilly, when you're older, I'll give you money to go wherever you like. I'll even go with you, but please don't go like this, sleeping rough and eating god knows where. How could I let him roam about with a giant rucksack on his back? It's alright for you, you're treated differently, you know. Sorry.'

'That's alright, Maryam, I know what you mean.'

'You don't know a thing … How, how can I carry this burden, this stain, this shame that you have cast on my womb? Disappeared is okay, a runaway is alright. A single, worry-less life without me is fine, too. A … what's it called … someone who sleeps around with loose women, I can live with that too. Maybe a druggie is alright too, but not what you all say … Okay, maybe not a druggie, what kind of life is that. If I think about it, maybe even dead is alright, lying in some morgue somewhere, or buried already, an unclaimed corpse somewhere. Allah toba, Allah, he'd be rotting then, my baby! What if he's lying in a hospital freezer right here, in Whipps Cross or King George, and you just haven't checked? I will take that any day but not—he cannot be the fucking Swordsman!'

'Maryam, I understand, I do … I understand your pain but hundreds have gone … from so many places. Disappeared from one life and reappeared in another. Some are known to the authorities … but there are some cases about whom we don't know much. I'm trying to say Dilawar's is not a rare case. This is what I do …'

'This is what you do? You can't stop those fucking worms from snatching my son, destroying my life, really, and then your boss thinks it's somehow my responsibility! How on earth does that make sense?'

Maryam sighed, casting a probing glance at Julian's face, unable to read what rested in his eyes. There were occasions when she felt she needed him to reassure her, tell her it would be alright in the end, that Dil would be back.

'I don't know how to make sense of anything, Julian ...' she said, slumping back on the sofa, her head hitting the backrest with a sound that alarmed Julian, but Maryam didn't seem to mind. 'I don't know how to think anymore. Whether to be sad or angry. You all even took my name from me. And what the hell was he thinking, leaving me like this ... I have no one to call my own now. Saffo and Zarro have their families, I can't ask them to babysit me! I'm going to lock him up in his room when he comes back.'

Julian leaned in, crossed his fingers, cleared his throat and said, 'Maryam, for a time there was such a mad rush, and it's likely he got swept away too. Many left their homes to fight, didn't they? Of course you know that. Some of them are now in refugee camps, some in prisons, I'm sure you've seen the news. Unfortunately, we have very credible information it's Dilawar in the video. I'm really sorry, and I can understand how hard it is for you to accept that, but I must tell you the truth—'

'It doesn't make any fucking sense, though, does it! You are an educated, reasonable man, so tell me this. Why would he do it? I'm not falling for it ... And why haven't you been able to find him? Zarrine and Saffina said I must go to the police so they can find him, and I did, I did! I want you to find my son, Julian, search for him, and tell me what happened to him. Who the hell took him? Is it not your job to find him?

'The truth is you don't know where he is. The whole lot of you can't find one little boy. Instead, your suited and booted boss comes into my home, scolds me and sends you to babysit me.'

'You know I'm on your side.' Julian shifted his weight and leaned towards her.

'What if he's just dead? Have you considered that? Will you help me, please? Can't you just put him in prison? What if he's just lost somewhere?'

'That's what I'm trying to do, Maryam. I am trying to help, help him, trust me … The question is, will you help us bring him home?'

'Why the hell do you think you're still in my house, drinking my tea, you silly man.'

TWENTY-TWO

Maryam felt drained, her throat parched. She wanted to open the curtains and let the daylight flood in. She looked around the room, at the photos on the walls and in the cupboard, at her own fuzzy reflection in the glass doors, her scarf resting on her lap, her hair, and then she found herself looking at Julian. She hadn't sat with any man for such long periods of time in years.

She became aware of the world outside, of her neighbours, of Tony's long vigil over the street, Sheila's loneliness, aware also of her sisters and their love, Ama's quiet faith and strength, and she became aware of her home world, shrunk, smaller than ever, pressing in. In this world, she had no one else, only her own mad reflection. She looked at Julian once more, caught his reflection in the glass door and felt his presence in a way she hadn't felt before, or perhaps she hadn't allowed herself to acknowledge fully until now. He was her one constant companion, he was patient with her, and attentive in ways she hadn't known in a long time.

She noticed he had moved closer to her on the sofa; a silence fell over the room, and her mind started to race.

The last few months and the years before then appeared in a sharp pass through her memory. Seeing Julian next to her, it struck her with a quiet, parching sadness that she had rarely thought of life beyond her husband and son, then just son. She hadn't had the room in her heart, nor time in her mind for such a thing. It had not occurred to her that she could think of herself, or of such things as second chances, companionship, getting old alone. Try as she might to push these thoughts away—why was she thinking of such things now of all times—she couldn't help herself. Her husband had left her suddenly, dying when he shouldn't have, and her son had literally abandoned her. Why must she be the one to give and accommodate and sacrifice all the time? If being in the same room with Julian gave her some comfort, or at least helped pass some hours of a hard, unrelenting time, there was no harm in it, was there? Though he came to talk about the *case*, he let her say anything she wanted to, listened to her, let her vent. And it was obvious he came to see her more often than he needed to, didn't he?

Toba! Why was she thinking like this? Her son was missing, for God's sake, he could even be dead! And she was contemplating seeking comfort from another man, a man such as this? It's alright, though, it's not as if she was planning on doing anything silly, it was alright to ease the tension in her head, calm the nerves a bit, get her stress down. It wouldn't help anybody, least of all Dil, if she developed some hypertension or blood pressure thing, god forbid.

And what had he been doing, coming to her home, if not to console and comfort her, to be with her. It was true he may have wanted to persuade her to say more about her son, reveal something about him they didn't know, but he didn't do that anymore. Something had shifted between them.

She spread her arm on the backrest and allowed her fingertips to lightly graze his shoulder; he stayed still for a moment, appearing as if he might shift closer, but then he paused. Maryam held her breath, her heart racing; she reflected upon this moment, looking at herself in relation to him, looking at the two of them together.

TWENTY-THREE

Christmas was approaching.

'What if we had presents on Eid too, Mums,' Dil had said last Christmas, which was what, eight, nine months ago? What the hell happened to the world after that, Maryam thought. Or was it the Christmas before last? Definitely two years ago, yes.

'Why, Dilly, do you want to open a gift store?'

'Oh, come on, Mum, don't be a spoilsport. Imagine all the presents, three times a year!'

'Three?'

'Two Eids plus Christmas, innit?'

'Alright, alright, I'll think about reinventing Eid just for you.'

'It's a cool idea, Mums, admit it, everyone bringing presents!' He had given her a gift bag from The Body Shop that year; she knew he must've had advice from one of his aunts.

She didn't want to be alone, and yet, she needed to be alone. She'd saved some presents from the previous two Christmases: a button-down Ralph Lauren collar shirt Aziz had brought for Dil after he'd finished at the polytech and started working at Britech, and a colourful PS4 Controller she'd put away in her bedroom. Why had she done that, what was she going to do with them now? She wasn't going to open the boxes, that much was sure.

—

The doorbell rang, once, twice, then again. She put her cup and plate in the sink, ran the tap over them and sat down in a dining chair, looking at the other two chairs. When her sisters came to visit, that's where they sat, and she sensed a resentment welling up in her, though she tried to suppress it. She missed them, their chatter, their touch, but she couldn't have them over too often. It wasn't good for them or for their families. The whispers in the extended family were like slow acid, she couldn't have them suffer the interrogations. The less they came, the less people would talk.

The doorbell rang again. She walked slowly to the door and saw Zarrine outside, putting on a smile, shopping bags in both hands.

Maryam told her about her dilemma. They'd always had Christmas dinner together; Ash had always loved it.

'It's nearly three months away, Baji, why start frettin' now, we are all here, innit? Do you want some tea,' Zarrine said, taking Maryam's hand in hers.

'Maybe I shouldn't do it this year, hun, you know, what's the point?'

'Look, Baji, it's totally your call, yeah, but if you ask me and I know you haven't, I'd say it'll do you good. Bhai Ash loved it, didn't he …' Zarrine flicked her fringe away.

'Yes, he did, didn't he, reminded him of his mum. Remember how he made the same joke every year: "I'm surrounded by Muslims the whole year but I shall have my revenge by making you all cook for me on Christmas!"' She smiled, then her face stiffened.

'But what good is making a mountain of food for myself, Zarro?'

'So don't cook a mountain of food, and who said you'd be alone? We always come, no? You just haven't asked, Baji …'

'I didn't know I had to send invitation cards to you.'

'It's not that, Baji. It's the family, you know … Oh, did I tell you Zak's been screaming he wants to go to Disneyland for Christmas? Fucking YouTube! Anyway, there's the in-laws, yeah, everybody makes plans for the holidays. I didn't want to make an announcement, oh, hello, I'm going to Maryam's, see you laters … Only to find out you have made other plans, with other people, you know …' Zarrine said, eyeing Maryam.

'Since when did I start making plans without you two?'

'Baji, look, I'm not going to lie and I wasn't going to say it, but you made it clear you didn't want to see us … and if we don't know what you're thinking, what do I tell Azy? As it is, with Dil gone, some people, you know …'

'So, what do you suggest I do? Invite everybody and their khala? My son's been missing for six months but let's have a bucket of biryani!'

'Not the whole clan, Baji, unless you're missing Baji Syedah and Lady Kulsumz! It's just me and Saffs, who else, and the kids maybe?'

Zarrine fell silent, sighing, then she caressed her sister's hands. 'Just tell us what you'd like to do, alright. Whatever suits … I talked to Saffs and she's cool too. Let us know, yeah.'

She unpacked the shopping and started stocking the fridge, the cupboards, the bathroom cabinet. Then she made tea and they had it in silence.

—

Later in the evening, as the light in the garden turned into the blushed pink glow just before it gets dark, Maryam spoke to herself in the mirror. She hadn't done it in a while, she was tired of her expressions—the imprint of a scowl, the aches of sleeplessness, uff, the stress lines here and there, the exhaustion around the eyes … She wondered whether she'd stopped talking to her reflection because Julian had been visiting more often. He had been a regular, frequent visitor, sitting with her on the sofa, relaxed, gazing at her. She regarded her face again and looked at the few grey strands that swept past her ears, the subtle sag in the skin under the chin if she went very close to the mirror. The discs under the eyes! At least they aren't too dark, Maryam, be grateful. Furrows on the forehead, come on, they aren't so bad, you've always had them, you're just looking your age, hun. Nothing a bit of concealer and rouge can't deal with, but yes, got to do something about these tiny hairs. Can't become one of those women, nope, not Maryam Ali. But what are the sisters for, they'll bring the world's bleach to me! It's only peach fuzz anyway. She touched her face, remembered her younger self, her youth, her face, her body, before marriage, motherhood and work subsumed her life. For a fleeting moment, she saw herself as she used to be and something stirred in her chest. What's got into you, Maryam!

A rising noise outside made her pause. She listened intently and guessed it was the usual Saturday football cheer at the Working Men's Social Club, the ground-floor drinking hole for the neighbourhood's older men, which had of late become an evening haunt for younger men and women too, after the Lordship closed.

They used to have a not-so-bad curry there at the Lordship, Ash and her, when they were younger, when Ash hadn't burned out, when Dil was old enough to be looked after by Saffo or Zarro. It was there in that side room Ash had taught her how to throw darts many years ago, holding her hand, landing kisses and whispers on her neck, making her blush. She remembered they'd had the longest lunch at the pub once, when Ash's estate friends had gathered for Christmas, taking over the whole place. She remembered Eddy, leather-clad local busybody, who for some reason had stared at them, Ash and her, all the time from his stool by the bar. She recalled she'd wrapped up some sausage-rolls for Dil because she knew he'd like them for breakfast. She had taken surprisingly well to darts, she smiled at the thought, they used to gather around to watch her, Ash's colleagues and some of the neighbours. Tony was good at it too, and they'd had a few matchups one year, Tony and her. Fags and pints everywhere.

It would be a bad omen to skip Christmas dinner because Dil isn't home, she decided. Would it be too much if I asked one or two of his friends? Andy might even come, he's nice, loves desi food. What the hell are you even thinking, Maryam? Why would they come to your house?

Saffo and Zarro, of course, and their children. And husbands? Aziz is alright, doesn't talk much, sits by himself mostly, fingering that giant phone of his, but he's a decent chap. Has been good to Zarro, listens to her, ah, well, who wouldn't? Saffina's mian can be a bit annoying but maybe not this Christmas. Educated man, Jawad, maybe even wise, but wants everybody to listen to him. It's not your classroom, bhai. Not a bad fellow at heart, though, not bad at all, but gets on my nerves sometimes.

As she ran the names on her fingers, the phone rang and kept ringing. She calmed herself, hands on knees, breathing slowly, before standing up to answer it. She clenched her teeth as she put the receiver to her ear.

'Oh, Saffo jaan, I thought who's going to call on the landline so late except for the—'

'What's up, Baji?'

'Nothing's up, Saffo, nothing can be up in this house. You know that well enough not to ask such questions.'

'I know, I know, I'm sorry … Erm … listen, Baji … I was thinking maybe we could come to yours on Christmas.'

'Don't you always come to mine?'

'I mean not just visit for a bit, you know, but be there beforehand, help with stuff. We could maybe drop in the day before, stay the night even, if you like.'

'Did Zarro put you up to this?'

'Come on, Baji. You know I always do my own thing,' Saffina said. Maryam heard her light a cigarette.

'You can come anytime, darling. Come along, all of you, talk to Zarro too. Oh, I already did … Anyhow, yes, let's have dinner together, if that's what you all want.'

'Yes, Baji, yes … You are the best, you know that, right?'

'Saffo, listen … I was thinking, what if Dilly appears at the door one day suddenly? What am I going to do? What if he's planning to come back home on Christmas, you know, give me a surprise? He knows his father loved it. What will I say to him? What will I do?'

'You will smack him, Baji, that's what you'll do, and if you don't, Zarro and I sure will, promise you won't stop us, yeah?'

'I promise, he-he.'

PART III

TWENTY-FOUR

In early October, just after noon on a sunny Friday, Saffina drove to Maryam's and parked behind her green Nissan Micro. Maryam seldom drove it. She had called Maryam the previous night and again in the morning, reminding her to be ready. Zarrine and she had been planning to take Maryam on a picnic since the day they'd heard her mention it, then noticed her abruptly change the subject.

'We should've thought of it sooner, Zee, kind of late for a picnic,' Saffina had said. 'She must go mad sitting all day worrying.'

'Let's just take her somewhere and make a day of it, Saffs. Remember what I said, though, don't give her cigarettes, please. I can see she wants to, won't be good for her, though.'

'She's a grown girl, Zarro, for God's sake, don't put it on me.'

'Well, you are the fucking chimney, love, not me.'

--

Maryam had left the door unlocked. Saffina saw her sitting at the kitchen table, a checked blue-and-white laundry bag and a rolled-up picnic blanket on the chair next to her. The kitchen was tidied up, breezy from the wide-open windows. For a fleeting moment,

Saffina felt she might well up seeing her older sister seated like this, silent, staring at the wall, but she reminded herself why she was here.

'Oh, excellent, someone's all ready to go. Salamalaikum, Baji.'

'Walaikum. Where are we going, honey?'

'You will see, not too far, I promise.'

'Yes, can't be gone for too long, you know,' Maryam said, expecting complete understanding from her sister.

'I know, Baji, I know.'

Maryam put her bag and blanket in the boot of the car and sat at the back, resting her head against the corner of the window. Saffina didn't object but couldn't help letting out a long sigh. She drove out of the neighbourhood quickly, past Tony's store, turned around at the corner of the church, and was soon headed towards the town centre.

She cut through traffic, overtaking a few cars and vans. Normally, Maryam would ask her to slow down, to be patient, but she remained quiet in the back seat.

Maryam gazed blank-eyed at the familiar streets. She usually took the W12 bus to the station, but Saffina turned in a different direction and made an exit towards Chingford Road, then merged with the streaming traffic on the North Circular. Zarrine called to say she was waiting for them at the Esso Petrol Station nearby where she'd stopped to buy drinks and snacks.

The three sisters then took Forest Road until they came upon a park area Maryam didn't remember seeing before.

—

It was open on all sides, without too much shade, perfect to get some sun on her tired shoulders, Maryam thought. Got to be grateful for what you get. She spread her blanket and laid a sheet on top and sat down. From her bag, she took out a thermos flask, plates, and Tupperware boxes with sandwiches, grapes and biscuits, arranging them haphazardly. Zarrine smiled at her.

The amoeba-shaped pond on the other side of the children's area had turned a radiant, porcelain blue in the sunlight. A family of swans had come ashore and stood lazily in the sun. Perhaps because it was a Tuesday, or perhaps because it was a relatively new park, there were not many visitors. Across another fence, on the far side of the pond, were rusted metal scraps, T-junctions, levers, engine parts, remainders from a disused pumping station. Maryam liked the stillness brought about by the steady sunlight on the pond.

She leaned on her elbow, her mind wandering to picnics of the past, debating whether to ask Saffina for a cigarette or not. She decided to wait, deferring the promise of a smoke until a later moment. As they were driving, she had wondered if it was a good idea to come with Saffina and Zarrine: what if it made them uncomfortable, put them in an awkward position? What if they didn't want to be seen with her in public? Wouldn't blame them. So it was probably better that they hadn't gone to Epping Forest or Victoria Park further into town, though she would've liked to be near the woodland or by the waterside in Epping Forest. They used to go there with Ash's office people once a year, so much food and drink, and Frisbee! Ash's boss was kind that way, wasn't he, she thought, taking his staff on picnics and the like. It was a good time at the estate back then—well, mostly good, at least in the initial years. Ash's boss had been particularly helpful to them. Must acknowledge the kindness of both friends and strangers, she thought, remembering they might not have been able to buy the flat without Mr Whiteley's help.

She recalled Mr Whiteley played bridge with the other owners every Thursday evening. They got together in his office and played cards and had drinks. Sometimes, they would ask Ash to stay on. She had thought it was probably because they were a player short, but Ash, bless his soul, believed the bosses treated him as an equal.

When they'd started thinking they could buy a little something of their own, Ash had insisted they must ask his boss for advice because he knew everything there was to know about property and finance.

Sitting in the boss's office one day, as he pored over the numbers Ash had prepared, they waited with bated breath. At last, Mr Whiteley said, 'I can't allow you to live too far from here, love. This young man here, your good husband … we can't let some city slickers whisk him away, can we? We'll have to find a place for you lovebirds in the neighbourhood, eh.'

'Oh, Mr Whiteley, I don't know what to say, that's so kind of you …' She and Ash spoke at the same time.

'That's alright, love. Have you seen those new flats with balconies as you get out of the estate and go down towards the church? I might know someone who's got a set of four there … No harm in taking a look, eh. What do you think?'

The following week, Mr Whiteley wrote a note for them to take to the manager at Nationwide, and in less than a month, they had a mortgage. They put every pound they had towards the deposit. In about five months' time, they were cooking a vat of chicken pulao and mutton korma for her family and friends. Ama brought gold-laced curtains for them, god bless her, as if she had bought a dance bar.

Ash, bless his soul, had no one in London he could really call close. His few relatives from his mum Lauren's side and his childhood friends were far away in Cork. He didn't have any friends apart from his work mates.

They stayed on Homecroft Street even after Mr Whiteley decided to shut shop like everybody else. None of them, not a single unit, Ash said, had been making money for a couple of years before the owners decided to close their businesses. The banks had had enough, Ash said, but thanks to Mr Whiteley, he worked until the very last day, afterwards too, helping his boss wrap up the books, tying loose ends …

They kept on with the card game parties, even after the closures; that wasn't good, she'd thought then as now, Ash staying out there every Thursday night. She suspected that's when he caught the habit.

—

Maryam stood up and started to walk back and forth by the pond. She seemed restless, edgy and teary, Zarrine thought. It was a bright day, the clear blue sky marked with dramatic splashes of contrails. Children chased each other around the slides in the fenced-off play area.

Maryam felt relieved, even strangely happy, that Saffina had brought her here. There was no talk of Dilawar, no questions about him. As long as they didn't say he was dead, maybe she could somehow carry on like this. Her situation was at least better than those mums whose sons had blown themselves up to kill other people, or whose boys had been caught with explosive materials, or Allah toba, beheaded people!

—

Remembering the last days at the estate had always been hard, the whole thing had been crushing, and still was, but that hadn't been the reason she had avoided talking about it—she could always do hard. It was because she hadn't wanted Dil to get any whiff of it. It had been too much for him to see his father die, so it was unwise to talk about what had happened before, who had said what … the ceaseless, hurtful gossip in the extended family. She knew her father and all the buas, the Finchley aunts and cousins, even Uncle Sharief who was supposedly a big lawyer, looked down on those who drank alcohol. You can beat your wife black and blue, you can torture your little kids, but Allah toba, straight to Jahannam if a sip of gin touched your lips! Maryam had ignored the much too obvious cold disapprovals but had felt wounded by all the barbs about Ash not being a proper Muslim. 'What with his Christian mother! Kaafir kaafir honda ae.' And then there was his supposed closeness with the estate owners, considered suspicious by both, her relatives and his co-workers. He's the one who does the books, the colleagues said, he's the one who does the sums, he must've always known. She remembered everything.

When word spread that the factories were to close in a year, or maybe even months, many of the staff began to resent the bosses' Thursday soirees. They were angry that the owners were partying while their lives and futures were at stake. Shouldn't they be looking to save the estate, relocate if location was the issue, organise a meeting with the council, ask for more time, go to Hadley the MP, beg and plead.

Instead, they were going about their days as if all was hunky-dory, as if factories closed every day. They sat in their offices and come Thursday, they played cards and drank expensive booze, while everyone else's jobs were about to disappear. 'Fucking unbelievable, the things they say at the pub,' Tony would tell her when she went to the shop.

And then they'd rounded on Ash who, quite suddenly, wasn't one of them anymore. The floor workers, the clerks and assistants, Tim and Gerry, Paul and Eddy, all those with whom Ash had broken bread and whose life stories he'd heard over and over, were now fuming at him.

He must have it all sorted, they said, he must've known all along. Of course he must've known, he's part of the plans, he's in on it. Can you fucking believe that? He's actually helping the fat bastards shut down our jobs. Bloody traitor. Thought of him as one of our own, didn't we, but I'm telling ya, these people—they show their true colours in the end. We welcome him, treat him as one of us, and look how he's repaying us.

That's the kind of stuff they had said about him, Maryam remembered with a parched throat. Tony, bless him, told her everything. Brought groceries with him too. It was heartbreaking not just because of what they did to Ash, but because of how some of them thought about Ash and her, and she had started to suspect—what if that's how they had always thought of them, from the beginning. But it couldn't all have been fake, could it?

Tony told her that one Thursday night, as Ash was walking home from Whiteley's office, some people from the estate cornered him, put a sack on his head and pulled him back in. They dragged him into a disused old unit at the back and strapped him to a lathe used to press leather swatches for briefcases. That's where the bastards hit him, spat at him. Fucking unbelievable, Tony said.

When Ash came home that night, he said he'd had an argument with some lads from the 'state, he shouldn't have, it was silly of him, he knew, but there wasn't any point talking about it, what had happened had happened!

'Which lads, Ashy,' she'd said. 'Give me their fucking names and I'll go and have it with their mums?'

'It's nothing, Maryam, just some bruises,' he had said. 'I don't want you to get involved. It's not too bad … You know I'm not used to this kind of stuff …'

'But you seem to have bled a bit, Ashy—'

'Yeah, just a bit,' he lied.

She could tell he had wiped blood off his face. She later found the brown jumper he had used to clean himself stuffed behind the coat stand.

She'd gone to the kitchen and brought a glass of water and medicine.

'Here, take two of these, they'll help,' she said, giving him the Ibuprofen.

'But I haven't got any pain, Em—'

'Take the fucking pills, Ash,' she screamed at him. 'You look like a sad little pup caught in the rain. Please take them, love. You will say thank you, Maryam Ali, thank you very much, in the morning.'

Then she'd fed him some chicken and mash and brought out his whisky bottle.

'Have a night cap, hun,' she said, 'it's alright, have a sip and go to bed.' She knew it wasn't a great idea to mix Ibuprofen with alcohol, but she thought he needed it.

At night, she had gone into the garden to be by herself. She remembered wrapping Ama's old Pashmina shawl around her and looking up at the sky, which was full of planes and city lights, all yellow and purple and pink. 'Shukr Alhamdulillah he is fine,' she said to herself. She found him snoring gently under the duvet when she went back. He'd had a few swigs from the Jameson's bottle and drifted into sleep, his bruises and scratches shining in the night light. She kissed him and whispered, 'I'm here, Ashy, always here.' The next evening, she'd brought his Jameson's bottle out again after dinner. 'Night cap, hun?' she'd asked.

--

Ash died suddenly, very suddenly, she remembered. Heart attack, they'd said at Whips Cross Hospital. Heartbreak is what she thought. Some in her family blamed this and that, the smoking, the drink, people like to talk, isn't it, but she didn't think it was any of that. Ash's heart just broke, like hers now.

Zarrine strolled near the benches where three old women were sitting, she paced lazily towards the pond and back. She looked at Maryam now and then to check if she was alright, if she wasn't straying too close to the water in her absent state. Saffina waved to her from the mat, signalling to her to let Maryam be.

On the day he died, she had found Ash sleeping on the sofa in the morning, his head on the arm rest, a beam of light on his neck.

There was some whisky in the bottle on the table, and she couldn't remember how much there had been the previous evening, but she was sure he wouldn't have had too much. She had put the bottle away quickly in case Dil walked in, and was relieved she'd done so because he came in a minute later and flung himself on his father. 'Wake up, zombie man! Come on, Dad, wake up … I have football today, remember,' he said.

TWENTY-FIVE

'It's no ordinary birthday, Baji, they turn into men at sixteen, yeah, have you heard his voice even! Like Tom Jones is gonna pop out of his throat any minute.'

'Alright, alright, do what you like, just don't bring booze into the house. He's too young for that ...'

'Are you also too young, Baji?'

'Get lost now. I've got a billion things to do.'

'Awright, general, byee!'

Maryam turned the photos from the birthday party this way and that, gazing at the faces. Dil looked dashing, she thought, although a bit thin, or maybe it was the clothes, one size too big. It had been her habit since he was about three. Anyhow, it was a fantastic party.

'We will do everything, Baji, don't you worry, for his seventeenth, eighteenth and twenty-first, alright,' Zarrine had said.

'But after that he's on his own.' Saffina slapped Zarrine's thigh.

'As if he's going to care when he's a grown man.' Maryam broke into a smile.

'Baji, by the way, have you thought about this? What are you going to do if Dilly brings a white girl home one day?'

'Oh, yes, what if he wants a church wedding,' Saffina said. 'What are we going to do then? Baroness Finchley is going to disown us, innit?' Zarrine opened her mouth wide in mock astonishment.

'Do you know what, Saffo, where's the problem with any of that? Have you at any point in your lives seen me live under a rock? The Finchleys can stew in their pious, know-all shit all they want. Dil can marry whoever he likes.'

'Oh, Baji, you get too serious sometimes, man. Zarro's taking the piss, you know … 'Course you'll go to the church in your humongous purple lehenga. It's like a camping tent, though …'

'And we'll take a cauldron of korma to the church,' Zarrine said.

'What fun!'

'Hmm … I might wear a sari, Ama's elegant gold-and-silver brocade sari,' Maryam said. 'She told me it was handmade by some legendary weavers from Madras.'

'Baji's going to dazzle everyone, even the bride, oye-oye.'

--

Maryam spread the photos on her bed and looked at Dil, at her sisters, at herself. She's standing in the doorway with a tray in her hands, she's probably looking at him. She wasn't sure now, but who else could she have been looking at? He's surrounded by her sisters' little ones like pups surround their mother.

There he is, lanky, plant-like, indulging his little cousins, letting them climb all over him, letting them pull at his clothes this way and that, grab his hair even. Oh, that's Shaye, Saffo's eldest, on his shoulders. Dil's got a big grin on his face.

There he is, happy at home because he's with his mum, his aunts and cousins. Think he'd only invited his best mates: Aiden, who didn't have many friends, Andy, his sometimes protector and guardian, and Rez, who'd been waiting for Dil to go to his house for a night spend but Dil had somehow always dodged it. Funny boy—there he is, in the midst of his cousins, aunts and friends, cake bits on his jumper probably, and that Ash grin on his face.

What does Dil's easy smile say? I'm happy you are all here, look at my mum and my aunts? Thanks for coming over, guys, and sorry for not throwing a big party someplace else, boys and girls only, no mum and dad, but you see, there's no dad, so had to do it for mum.

Did he do it for me? I never said anything, though. It was Zarro and Saffo, they planned the whole thing. Did he secretly hold it against me, resent me for making him stay home on his sixteenth? Although I didn't make him. Or did I?

But he looks genuinely happy in the snaps, he does, or was he feigning it for my sake?

There's so much I don't know about him. So much I didn't know, now that I think about it. He does look happy in the photos, though. Look at that Ash smile again—it can't be fake! Get a grip on yourself, Maryam Ali.

She brought the photo closer to her face, then chose not to kiss it.

She remembered the first time he had flinched, put distance between himself and her at the school gates. He was in Year Five then, and had started to shoot up a bit, the earliest version of the lanky boy he would become. She noticed he turned sideways as she tried to put her arms around him; he had probably meant for her to notice. From then on, she had only flicked his hair at drop-off, like Ash used to.

'That's the way it goes, Em, that's the way it goes,' Ash had said. 'Absolutely nothing we can do about it. They don't like to be hugged in public as they grow older—mummy hugs in particular.'

'Alright, alright, no need to go philosophical on me. I know. But do you think he's embarrassed by me? That his mother is a school chef? Do you think he'd prefer it if I didn't go with him?'

'Do you think we've brought him up to be like that, Maryam? I don't think so.'

'I still wish you dropped him off, though.'

'You know I can't do it. Mr Whiteley wants me to come in early. All these years, it's never been a problem. You go that way anyway, we've talked about this, we decided on this, Maryam!'

'I know what we decided, Ash, for God's sake, I'm not a moron. I thought maybe he'd like it more if you go with him, he's growing older.'

'Then he will grow up some more and see the silliness of what he wants. He's our son! You're overthinking this. The simple thing is, he's become a bit self-conscious about his mother walking him to school. That's normal, and maybe he's embarrassed about the hugs. You can't do that to a growing boy in public.'

'Oh, yeah? Now I don't know how to hug my own son. What is a good hug, Ash? What in your vast experience as a father and expert hugger is a safe, not-embarrassing distance between mother and son when mummy wants a hug?'

'Come on, that's not what I meant, you don't need to go all sarky on me …'

'Alright, alright, not your fault. I just felt a bit sad when he turned away the other day, didn't even look back, yeah.'

'It's alright, Maryam, he'll be fine, you'll be fine.'

TWENTY-SIX

Turning over Ash's words, Maryam noticed she had bent the photo in her hand, so she relaxed her grip. Then she wiped it with a tissue paper, turning it against the light to look for smudges and scratches, and put it back in the heavy photo album she had bullied Ash into buying.

'Why do we need an album that is larger than a door, Em,' he had said.

'Because an album is for life, even for after-life. Have you even seen Ama's? It's as big as a garden shed.'

Where is he now? Why isn't he here, in this room, looking at these with me? Where are the cheesy quips, Ashoo? Why aren't you here, looking for Dil with me? Why aren't you running to every corner of the country, the whole fucking world, and bringing him back by the scruff of his neck, scolding him, where the hell have you been? How dare you disappear like that? You're grounded for life.'

And where is he now, the new man of the house, eh? Dependable, reasonable boy, huh, man to take care of everything! It must feel good, yeah, liberating, leaving your mum like this?

—

'Mum, Mum … you worry too much sometimes, innit? I'll take care of everything. Chill, yeah, look at Zee and Ess, always crackin' jokes, laughin', innit … We're going to be okay, you have to stop fretting over everythin', yeah, and you don't have to do all this shit anymore. Sorry. I mean, you can stop anytime you want. Times have changed, Mums, big time. I can work anywhere I like! I can work remote, on site, off site, in a flippin' bus, fam. I don't have to go to an office, I can sit right here and make enough dough, yeah, so don't worry. I don't even need a job! Hang on, don't freak out, yeah. I'll do proper contracts, signatures and all, alright?

'You remember Jenny, the intern coordinator at City? She told me about this giant new mall near Ilford, a bit outside … It's a new place, so obviously they're all on the same network, but, wait for it, some of the storeowners don't want to pay the IT vendor all the time. Not for every little thing, innit! Jenny says they don't want to fork out shitloads in contracts, one G a year for a 300 quid Dell, Mum! All that the IT guy with a cheap lanyard round his neck will do is reboot the thing, run a diagnostic, update network profile, update security … I know that shit like the back of my hand. Long story short, Mums, Jenny puts in a word for me, and guess what, her contact got back the same day, says she likes my CV and wants me to start asap. Justine Bradbury is the name, Mum, *Justeene*. So, if all goes well, I will set up a company to do this. So I was thinking … I want to register the company in your and Dad's name, you know.'

'Oh, that's very sweet, Dilly. You don't have to … Tell me something, don't you think it's a bit early to be starting a business, though? Don't you want to get some, you know, work experience for a couple of years, work with other people, and then start on your own? Of course you can have your own company, I'm just saying there's no hurry …'

'Mums, there isn't a lot I don't know about the, umm, network side of things, yeah. It's like you make computers talk to each other, share stuff across terminals, you know what I mean. They could be in the same office, same building, or they could be in different countries, and I know how to keep them hooked up without a fuss. Think of me as a PC plumber, Mums, I keep the pipes, the joints between the pipes and the boiler all working together. How's that?'

'I'm not that daft, Dilly, I get it, you know your stuff. But what if you don't get a lot of work, you know? What if you don't find a lot of … clients? That can happen, right?'

'Oh, there you go again, Mum, worrying about something before it's even started. Can't be negative all the time, fam! It's so frustrating. You do it all the time!'

'All I'm saying is, shouldn't you think of all the pros and cons beforehand?'

'I get it, Mum, I get it. You are a risk averse person,' he'd said with gritted teeth, 'afraid of trying new things, innit? Maybe I know why … How about we start a … a catering business then, what do you think of that? I dunno, Mum, I don't want to work in an office, you know … I don't want to slave away for someone else. You can look after the production, and I'll do distribution and delivery. How about it, yeah? But it can't be called Mad Networx … How about Maryam & Son?'

Why had he used that name? Was he trying to do something for me because he knew he was going to leave, she wondered, remembering what she'd asked him then.

'Dil, why call your company mad, though?'

'Oh, MAD's for Maryam, Ashfaq and Dilawar. Simple!'

'Ah, I get it. So why have a different name for this other company?'

'Because it's your thing, Mum. You've worked so hard all your life, innit? You know everything about food, and with a little bit of help from me, online and data side of it, we can start a food business right here in da stow! You have all your school contacts, right? They know you, they know your food, they know the kind of person you are.'

'And what kind of a person am I?'

'You're not too bad, Mum, you're alright, yeah … Okay, okay, it was a joke! You're a nice person, Mother, you're the best, happy now?

—

Maryam felt she might well up. She struggled, trying to hold back the tears, then gave in, moving the photos away. She had read somewhere that grief is not a state of mind, it is not something you do or don't, nor something that fades away with time, but that it's a living, breathing thing that resides within you, somewhere behind your eyelids. You close your eyes and you feel the shadow of the lost one flit across. It's best to let it live there and make peace with it. Carry it with you.

She lay still, aware of the room, of the bed, of Dilawar's things, of the many frozen glimpses of life, life thus far, life with Dil, life with Dil and Ash, life in this house with the two of them.

It had been kind of perfect, the three of them behind these doors, on this street, away from the overwhelming, maddening bustle of the city but not too far. It was a good thing to have London throb and pulse near you, but you didn't need to be inside it. When she was young, working in the city had been a dream for so many of her friends and cousins, but while she wasn't opposed to the idea, she had no burning passion for the big city, and as she grew older with her husband, then with husband and child, she felt it had all been written in the stars. A small, quiet life in a small, quiet enclave in the suburbs, on the fringes of the city, was just the thing for her. A dream she'd never dreamed but cherished all the same, probably all the more.

As she looked around Dil's room, his chair, his desk, his computer, the clothes which she arranged and rearranged on the door hooks week after week, the charts of peer-to-peer networks, server architecture and network encryption, Maryam was filled with an intense, seething anger.

'How dare you, Dilly.' Then, struggling to keep that old worm away, that he may have inherited some of his father's bad traits, she felt angry at Ashfaq too.

Did I just give, give, give all my life? And the boy and man take all the time? Did they take me for granted? My understanding and my accommodation, my fucking resilience!

'She can withstand anything and laugh about it all,' Sugra Aapa, Maryam's eldest aunt, used to say about her when she was young. Sugra Aapa, who had helped her sometimes, and once shared her wisdom about 'the obstinate world of men'.

They are always full of self-regard, every cell choc-a-block. Ignore the neediness at least half the time and show love and care the rest of the time. That's all, Maryam, that's all you need. Another thing: they will love you, admire you, but they will always look up to a man. They will praise you and honour you. But they will not want to be like you. Remember that, jaan.'

I showed a lot of love and care, Aapa, but look where that's landed me. Both my boys have disappeared!

'Where the hell are you, Dil?'

She listened to her echo for a few moments, called to him again, the name ringing faintly, then became quiet. A housefly had been buzzing annoyingly by the curtains for two nights. She stood up with determined lips, picking up *The Complete Guide to Networking* from Dilawar's desk, and chased the fly around the room, swiping wildly at the curtains, jumping from floor to bed and back with speed.

'You pesky little monster, I'm going to get you today, behenchod makhi, you nasty little bastard, you have no idea who you're messing with. My name is Maryam Ali. You have the audacity to buzz-buzz-buzz here. You are an abomination, you brainless pest.'

Armed with Dil's fat manual, she flung herself after the circling, droning insect. She ran from wall to wall, from floor to bed, to the corner with the curtain holdback. At last, she made her kill. Not at the sill, which she would've preferred, nor against the wall, but bang in the middle of the windowpane.

She considered the map-shaped smudge on the glass and kept looking at it for a while, then dropped the book on the floor. On its glossy front cover, across bits of black-and-white lettering, shone a glistening bright red orb.

What if they have hearts and it's burst open on Dil's book, she thought, but didn't bend down to take a closer look at the entrails of the creature that had been flying moments ago.

TWENTY-SEVEN

Zarrine exchanged pleasantries with Tony as she bought Polo mints and cigarettes. 'So, how are things in the neighbourhood, Tony?' She smiled at him. This was a more or less mutually understood and rehearsed routine. He knew she didn't smoke; it was the other one, the middle sister, who did. He had known Maryam's sisters since they were teenagers.

'It's the same routine, darling,' Tony said. 'Your sis is lonely but that's what she wants, can't do much about that, can we, and I have the shop to mind … When your sister decides on something—'

'Yes, tell me about it … Those government people, do they still come around—?'

'Naah, darling, haven't seen any of them in a long time. It's the other bloke, the tall, posh man, some high-level official, isn't he, he's the one who's been about a bit, you know. What can I say? My guess is he brings news of Dilly …' Tony shrugged and closed his cash register with some force. Its tinny sound rang in the store for a bit.

Zarrine put the pack of cigarettes in her bag and said, 'Thanks a ton for keeping an eye, Tony …'

'That's fine, darling, that's fine, wish there was more I could do …' He left it at that and sighed, watching Maryam's youngest sister walking out of the store.

Zarrine called Saffina as soon as she was out of Tony's earshot. 'What the hell, Saffs? Guess what, that fit guy, bet he's some kind of high-level spook, he's been to see her more than we have! Like regular meetings and all … Can you believe it?'

'You know how it is, Zarro, but think about it, Baji obviously sees something in it, isn't it? I think so anyway … Just don't bring it up, please, stick to what we discussed, alright? Just chat with her, yeah.'

'But this is insane …

'You really want to pick a fight with her now, Zee?'

'Alright, alright, Saint Saffina, I won't, but I'm telling you, this is not normal. What the hell's going on, what if people find out? Has Baji lost it?'

'Yes, she may have lost it a bit, but who wouldn't! Now please go and give her a hug,' Saffina said and hung up the phone.

Zarrine didn't have to wait for Maryam to let her in, it was as if she'd been waiting behind the door. Maryam gave her a quick sideways hug and walked back quietly. Zarrine spoke behind her. 'I'd love to see you at least as often as the posh police, Baji, but I know it's a bother … Anyway, how've you been?'

'You silly girl, don't you understand anything! You have families to worry about, isn't it? I don't want you to think you need to babysit me and neglect your own children. God, must I spell out everything! I'm as well as I can be in my limbo world, Zarro, what do you expect? I wait and live. I live and wait. For what, I do not know … One day, Chapman is going to walk in through that door and say, "I'm afraid I have rather bad news, Mrs Maryam—", and I don't know what I'm going to do then. Grab him by his collar and throw him out of the house? Curse the day they walked into my home? Shout at him, shake him by his shoulders, damn it. "Leave me alone, for God's sake, you've done all you wanted to do, take your sympathy and please go away."'

Maryam couldn't bear the thought of Dil's disappearance causing tension among Zarrine and Saffina's families. Who would want to be constantly asked about the Swordsman on TV and YouTube—it was a subject they must avoid at all costs. Can't blame them. At some level, they must feel shame, embarrassment and guilt at being aunts of ... They probably lower their eyes when out and about, trying not to meet people's eyes. And yet, here Zarrine was, come to talk to her. Was there nothing one could do to stop Zarro from talking, she wondered, looking at her sister.

'Oh, Baji, Baji, you're overthinking too much, no, why be so negative? There's no reason for us to feel like this.'

Maryam stared at her sister, her lips moving over her teeth, as if she was struggling to speak. Outside in the parking lot, a Sainsbury's delivery van was trying to manoeuvre a U-turn, blowing puffs of smoke that Maryam saw through the open kitchen windows—small blue clouds floating, dissipating one after the other.

Zarrine readjusted the pin in her hair for the third time, conscious it annoyed Maryam, then she put her hands in her lap.

Maryam stood up and went to the kitchen where two half-eaten scones rested on a plate. She had been allowing herself this indulgence—scones and strawberry conserve from M&S—in a mostly futile attempt to lift her mood. This morning, they hadn't done the job at all. She'd lost some of the calm she'd cultivated in the last few weeks and had been feeling more frightened than usual, and at three days old, the scones had become dry and powdery. She supposed they might taste better with tea. 'You make the best tea, hun,' she said to Zarrine.

'Why can't they have a small store nearby?' She had found it daunting to go to the high street where the nearest M&S Food was. She had to take the bus, then the tube for two stops, which she hated, then another bus to get to the store, and she wasn't too fond of the area around the underground station, with its grime and smell and the blast of foul hot air that hit her in the face. So she'd started going round through the side entrance, via a paved compound where a tall red-brick-and-glass tower had come up, she didn't know when. She saw young couples seated across each other in the coffee shop that was part of the new building. Steam, conversation and hand-holding behind brown tinted glass.

'You want me to make more tea, just say so, Baji. What's with the gold medal for best tea?'

'Yes, Ama, can you make some more tea, please,' she said and broke off a piece from the crumbly scone.

She started chewing it softly, eyes closed, intense contemplation on her face, as if willing something into reality.

Zarrine looked at her face, noticed faint cracks here and there, a fuzzy paleness over the cheeks, and concluded that her sister hadn't used face cream in some time. She decided she must remember to bring a new moisturiser when she came to see her next.

'I am so tired, Zarrine, I just want him to come back home, that's all …'

'Oh, Baji, 'course he will be back, he will have to … Let me get some fresh tea for you.'

TWENTY-EIGHT

It was the first time in months that she did not feel a twinge as she turned away—determinedly—from Dil's photos and clothes. She felt alright about it, tired, resigned, but alright, kind of alright anyway. Until recently, it had been a drug addict's cycle of want and self-reproach. But of late, leafing through the photo albums, touching his clothes and things, had started to fill her with exhaustion; it no longer carried the satisfaction she derived from seeing him at various stages of his life; the propitiatory after-effects of longing had started to fade.

'Give it a break, Maryam, give it a break,' she said as she went round the flat, opening all the curtains in all the rooms, including the bathroom.

Looking out of the living-room window, she saw that the lights from the houses on the other side of the garden had cast long, jagged columns on the grass outside her balcony. Shadows of those living in the houses leaped across now and then, elongated human forms breaking into the garden, reaching up to her windows. Families going about their night chores, chatting with each other, getting up from dining chairs, washing up, people making their last movements before settling down for the night.

She ate a dinner of chargrilled chicken and mixed-leaf salad that Zarrine had left in the fridge. She was surprised by how much she liked it, perhaps because she'd grown tired of her own dishes and the korma, dal and rice tiffin boxes Ama dropped off or sent with either of the sisters from time to time. Or maybe she had simply started to enjoy eating again, rediscovering her tastes.

Later, when she went to the bathroom, she noticed many smudges on the sea-foam blue tiles—or perhaps there were only a dozen or so—then some on the rim of the bathtub, on the stainless-steel effect Mira shower that she and Ash had bought together because she'd been unhappy with the 'drought-stricken' showerhead the plumbing company had put in.

'What is this, Ashoo, you really think a fully grown woman with a massive head of hair can bathe under that toy? No, really, love, what were you thinking? That your wife's going to be over the moon, give you a trophy for bringing home a Barbie shower? It's for dwarves, not for sexy women with long hair. It takes me half an hour just to wash the shampoo off, darling. What the hell were you thinking?'

'You know I didn't put it in, Em. I had absolutely nothing to do with it.'

'Here's what I think. They showed you a glossy brochure or pictures of someone else's bathroom and you said it's perfect, isn't it? You must've counted the forty-five hairs on your head and thought, oh, that's wonderful, there's definitely more water in that thing than I'll ever need. I'm sure they sniggered behind your back. We sold him a toy, mate, give me five.'

'That's not funny, alright, maybe a tiny bit funny, but seriously, man, come on, I didn't do it. Yes, I looked at the fittings because they were the same as the other flats. So I said OKAY, it's fine by me … you weren't home at the time. You used to leave at seven and come back after six in those days. Remember?'

'And why did I do that, Ashfaq mian? Go on, take a guess.'

'I know, Maryam, I know. I live with you, for God's sake.'

'No, let me jog your memory, darling. I was doing overtime, breakfast *and* after-school club! Because we didn't want a giant mortgage hanging on our heads, remember? Because you, our in-house financial advisor and personal accountant, said it's best to chip off the loan so we'd have an easier time later. It's prudent to reduce the *El to V*, you said, darling, didn't you? So we can pass on some equity to Dil when he's grown up, so he doesn't have to struggle the way we did, you said. Maryam Ali works her butt off, making thousands of meals, Ashy, thousands, so we could have an easy retirement, and what does my dear hubby do? Bring home a shower large enough to wash a rat's ass.'

'Funny girl … you said your piece? You've forgotten I did overtime too. It's not my fault that the estate shut down, is it now?'

'That's not what I meant, you know I'm not the kind … I'm just saying Maryam Ali deserves a proper shower, one that releases nice, satisfying jets of water, not threads of drool!'

'Alright, alright, you've made your point. God! Can I get a hug now?'

'Booby hug?'

--

Maryam scrubbed hard at the tub and the tiles, first with Cilit Bang, then with Dettol. With wire mesh, with gloves on and off, with her palm and nails. She bent, curled and reached, trousers and sleeves rolled up, hem tucked into her trousers. She worked up foam the size of a cloud, lather like a barber's hot shave, soap suds as though made by a giant bubble gun. Then she stepped out to admire her work.

All these months I didn't see the dirt, haan, all these fucking months, because I've gone blind with stress. Now watch what I'm going to do!

She went to the bedroom and brought out the old red Sanyo stereo from Ash's cupboard and inserted the mixed DVD Dil had made for her fortieth birthday. She waited for Sabri Brothers to come on, for that haunting old qawwali recounting Prophet Muhammad's ethereal journey to see his creator on the night of Mairaj:

Sar-e-la makaan se talab hui
...
Koi had he unke urooj ki
Balagal ila be kamal hi
Sar-e-la makaan ... *Sar-e-la* ... echoed in the bathroom.

She recalled watching one of the Sabri Brothers rocking left and right in a YouTube video as he chanted the many titles of the Prophet—'an epic, memorable sequence' (Ash's words came to her mind)—before closing with 'Yaane Muhammad-e-Mustafa!' She scrubbed and scratched and polished.

Koi had hai unke kamal ki ...
Hawas thhi deed ki ...
Mairaj ka bahana thhaa ...

As the chorus picked up the tempo following the lead's extolment of the Prophet's virtues, Maryam paused at the mention of Buraq, trying to visualise the heavenly flight of Prophet Muhammad and his steed. She sighed at her inability to understand the high Urdu words.

'If only I had taken those lessons seriously,' she would say to Dil because he, too, had stopped going to the Urdu classes Mrs Mirza ran in Chingford Mount.

'It's too far, Mum, and I feel sleepy, the bus takes forever and there's yobs on it. You don't want me to get into a fight, do you?'

'But you don't have to get into a fight, Dil, you know you don't have to.'

'Even when they stick chewing gum on the back of your head? Even if they pour Red Bull down your shirt from behind?'

'Okay, don't go! But stop making lame excuses. You know they don't cut it with me.'

'But it's true, Mum. Why don't you ever believe me? I swear I'm not making it up. You remember Zaid, that wicketkeeper guy from school? They poured warm beer down his trousers once, Mum!'

'No, honey, I'm not saying you're lying. Just make cleverer excuses next time.'

'I didn't make up the effin' yobs, Mum! Can't even fight back, yeah, they're effin' huge.'

'Language, Dilly, what the hell!'

'Ha, ha …'

'Alright, you got me, come here, my yob.'

'Mum, stop it!'

--

Maryam wondered if Dil had ever liked Indian or Pakistani music. Probably not, although she felt he would find Nusrat Fateh Ali Khan or Asha Bhosle catchy as he grew older. She had decided not to push desi music on him, supposing that playing it in the house now and then would draw him in one day, as it had drawn her.

--

As the qawwali boomed, she started to pray, chant for chant, line for line, entreaty for entreaty. It felt to her that the lyrics had been composed for her. Every word a spear, every beat a clutch at the heart.

She worked up more lather and wiped surfaces that were already shining. Am I waiting for him to die? I am waiting for my son to be killed, aren't I? And is he out there, hiding somewhere, preparing to kill? Tajdar-e-Haram, how will I live through that?

Is Dil, a piece of my heart, really not a computer specialist but a terrorist? A T E R R O R I S T?

She turned the mixer tap in the tub to full and watched eddies of foam swirl and circle. As the white water rose, she recalled how Ash used to bathe Dil in the old tub. As with the shower, she had never liked it and had replaced it with a porcelain one three years after they took possession of the flat.

'The little man likes lots of lather, not so much the bubbles.'

'Ashoo, most children do, it's all bubbles for them.'

'Yeah, but ours seems happy rolling in the dirty froth. Look at him!'

'Of course, he's your son.'

Maryam watched the pool of water rise and imagined herself lying down in the frothy tub, stretching full, the water surrounding her chest, her throat, her chin and face. She wondered if she'd gasp for breath and splash out or stay under forever. Must have some clothes on if I do, though … Can't have them discover me naked. What will people say? That Maryam Ali hadn't been looking after herself in her last days? Definitely can't have Saffo and Zarro embarrassed about it. What will *they* think? That Baji had become a slob, wish they had seen the signs and done something about it? That Baji's house was full of stains and smudges, her bathroom damp and mouldy, and she smelled a bit odd herself too?

At this, she quickly sniffed at her sleeve, was pleased to not find any body odour, and felt a little less of the embarrassment she'd felt looking at the few stains and bits of flaked paint in the flat, the tiny patches of scum in the bathroom corners, and the mites of dust and carpet hair that floated here and there sometimes. She missed the old Maryam but she knew that woman belonged in a different world, and that this Maryam, Mother Maryam, was the one left now.

She felt wet around her ankles and unplugged the drain hole with a jerk. The plug chain broke off and she gazed at the thing in her hand.

PART IV

TWENTY-NINE

The chill of late autumn evenings had started to infiltrate homes and offices through the slits in windows and shutters, from under doors in through the partially open bathroom windows and through the cowls of exhaust fans. Across the wide, tree-lined avenues near the Joint Section offices in London, pale, blonde, scarlet, yellow leaves gathered on well-attended pavements and neat gutters.

The day hadn't gone well for David. He was frustrated that the video call with Washington had been moved for the second time in two weeks; he attacked his salad with the restlessness of a hungry cat.

The campaign in Iraq had picked up steam, and it was clear to him that the Americans wanted to claim a victory before the president's exit. He was also aware that sometimes operational protocols took time, and that those at the helm in the other half had to tick procedural requirements on their grid. He knew he was expected to wait, but a state of dissatisfaction remained. The lunch fare didn't help to take the edge off either.

Last year's David would've ordered a gourmet burger at a time like this. Comfort food often took the bite off prickly work issues. But he had to defer to Oskar and co., he reasoned once again, they were the ones who determined the date and time of their exchanges, even as he'd had a recurring suspicion that he often gave more than he was given during these meetings.

He turned up the dial on his tabletop speaker, which was playing 'Soothing classical' from his playlist, but after a short while he closed the app.

Sunlight filtering through the slats in the blinds cast long rails on his desk and the floor. These criss-crosses of light reminded him of the plastic model suspension bridges he and his brother James used to build in their long garden in Beckenham when they were boys. During his visits to DC, he sometimes went over to New York and stayed at James's apartment—he liked driving across the bridges in the city. Once, as he slowed down while crossing the Brooklyn Bridge, he had been hypnotised by the strings of light and shade filtering into the car, the long cables of the bridge chasing him as he drove. He remembered how James used to cover their under-construction projects with tarp at night, and in the morning, he would see his younger brother wiping off dew from the engineering models they built together.

Occasionally, David wondered whether he might have been better off working across the ocean. Then again, life for high-level intelligence consultants had become quite complicated lately. There was much more paperwork now, and he loathed the idea of sitting for a lengthy interview during which a smug psychologist nodded knowingly from the other end of the table. He'd done it once and sworn he'd never agree to another. It might, however, be vastly different if he applied for citizenship, his friends at the D Wing had suggested.

David wasn't, however, entirely sure it was a good idea to set up house in a new city once again. He was getting too old for that kind of thing, so, on balance, he was probably alright working at home. Brits weren't so bad after all, yes, there were a few hoops to jump through, but short of a total carte blanche, he'd been given everything he needed, which wasn't too bad given how some of his countrymen remained obsessed with amassing cupboardfuls of paper, lifelong love affairs with filing cabinets, even at such an extraordinary time. Then again, as long as they stayed out of his way, which he'd been assured of several times, the paper trail people could have all the paper they wanted. And his superiors owed him, after all—he had given them precisely the kind of 'concrete deliverables' they'd asked for. He'd brought back more than a few boys and girls from the caliphate and dealt with some others in the best way possible. Sometimes, when he chanced upon a news broadcast at night, he found himself on the verge of breaking into a smile but then fixed his face promptly.

As someone who ran his own department, someone who had complete and, he liked to believe, unquestionable authority over matters such as that of Maryam Ali's son, he was certain he would never waver in his objective. Accounting for those who had left their homes to fight alongside people whose primary goal was to kill, torture and capture anyone who didn't agree with them or their ways, was a matter of great and everyday urgency. It was also clear to him that, if the subject came up for reflection, he wasn't required to dwell on how people from faraway places had come to exert such magnetic power over young men and women in his own backyard.

No matter what, though, it was his duty, above all, to pursue those who had disappeared from the country and surfaced in terror camps in the desert or morphed into mysterious actors in the dark underbelly of the internet. He had been highly successful in this venture so far, because he did whatever it took, and he knew his methods were right because he had been so successful.

If only there wasn't this matter of the Swordsman, he would be more at ease reminding the Chief SpAd on ISIS that it was perhaps time to revisit his terms. 'Make a start, David, give me something solid and the sky's whatever the fuck you want it to be,' the big boss had said.

He hated Maryam Ali's son for getting in the way. And the fucking eyeball media, timeline shits, attention piranhas, they had hyped the Swordsman far more than the boy deserved. Of late, he'd also started to doubt whether Julian was the right man for the job after all, although he had seemed perfect at the start, especially after those first meetings with Maryam Ali. He was the one who had established some rapport with her. Julian this and Julian that! And it was he who had kept the family calm and under control. Had to give him that. It was he who had persuaded Ali to call off that Hampstead lawyer of hers. Self-important old prick.

But the Swordsman was still a pain in the ass, and his partners weren't giving him much either. What were Oskar and his boys playing at?

He looked out from his office, at the analysts resting on their bean bags, at the large screens aflutter further back. He saw each lit screen and imagined a file being processed and updated; a case opened; a case closed. The more files closed, the fewer lit screens, the better; a hall full of dark screens would be nice, he thought, scooping up the juice left in his bowl. He revised his terse message to Oskar, leaving it formal enough to indicate his dissatisfaction at not having been sent the dossier on 'Ali of London' yet, which he'd been told was 'invaluable for all concerned'. Signing off as 'Dave', he paused, changed it to 'David', and closed his laptop. As he left the office, he saw Julian bent over his screen and scribbling something on a notepad.

'Must be rehearsing his lines to his girlfriend.'

THIRTY

Maryam started throwing the flowers in the bin because she didn't like the misshapen ones, and one by one, she decided all of them were of odd shapes. Crinkly red, orange and pale bunches landed on the rubbish with a low rustle. She saw a shadow spread over the petals as she closed the lid.

It was early November, dry and cold, the sunny interludes a balm for her shoulders. She positioned her back at an angle by the kitchen window in the first half of the day and near the sitting-room window in the afternoon. Thinking and then trying, determinedly, not to think of Dilawar had instilled in her the kind of fatigued patience known to people who spend long periods in hospital waiting rooms. There was nothing to be done about the waiting, and there was nothing to be done about not knowing.

In her scheme of things, everything would be restored to normal the moment Dil walked in; it was this image, this constantly imagined moment that gave her hope, for which she prayed during every namaz. She asked for forgiveness, too, for not having prayed five times a day in the past and sometimes worried she might still have missed a prayer. She had, she suspected, started to forget things on occasion. Then she told herself she was far too young for dementia and suchlike. 'It's just a lack of sleep, Maryam, what else.'

She looked forward to seeing Julian, and yet, she tired of him sometimes, not his person, but what he represented. But she needed him, his company, the comfort she felt in his presence.

--

He was late that day. She had left the door unlocked for him while she tidied up her bedroom, the bathroom and Dil's bedroom. She should keep him waiting a little longer in the living room, she thought.

After pacing around for a few minutes, Julian found himself studying the photos in the cupboard. He felt as though he knew the people in them. A familiarity grown out of habit, out of seeing these faces regularly for the last few months. He couldn't help wondering what it might have been like if he had actually met these people, known them: Ashfaq, Dilawar, Dilawar's friends, the people he hung out with. What were they like in everyday life? Then it struck him that if he had known them, he wouldn't have come to know Maryam in the way he had. At home and work in recent weeks, he had been reading about British Muslims, their lineages, families, their boys, and making notes. He read think tank papers on radicalisation, domestic politics and marginalisation; he underlined passages from in-house documents marked 'highly confidential', he bookmarked or downloaded university research projects on radicalisation, social media and the patterns of online recruitment.

When Maryam walked in, he asked about Dilawar at once, without thinking.

'What was he like when he was younger,' he said.

She felt a stab when she heard him speak about Dil in the past tense, even though she knew it was meant in the context of his childhood. She paused, drew in her breath, heat rising to her face.

She thought about what she wanted to say and, in the end, simply said, 'Normal. Like most boys.'

'Did he, you know, show any signs, Maryam, you know what I mean …'

This was a different Julian from last week's Julian.

'You mean did he show signs of being radicalised, like they say on the telly? You forgot to ask what mosque, which imam, what school of thought? Some of your mates probably think I don't understand these things, Julian, isn't it? School chef woman—what does she know!'

'I am sorry, Maryam, you are right … It's just that I have to ask, part of the job, you know, and sometimes it may not be easy to find the right words,' Julian said.

'There are no right words, are there. You ought to know … you went to Oxford, didn't you?'

'Cambridge, actually.'

'Same thing … Anyhow, no, Dilly wasn't part of any mosque—since you all think we live in mosques and do bad things there. Dilly said, "Mosque visits are special, Mum, can't do 'em every day."

'There was no mullah either. We call them Imam Sahib, by the way. I don't see any hate preachers with snarling faces roaming around here. Have you even looked around? You know me well enough, Julian, do you think I would've allowed any such character within a hundred miles of my child? Why do you think I didn't mind it when Dilly stayed in his room for hours? You're barking up the wrong tree here, your uppity boss will never get it.'

Julian cleared his throat, smiling inwardly at the mention of his 'uppity boss'. He leaned back in the armchair, its back to the door.

Maryam reclined on the sofa near the windows, streaks of soft sunlight lighting her face and neck. She looked at the evil-eye trinkets hanging from the balcony roof and turned to Julian.

'I don't have a radicalisation story for you, Julian, I really don't. I've got a sad-mum story, a pissed-off mum story … I don't know any more than you do. I don't know what happened to my son, I don't know where he is … If I knew, you'd know. If he had sent me messages, you'd have seen them. If he had been in touch with Saffo or Zarro, you'd have known. If he was, you know, putting photos on Facebook, you'd know before me. Dil left because he was fed up with me. What can I say, it's my fate, my bad kismet, my misfortune. I've lost my mind thinking about it, I have, and I'm tired of it—' She stopped abruptly.

'Maryam, I didn't mean to, but you know, I have to ask …'

'I know you have to ask, and I wish you didn't have to. Or chose not to. I know you must, yet it feels hurtful that I must explain myself. Sometimes I feel I will always be under suspicion, you know what I mean? I feel eyes on me even when no one's looking, and it tears my heart,' she said, rubbing her thumb over a closed fist. Julian felt a wave of sympathy for her, an urge to tell her that he knew what was in her heart, that he believed every word of it.

'A part of me understands and that's what hurts: that you must ask me. I'm not them, Julian. I can't believe it needs to be said, but maybe it always needed to be said.'

Maryam fell silent and turned to look at the trinkets in the balcony again.

Julian stood up from the armchair and moved to the sofa, sitting down at the other end. Then he shifted to the middle, next to her, hands in his lap, eyes on her face. At that moment, he knew if he were called to speak for her at some point, he'd vouch for her truth, the truthfulness of her character.

'I gave birth to a child, a boy, and brought him up as best as I could, Julian. I know what women mean when they say, I gave birth to that child! But it's not just about the birth, is it? It's beautiful, painful, memorable and life-changing, but it's just one event, a big one, yes, but one among many, isn't it? There's an entire life afterwards, isn't there? If you ask me, I'd say the mystique around childbirth has something to do with how men think about it all.

When you give us credit for bringing that beautiful baby into the world, you also hold us responsible for how they turn out to be.

'What was I saying? Yes, birth's just one thing! I don't mean that in a bad way. I brought my son up as well as I could, in the best way, in the way I am, and then, and then, if he has grown up into this—this unimaginable thing ... I am as crushed and furious and mad as any mother would be. A mother whose son has knifed someone, a mum whose child has stolen something from the supermarket, a mother whose child has harmed another child, a mum whose boy has misbehaved with a girl on the bus, do you know what I mean?'

Julian touched her hand.

'You think I don't know how my life is under the microscope all the time, discussed on TV, my life choices questioned by strange men?

'I don't know why I'm telling you all this ... Have you thought about Christmas then? Not a lot of time left now. I might make biryani ... Saffina and Zarrine like it, you know. I am going to miss Dilly, obviously, so I thought we will miss him together. Allah knows what all he must eat these days. Allah only knows.'

THIRTY-ONE

Aunt Sugra said this every time she remembered her husband, Syed Uncle, who had died at Whittington Hospital as she was cleaning his face with cotton wool and spirit. His lungs had given up at last, she said. 'I felt Siddi's presence more when there was silence in the house, it was also then that I could talk to him. His shadow lurked here and there. I saw him standing in the doorways, sitting on the windowsill, walking past the curtains. Siddi chased me around, Maryam, I could feel him.'

Perhaps it becomes easier to feel the presence of a departed one, Maryam thought, remembering Aunt Sugra's words, because it's thrown into contrast by the pitch-dark impossibility of return. Death makes absence tangible, its edges fuller and sharper. When Ash died, she had closed herself off, not let grief take over, willing her legs on so she could do everything they would've done together for their son. Now she felt a stab of guilt at the closure she might feel if Dil was declared dead on TV. Among the dead is—

Why TV, though? She didn't have an answer to this. She had rarely watched the news before, and it was only after Dil disappeared that she'd started to switch to News at 10. Was it because they made important announcements on TV?

The Queen always spoke on TV, the PM too, but so did Anne Widdecombe.

She had spent the week returning to the news bulletins at night. She dreaded the broadcasts and yet couldn't keep away for long, fretting, gloomy, biting her nails.

When Julian came the following week, she watched him suspiciously, nervously, as he spread printouts of ISIS travel maps on the coffee table. She swallowed, trying to act normal. She was distracted by a grey-scale printout with arrowheads curving over it. Why had he brought these? She flinched.

He had come early in the hope that he'd avoid being seen by her bulky shopkeeper friend whose unflinching glare made him uncomfortable.

'You see here, Maryam ... thousands of people travelled ... from all over the world,' he said, his index finger hovering over the trajectories on the first map. 'Many have ended up staying in Syria, Iraq, some are stuck in Turkey, some in between, and many, you know ...' He took his finger away from the printouts.

'You mean died, Julian?'

'How shall I explain this ... It's a very different world over there, Maryam. It's hard for people to come back—'

'Different from what, Julian, from my British-Muslim woman of Indian slash Pakistani extraction world?'

'I meant it's not a conventional war, Maryam, how shall I explain ...'

'I was joking, Julian, do you not remember? That's how that posh lady professor on TV described me after you printed my photo on the front page! Zarro was in splits, said, "Baji came out of a garlic press, innit?"'

'I didn't leak that photo,' Julian protested, smiling, pleading with Maryam. 'But yes, I remember ...'

She pulled the map away from the table with the tips of her fingers and dropped it on the floor, watching him.

'I know what you're trying to tell me, Julian, but I'm not dealing with any kind of war, am I? You all are. All I'm dealing with is my missing son, and I'm dealing with you.'

'Maryam … about Dilawar, what I meant to say earlier,' Julian said, sensing an opportunity, ' … is that it's become quite complicated … They have a dossier on him, it's like a detailed report on a person, a profile … As family liaison, it's my responsibility to keep you informed—'

'I know what a profile is, Julian. I went to school, you know … You said "they", who's they?'

'I'm afraid I can't say more.'

'You just said it's your job to keep me informed.'

'If I'm honest, Maryam, I am not really at liberty … There are rules. But I know you—'

'Do you know me?' Maryam said, leaning back.

'Well, as I've been seeing you … I feel I must tell you the gist at least. I know you wouldn't tell anybody.'

He rolled around a few more sentences in his head and yet he couldn't bring himself to say more. He had, in recent weeks, detected a kind of stillness on Maryam's face, an occasional quietness in otherwise intense, restless eyes. He had earned trust with her, he knew that, but he also knew about her son, where it all might lead. It made him feel sick.

'Who am I going to tell, Julian? Tony, Sheila, Gemma … they don't see me anymore. Tony has become hard of hearing in both ears, I think. And Sheila is as mad as a box of frogs. Still hopes I will take her rubbish out like I used to. It was nothing, though. Poor Sheila, she's seen better days, you know, you should've seen the photos on her walls, the places she's been to. You wouldn't believe it seeing her now, filthy nightrobe-wearing beauty at her doorstep, crumpled garbage bag at her feet. She's been on cruise ships in her day, you know, red swimsuit and fancy sunglasses. God bless Dil, he printed some of her holiday photos, copied them from her ancient album and made large prints for her walls. You see, Sheila's memory is not what it used to be. Dilly got that …'

—

He watched Maryam's face as she talked. Her eyes shone when she spoke, her face glowed, she was beautiful in a way he hadn't encountered before.

Had Maryam been on a cruise holiday? He realised with some embarrassment that he had momentarily contemplated whether or not Muslim women went on cruise holidays.

Had they gone on a holiday together, Maryam and Dilawar? She would've been happy if they had. But the son had now gone on a different sort of vacation, hadn't he, to pursue some crazed dream, some incomprehensible resentment. He recalled Alexei saying the Americans had found thousands of images from Iraq in Dilawar's cloud folders. 'He's lived with photos and videos from Iraq all his life … Gitmo, Abu Ghraib, Faluja, corpses in white phosphorous … the works. He's been following it all the time, like a favourite pastime.'

There was no point telling Maryam about it and he had not seen anything himself. He sighed.

Maryam turned to look at him, then shifted her gaze.

This man had been brought up well, he was considerate, she thought. But what did that mean? Had she done a bad job with Dil? Saffina and Zarrine didn't think so, neither did Tony. Aunt Sugra was properly proud of her, she had said so often, and Ama acknowledged it in her own way. They all loved Dil, they all believed he'd be back, didn't they?

But this man in front of her, this man who looked at her fondly, keenly, and of whom she'd grown a bit fond too, wasn't sure he'd come back. Or maybe he knew where Dil was. He didn't care for her enough to lie to her, or he liked her enough to owe her the truth. She wasn't sure which it was.

'Do you know what,' she said, 'I still think of Dilly as a missing person. As if he's lost in some mystery place, you know, trapped, unable to come home. At other times I think maybe he's in a morgue somewhere, waiting for me to identify him, you know. Cold, frozen in a box, like they show in the films. What I'm trying to say is, when I think through it all, Dilawar as the Swordsman, Iraq, war, ISIS, my heart says, no, he cannot be what you say he has become. I know what a dossier means, Julian, I'm not illiterate. I know the sound of that word. But he's a boy from Walthamstow.' She glared at the map on the floor and imagined burning it on the gas stove.

'They are put together after a lot of work, Maryam. I wanted to tell you earlier but I just couldn't … I'm afraid it's not good news.'

'There's no such thing as good news for me, is there! There's only bad news and worse news. I want you to be honest with me, Julian. Is this what you believe to be true or is it what David has asked you to tell me? Why can't you just find Dil, though? You know where to look, don't you?'

'It's true that a lot of this comes from David. But I also work in an office, with other colleagues, Maryam, you know …'

Maryam had the impression Julian was trying to suggest he was doing her a favour or, at least, he wasn't making much effort to disguise the suggestion.

'We have partners in the US, Maryam, and you didn't hear this from me, but they, the Americans, have a profile on Dilawar. And it's not looking good, Maryam, I thought I should tell you before—'

'Before what?'

'Before you find out anything in the press.'

'Oh, so your boss is going to leak it to the press? Which photo is he going to use this time?'

'Let me finish … As it turns out, Dilawar is one of the more serious cases the Section has been investigating for some time. It's part of our job to …' Julian felt a nervousness, an indecisiveness he hadn't felt before. His throat tasted dry, words felt hard, rough.

When he didn't speak further, Maryam said, 'What does it mean? What aren't you telling me? What am I going to do!' She clutched a corner of her chadar and twisted it around her finger, pulling at it. A cold, sharp spasm ran through her chest. Her face felt warm; she gritted her teeth, trying to keep her breathing down. She wanted to stand up, go through her breathing routine, gaze at Allah and Muhammad in the cabinet, but she remained seated.

'No, Maryam, that's not what I meant at all. I don't know what the office is going to do with this new information, and not everything is confirmed, so please don't worry.'

'Can you stop saying don't worry, don't worry … I'm sure your mates are going to send Dil's bearded photos to the newspapers!'

'Please, let's not rush, Mrs Maryam, a dossier is just a lot of paper sometimes. I'll try to find out more, I promise …'

'Alright, alright, I believe you, Julian. I do, I trust you … Have you noticed you revert to Mrs Maryam sometimes?'

'Oh, you know …'

Maryam thought she might feel dizzy, loops of thought coursing through her head, as she gazed at Julian with a prayer in her eyes.

'Can't you try and get Dilawar out, please,' she said, swallowing.

'I will do everything I can, Maryam … I will do everything in my power,' he said, looking back at her. She met his eyes, then looked down, struggling to keep the tears locked in.

--

At night, she felt a dense, stifling weight on her chest. She thought it was pain and that it was growing. She stayed still, hands grabbing the edge of the mattress, and thought if she died like this, she'd be happy to pass into oblivion while no one knew—that would teach you, Dilly, Mums gone while you're prancing around with murderous pricks somewhere. And then she felt a sweat coming, so she sat up and drank the glass of water on her bedside table. She ran her palm round and round over her breast and thought maybe it wasn't pain as much as a heavy dread, accompanied by a sensation of hollowness in her legs. Weight on the chest and a weightlessness in the legs, this isn't how heart attacks come on, she reasoned and stayed still, not moving from the bed.

It was 3.30 a.m. and she wasn't sure if she had slept much, if she had slept at all. She recalled she had tried stalling the panic after Julian left; she had made an aloo and onion dish, and she'd eaten it with the rice left over from the previous night or the night before … She had watched TV, flicked through the channels—*EastEnders* had turned violent, and she didn't see the point, or maybe some violence had always lurked in that pub, on that street. Then she had smoked a cigarette, a remnant from the Benson & Hedges pack Saffina had left behind some time ago, she hadn't liked the taste of it but had finished it, leaning into the kitchen window where the neighbours wouldn't spot her, if at all anyone still cared to spy on her. How they had watched her from behind curtains and partially open shutters! Then she had made a cup of chamomile tea, more to take the edge off the acrid taste in her throat than to help her sleep because it often didn't make a difference. She had lain awake in bed, going over Julian's words.

He certainly knew more than he let on; he was a nice person, but he was also from the security services; he fancied her, she liked him too, but she needed him to find Dilawar. He had talked about his colleagues, people who knew these things, and he had talked about their *partners* in America, and the dossier on Dil, it all made sense now—always together in these things, America and Britain, isn't it, wars and terror and whatnot! It made perfect sense, though, they had waited all this time to find out more about Dil so they could charge him or whatever, but they had nothing apart from that strange video, so they had to bring him back! Julian knew about it. He was trying to tell her something, and he was right, of course, it wasn't possible for him to share everything with her, he would get into trouble if he did, but didn't he say he would do everything? 'Everything in his power', that's what he said, and he couldn't tell her more, she was a common man after all, common woman, that is, but he wasn't. He was privy to secrets she didn't need to know. All she needed to do was keep reminding him, beg and plead even, so he would do something about Dilly, she just needed to be on it, time was running short, something was definitely going on, she could feel it, so she needed to do something and leave the rest to Allah. It was possible she might even see Dilly soon!

She felt such fear and loneliness that night, and a fear of loneliness she had not known before.

But what if it didn't work out? What if it was all talk, Julian being nice to her, managing his case …? That's when the dread had come sweeping, filling her chest with a pressing weight.

Perhaps the panic was rooted in her own thoughts. She had to try; no matter what went through her crazy head, she had to try; despite all her horrible imaginings, she had to do everything to get Dilly back, Ash would do the same, wouldn't he, together they would do everything to bring him back, but it was only her now, so she had to do everything she could, and leave the rest to Allah.

THIRTY-TWO

The next day was a Sunday, so she stayed in, relieved she didn't have to face anybody. If Ama calls, she told herself, I won't pick up. She spent much of the day in a determined, reflective state. She smiled to herself on thinking she had grown up in these last months, become more herself in a way, even if life had come apart because of Dil.

On Monday morning, she was walking down Enfield Town high street amid a steady stream of shoppers, people who'd come to the Palace Gardens for an early purchase; like most shopping estates in the suburban sprawl of the city, Palace Gardens catered to all—those in search of last year's discounted fashionwear at TK Maxx and budget clothing at H&M, or those shopping for their favourite brands at the old Enfield landmark, Pearsons.

She felt an old freedom walking amidst the people she saw around her; among the many walkers and those getting off buses were all colours and tribes, black, brown, pale, white, and all the shades between. For once, she even liked the smell of the exhaust from the many buses that poured into Church Street, and she liked walking on the coated black asphalt of the road. She was wearing her long brown coat, she'd tied her hair up so she could fit her hat tightly, and she'd put her old sunglasses on.

Earlier in the day, she'd wondered where she could go, then decided against going anywhere near her neighbourhood. She didn't want to bump into someone from the school, and she didn't want people gawking at her.

So here she was, walking down Church Street, taking in the smells of old Enfield. 'This is where the world's first ATM was installed,' Ashfaq had said to her many years ago, pointing to the Barclays Bank building on whose front wall was a large black-and-white photo showing a crowd in front of a cash machine. They had come to buy curtains for their flat. The moment had passed unremarked, and now, so many years later, she knew what it was about cashpoints that she found peculiar. They were places of loneliness, designed to encourage distance: you were meant to stay aloof, keep your distance ... What if they had never been invented, she thought. Then people would queue up next to one another, talk to each other or to the bank teller at least, maybe even bump into Sheila with her giant cheque book. Yes, these were places of loneliness. She hadn't said any of this to Ashfaq then.

Even though she was certain she'd disguised herself well, she bent her head when people passed by, trying to appear casual at the same time. Now and then she glanced at her reflection in the shop windows and was satisfied—who was this stylish woman in a dark brown winter coat, her head covered with a round hat, a large, coloured jute bag in her hand, walking alone in front of the shops? Not many would be able to tell it was that Maryam Ali, she reassured herself, even as, looking at the reflection keeping pace with her in the glass fronts, she felt a certain sorrow.

Maryam walked all the way to the end of the street, past the old Sunday market, past the Barclays building where the first cash machine had sprouted currency in 1967, and stopped at the busy crossing that led to Great Cambridge Road. There was a wide pavement in front of the pub and restaurant across the street. She crossed over and sat on a bench. When was the last time she'd sat on a roadside bench, she wondered. Hope no one thinks I'm a homeless person—you're not in those kinds of clothes, what are you thinking, Mams! She looked at the pigeons stuttering in front of her and lit a cigarette. She didn't really like smoking, she'd decided a long time ago, but these days she sometimes felt she needed it. Cars, pedestrians, young mums in stylish pink-and-beige tracksuits, with over-accessorised push chairs gliding in front of them, and old women with shopping wheelies passed by. She blew smoke as a group of youngsters with JD Sport and TK Maxx shopping bags walked past: loud, gesticulating, animated, a few smoking like her. She liked them.

She was prevaricating, she knew, but she wanted to buy these things she hadn't bought for so long. That's what she'd come for. She crushed the cigarette with her heel and got up, looking left and right to check if anyone had been looking.

She walked back halfway and took a left turn near the Waterstones where a pedestrian path led into the shopping complex. Ahead of her was a glass-panelled bridgeway that probably connected one part of the building to another. Further up to her left, there was a WH Smith, and a few pop-up shops in the centre of the path, which sold jewellery, perfumes, watches, wallets and glittering phone cases. She walked past a bright pedicure booth and thought of Zarrine and Saffina—they didn't know about her shopping trip. She didn't want them to know.

She arrived at the M&S store after three more turns and at once felt intimidated by the revolving door in front of her (there's nothing wrong with straight doors, you know, she muttered to herself), but she braved it, anxious the doors might close on her too quickly.

She made it in and gazed at the bulging food aisles everywhere on the ground floor, the cheery, colourful Fruit & Veg aisles, and shelves and shelves of juices and health drinks and sandwiches and whatnot. She stopped near the flowers lined up against the wall to her left, breathing in the fragrance from the bouquets of jasmine, lilies, roses, carnations, rhododendron foliage, iris blue, narcissus, white protea, and the many potted orchids. Flowers should never have become expensive, she decided, and walked on.

She took an escalator up to Womenswear, nervous suddenly. Not too many shoppers at this hour, she thought, that was good. A senior looking M&S woman was talking to a young attendant behind the till. Dresses, skirts, shirts and trousers everywhere, scarves, hats and bags here and there, on mannequins, hangers, racks and shelves. Line after line. She touched the front of a tea-coloured cashmere jumper, its top lined with silver threads, and it felt very soft but the colour was dull. Then she looked at New Arrivals: coats, jumpers and jackets, all bright and shiny, purple and green and red, orange even. When she was a young girl, most stores around her sold black, brown and navy, didn't they? She wondered why. She would like the beautiful bottle-green overcoat on the mannequin with stunning eyelashes, the matching scarf and hat too.

But that's not what she'd come here for, she thought, as she hurried off to the far corner where the lingerie section was and strolled lazily, taking in the scene as if she was on an inspection. It was exceedingly bright in this section. What am I doing here, why am I doing this? Maybe they're right, after all, maybe Maryam has lost her mind. Maybe I have. Lost my mind.

With these and many other thoughts running circles in her head, she crept close to a table with a laminated card that read 'New'. She looked at all the display bras hanging fruit-like from a tree stand: pink, red, purple, sea-green, maroon, chocolate-brown, fawn, pale, sunny yellow, dark blue, black and white. A half mannequin hoisted on a stool wore a golden bra with a subtle lace pattern lining the border on the cups. She thought it was astonishingly beautiful. There was an outline of a dried water drop on the mannequin's collar bone. The lace on the bra was a darker shade of the main colour, she noticed on closer inspection, and went back to check other bras from the same line. She couldn't recall the last time she'd felt happy in this way. Then she remembered. Of course!

The last time she'd bought pretty underwear was a long time ago, a few years before Ash passed away. Saffo had given her a spa coupon for her birthday, after which they'd gone shopping together. 'You've got to look after yourself, Baji, you work so hard, what's all the money for, haan?'

She'd bought two then, a blue silken one and a black bra with no wires. That life was over when Ash left, although ... although, should it really have? But it did, maybe that was how it was meant to be. You became Mums, do-it-all parent, isn't it, the mother woman. Or maybe that wasn't how it was meant to be.

She sensed a liberation, as though she had been freed from chains, and at the same time, she felt guilty. With a growing and then a grown son at home, she had felt tied down, in service of his needs and life, and although she had been happy to be this person, the mother woman, now that he had betrayed her, negated her, she felt those suppressed, unacknowledged parts of herself come to the surface—to her great agony, confusion, and an excitement which she didn't want to name. She felt freed from a past burden even as she was weighed down by present worries.

She picked a peach-coloured set, checked the label for the size, momentarily unsure because she thought she had put on some weight since, since ... she couldn't remember, then grabbed two skin-coloured vests, three pairs of socks, and a bag of scrunchies for her hair. She hadn't bought these in a while either. £5.99 for velvet green, purple and maroon scrunchies inside a plastic case, nice and soft, in the nice way they always make them. Wish they did halal food too, but they don't, I wonder why.

With the little things in the basket near her feet, she checked herself in the life-size mirror attached to a pillar and turned this way and that, looking at her body, her sides, taking her hat off, putting it back on. She picked up the bra and placed it in front of her in a way she thought was sufficiently surreptitious. Then she imagined how she might look in the peach panty, but while she liked its style and texture, she was unsure about the colour, so she went back to look at other colours. Something brighter, bolder maybe, she thought as she strolled amid the racks. She sighed. She smiled.

At the till, the young black woman she'd seen earlier gave her a broad smile and started scanning Maryam's purchases. Maryam thought she approved of her choices and stood quietly in front of her, thinking, thinking, picking bits of skin from the inside of her lip with her teeth as if plucking and crushing tiny seeds. She hadn't bought much for herself in quite some time, she thought as she left the pay counter, feeling the cool green M&S bag to check everything was in there. Then she took the down escalator.

As she was walking down the red-tiled footpath out of the shopping complex, she suddenly remembered Aunt Kulsum talking about Pearsons of Enfield once, how big a deal it was that her husband Showki had signed a contract with the store to supply carpets or rugs or doormats, she couldn't recall exactly. 'We are basically the main supplier only,' Kulsum had said. 'You must go there with Ashfaq, no, nice rooftop restaurant they have on the top floor only.' *Where else would they have a rooftop restaurant, you thick woman, on your backside,* Maryam remembered thinking at the time and sharing the joke with Ama on the phone later that day. Silly old Aunt Kulsum, she said to herself.

She went back in, found the side entrance to Pearsons, and was soon looking at the lunch cart in the Skylight restaurant on the top floor. She found a table by a window and sat there, plonking her shopping bag in the opposite chair. What would she not give to have one hour, *one hour* with Ash in the seat in front of her. But then, she didn't have much to give now, did she, hardly anything. But really, what would she not do to have Ash with her, right here, right now, at home with her, the two of them searching for Dil together, fighting to bring him home somehow. Together, they'd do anything to get him back from Iraq, that's where they said he was. There was still time to find him, to bring him home.

She had a lunch of vegetarian pasta bake with peppers and courgettes sticking out at the edges, a side of hand-cut fries, and salad in a small plastic case. Could you not find a smaller bowl, she thought as she tried to fork a slice of cucumber. We gave larger bowls to the kids at school, for god's sake. What's happened to England? Ek toh poori duniya behenchod vegetarian ho gayi hai, and then you serve salads in these squirrel pots, she thought as the cucumber slice jumped out and fell into her lap, leaving a wet spot on her shirt. Then she saw that the wet patch was reddish, so she peered into the bowl and noticed that the cucumber slices had turned purple and soggy at the edges because of the red cabbage underneath. Keep your fucking salad, fellas, take it home to your naani.

Outside the window, long beams of blue light shone on the mouldy, brown-grey rooftops across the road and slid down to the streets below. The well-groomed tops of the hedges separating the driveways in front of the houses flashed silver. On the pavements, there were patches of shade and light, shadows or wet patches left from car washes or from the rain overnight. She thought of Aunt Kulsum again, and laughed a little.

THIRTY-THREE

Maryam lay still in the bathtub, the water calm around her as she watched soap bubbles circle slowly. She closed and opened her eyes, took a deep breath, watching steam gather in the corners and dim light filter through the frosted window. As she stood up, she looked at the thin streaks of water running down her breasts, her belly, along her hips. She ran her palms down her sides and front, and watched the water collect near her feet and trickle towards the drain hole.

As she stepped out of the tub, she caught a glimpse of herself in the clouded mirror at the wash basin, her wet hair splashing past a corner. Then she turned to look at herself in the long mirror on the opposite wall, considering her body, turning at slight angles, admiring herself. As she dried herself with the bath towel, she felt she smelled nice. She sprayed some perfume from the red glass bottle she kept at the back of the cabinet and left the bathroom. It was a present from Ama, an expensive sample from a perfumery in Marrakesh, her mother had said. 'Jasmine, aloe vera, orange and rosewater!'

—

She brought out the pale pink, embroidered shalwar kameez from her cupboard, the creases and pleats on it sharp from the steam press, and spread it on the bed to let it breathe. She put some moisturiser on her face, applying it twice around her eyes, rubbing it into the creases. Then she put on the new deodorant, looking at the blue waves drawn around the name, Ocean Mist. She tore off the packaging of the panty and slipped into it, pulling it up, letting it relax around her.

She clasped the bra on her back, then adjusted it around a few times, her bust full under it—had she picked a size small, she wondered. She put on the new vest next but took it off promptly. It was thick, too much fabric, she thought. She folded it into a compact square and shoved it under her clothes on the middle shelf. As she pushed the pile back, the old blue bra poked out of a corner. She had bought it years ago to surprise Ash; should've seen his eyes! She thrust it back before she could sink further into thinking about those days. Her hair was still moist, and it made the neck of her shirt wet too, but that was alright, she decided.

She draped her chadar like a long V-neck, pressing the fold onto her chest. She looked at herself in the mirror and saw droplets of perspiration on her chin; she felt some wet patches on her body too, the kurta sticking to her skin. She sighed, exhaling a few times; her stomach turned cold suddenly, so she sat down on the bed. A chill ran through her, rushing in her heart. She tried to calm herself, breathing slowly, telling herself to relax, hands on her hips, a prayer on her lips.

She stood up to look in the mirror once more, turning left and right at slight angles. She was right not to apply lipstick, she thought, it wouldn't work well with this kameez and chadar. She dabbed at her cheeks, ran her fingers through her hair, pushing back a few strands behind the ears, and started for the door.

Then she stopped and picked up Ama's perfume bottle from the table where she'd left it, tilted it against her palm, and ran her hand over her throat and shoulders. She left the bedroom.

--

Julian was waiting in the living room, unable to stop himself from thinking about the first time he'd come to this house. Back then, he had come to Dilawar Ali's address, to 22 Homecroft Street. The address was part of the police summary, along with a few lines about the Missper case: 20-year-old Muslim IT worker/Freelance jobs in East London/South Asian, Mixed-race, lives with mother Maryam Ali/Father Ashfaq Ali alias Ash Ali, deceased. Friends and family spoken with/No red flags/Presumed missing/ absconding.

He remembered being struck by the word 'absconding': how does one abscond from living with your mother, how does one abscond from life? He also recalled that the phrase 'clean history' had been crossed out in one place.

There was that, and then there was the J-Sec version in which Dilawar Ali was the IT whiz who led a parallel life online, working with an ISIS chapter all the way in Iraq, setting up and running their transnational internet networks. One of the networks, Alexei had said, was hosted from a defunct gaming chatroom, which Dilawar Ali had reengineered to function as a 'recruiting sauna room', facilitating the flight of men and women from the US, the UK, Australia, Canada …

--

Maryam walked in with a glass of water and put it down on the coffee table. She sat in her usual corner on the sofa and flicked back strands of moist hair from her face. Julian noticed she was wearing the striking pale pink shalwar kameez he'd seen her in a few months ago.

She was silent, calm, pretty, a hesitant, enigmatic look on her face. She looked like a girl.

No, he can't, he shouldn't, he must not.

He had imagined kissing her many times, holding her, touching her; he'd imagined seeing her body. There was something about her today, something that suggested an openness, her fragile loneliness an invitation. He didn't want to dwell on it; it was fraught with danger, time pressing on the moment with a brittle force. There was no coming back from such a moment. He sat motionless, feeling as though he was in love with her, swallowing nervously like his younger self would have—unsteady hands, shallow breath, conscious of every movement and yet unsure. All these sensations made more acute by his feeble attempts at concealment. What a tangle he had got himself into, he thought as he watched Maryam, her beautiful face, her liquid dark eyes, the deep sorrow in them, her scarf hanging loosely on her shoulders, her bright skin. He took a long breath as he watched her face in the streaky sunlight filtering through the gaps in the curtains.

Maryam wanted to forget. She longed to cast off the erosive shadow of pain that had resided inside her since that doleful morning in February. She wanted to be herself, for herself; she had been that other person for too long. She felt a flutter of anticipation that she hadn't known since Ash, and it frightened her. Taking a deep breath, she stood up and walked to his chair. She felt a warmth rising to her face as she looked at him. Then she stopped, touched her hand to his wrist and said, 'Come, come with me.'

Julian felt a burst of happiness, nervousness and fear as he walked behind her, his pulse racing. They were in the hallway now, and he was unable to take his eyes off her back and waist, where, perhaps because of the angle of the light, he could see through her shirt how she'd tied her shalwar. As he took a long breath in, he smelled those flowers again, lavender and orange probably, summer breeze in the park, and a hint of her own scent perhaps. It was this last whiff, he would try to remember its specific tinge later, that took him to a place where he knew without a doubt that he wanted to be with her, no matter what.

Maryam nudged open the last door on her left, opposite Dil's room, and walked into her bedroom. She led him to the armchair near the bed and turned back to shut the door.

Julian rested his hands in his lap and watched her turn the doorknob. Her hair had left a wet patch on her shirt at the back, a small map clinging to her skin. He closed his eyes as she came back and stood next to him. He could hear her breathing.

Outside in the garden, a steady breeze skimmed through the bamboo reeds at the fence, creating a low hiss and a rhythmic flutter. Maryam heard its echo against her window. It was late afternoon, the early winter sun's long arms wading through the trees in the garden, reaching across the grass and the flower beds, then sliding up to her curtains where they created a pattern of light and shade. She knew this light well and it brought her a sense of calm.

The bedroom felt warm and secret to her, the latter a sensation she hadn't known for many years. She sat down and adjusted her chadar, tugging at it. She ran her fingers through her hair, looking sideways at the mirror where she saw a glimpse of herself and Julian sitting, she on her bed, he in what used to be Ash's armchair. She leaned forward and touched the hair on his forehead, swallowed, smiled.

Then she took a deep breath, as if about to launch into a dive, and took his hand in hers.

Julian saw that she was trembling, her chest rising and falling against the beautiful pale pink fabric. She took his right hand and placed it on her chest. She could feel her heart pounding against it.

He let his hand stay there, feeling the heat of her skin. For a moment, it seemed unreal, something from the depths of his mind rather than real life; he couldn't believe his eyes, so he closed them.

He had imagined this moment often, probably every day during the last few months, but hadn't allowed his imagination to soar higher, run too far. There was some dampness under his fingers, and he opened his eyes to look at her face, to understand her. He saw thin strings of perspiration on her upper lip, starting to run down.

Julian saw himself tower over her, his shoulders covering hers entirely. Then he kissed her, lightly, quickly. The shalwar kameez looked beautiful on her, and he wanted to say that, but something held him back. He didn't need to. She rested her chin on his chest, her eyes still closed. He sensed an edge of tension or unease—he couldn't quite put his finger on it, but he ignored it.

His hand ran down her back, his fingers tracing the valley of her spine, her skin smooth and warm.

'Would you like to see me,' Maryam said suddenly. When he didn't answer, she withdrew and stood in front of him, her arms crossed. She relaxed her hands, tilted her head and gave him a smile, her upper lip curving. Was that forced, Julian wondered, but he was distracted as she rested one hand on her waist. Maryam stood still, waiting, he thought, inviting him to admire her.

'What are you thinking,' she said, smiling.

'That you are … absolutely gorgeous … Maryam,' he said, drawing in a long breath.

Glitter-like beads of sweat had collected under Maryam's chin. A thin thread ran down the side of her throat and there were wet smudges on her midriff. The bedroom door was locked, he knew.

--

Standing by his cash register, Tony looked at his watch again. By his calculation, the lanky blonde man from the government had been at Maryam's for more than an hour already. Same as usual, or was it longer, he wondered, and rolled a cigarette with his brass brown fingers. He mostly came on the weekends, this young man, didn't he? He hadn't seen the other two men in a long time, but the smart, fit woman still came, every few weeks. But not today, eh. He drew hard on his cigarette and exhaled towards the peninsula of stains on the plaster-board ceiling. He really should think less of Maryam and those who visited her, he thought. It's not as if he himself had been to see her ever since ...

Maryam found herself sweating next to Julian, teary-eyed, startled by the realisation of where she was, what she was doing, at the smell of this man, at the knowledge of who he was, but she stayed where she was.

As Julian felt her breath, her body, he sensed the peculiar warm singe of lust in his nostrils as he breathed.

He drew her face up and kissed her carefully on the lips, then let her rest her head on his chest.

A moment later, she grabbed his arm with some force, her breathing heavy. Then she spoke. 'Julian, tell me something ... I know you've said it before, but I want to hear it again. Will you bring Dilly home? I want you to promise me.'

'What?'

'Will you promise you will bring him back? I believe you, all of it, so please bring him home. Please ...' she said.

'Well ...' Julian touched her shoulder. 'I'm doing everything I can, Maryam ...' He pulled away slowly so he could see her face. 'I will bring him back.'

As he pushed her away gently to let some light come between them, Maryam gripped his hand. 'Thank you. You are the nicest man I've met,' she began, then stopped, liquid gathering in her eyes. She breathed in a few times, looking up at the curtained window.

She became aware of the sounds from outside, the leaf buzz from the garden, the filtered drone of TV, radio and chit-chat from the other flats, the static from the houses on the other side of the garden, the distant hum of motorway traffic, the sound of life in the world outside.

She sighed, then turned to look at him, and said, 'We should stop, Julian, whatever this is … You have been nice to me, and you know I like you, but let's just stop … I'm sorry, I'm …' She lost her bearing, her breath shaky. 'What am I doing, what the hell am I doing? This is wrong, Maryam, stop right now … Allah toba, Allah toba!' She put her hands on her chest and leaned back, her eyes downcast, almost folding down on the bed, curling into herself as if she wanted to get back to a self she'd walked out of, leaving Julian silent, stunned, his face like stone.

'I did this. I did this,' she said in a dry voice, a fleeting sense of loss washing over her.

She gathered herself up as fat tears rolled down her cheeks; she wished they wouldn't. She didn't sob. Sitting on her bed, she felt sad and crushed somehow. She bent her head and, catching a glimpse of her legs which she had shaved the day before, felt a deep mortification, like a cold hard brick in her gut. Not only at what she'd tried to do, but at what she had wanted. Then some resignation, relief, and a kind of satisfaction.

'I am so sorry, Maryam, I couldn't resist—'

'Yes, I know, who could … I am irresistible,' she said, sniffling a little, her eyes filling up once more, but she was determined not to cry, not now, not again. And she didn't.

'I feel as if I have …'

'Can you not make it worse, Julian, please? Can you not talk for once, can you just shut up.'

PART V

THIRTY-FOUR

It's a hot, sunny day in the park grounds, faces flushed salmon pink. Long beams of sunlight, like those behind Mecca and Medina in Islamic calendars, descend from the field maple visible in the photo. Zarrine has a green plastic bat in her hands, pretending to acknowledge applause from imaginary spectators after having reached some milestone. Saffina has her hands on her waist, waiting for her sister to settle down at the crease. Dil is captured waving his arms, ball in one hand—he's laughing and he appears to be approaching Zarrine. What had made him laugh in that manner, walking towards his aunt at the other end? It was some dispute in the game; the sisters had probably had an argument that Dil found amusing; or was it something she had said?

Maryam had taken the photo while sitting on the picnic blanket, she remembered. She drew it closer and touched Dil's face. The light from the ceiling lamp in his bedroom cast a shiny gloss on the faces. She put the photo in her lap and looked at it again, considering the scene from a distance. 'That's alright, Maryam,' she thought. 'It's been a while.'

--

Maryam had spent the last few days in quiet reflection, pacing now and then in the flat, rewinding what had happened with Julian, or seated in front of the TV, listening to the recitations of naat on one of the free-to-view Islamic channels. A young woman with a sweet face had a sonorous, affecting voice, but she found the others boring. Though a part of her couldn't quite believe what she had done, and wanted to do, she had arrived at some sort of peace with herself, recurring pangs of guilt notwithstanding. And yet, in her conscious deliberations, she found herself asking, what's wrong with it? She had allowed another man to touch her for the first time in years, and she couldn't lie to herself—she had liked it. When had it been written in her destiny that she couldn't?

Julian hadn't been to see her since then, but it hadn't been too long; she was overthinking it. And did she really want him to come? The time before last, he'd said, 'It's not looking good, Maryam ...' But he'd also said, 'I will bring him back'. She did want to see him, though, if she was being completely honest, despite everything ... It was always nice to see him.

Perhaps because she didn't want to dwell too much on it, or perhaps because she was frightened of what she might do next, she had gone back to the photo albums.

—

At the picnic in the wetlands, they had sat under a large willow, some of whose branches dipped into the water; Dilawar had helped her spread the blanket and sheet she'd packed. 'I'm going to lie down a bit ... Where's my cushion?'

It was a clear day at the waterfront, with wildfowl swimming near the leaf-shaded banks, the water a bright screen of green. She had stretched her legs, with the cushion under her arm, and felt a calm she had rarely felt after Ash's passing. This is good, we should do this more often, she'd thought, as she looked at Dilawar and Saffina and Zarrine.

Maryam had come here once before, on a school trip a few years ago for which she'd volunteered. This part of the wetlands had just been opened to the public after improvements. She'd liked the long walkways, the wooden bridges, and the old brick buildings in which she had found a likeness of the pastel houses she would see in the children's books she sometimes leafed through at school. She'd heard two teachers separately tell the children that it was the largest or one of the largest wetlands in Europe.

THIRTY-FIVE

Tony looked at the damp front pages of the newspapers and sighed. He grabbed the two stacks and brought them in. The van turned the corner at speed, pressing on the road, screeching, as if running away from a crime scene.

He untied the cords and picked up the two papers one by one. Fucking hell, he muttered to himself. Skimming the banner headlines, he thought of Maryam at once. He missed the way she used to say 'Tony' every time she came into the store. She stretched the 'O' in the nicest, sweetest way. No one did it better, no one. Taownay, she'd say! He put the kettle on and flipped through the inside pages. He hadn't had his first tea yet and it wasn't possible to think straight without. He took the PG Tips bag out of the cup and started to laugh. 'It's disgusting to keep it in there for so long, give it to me … Do you have a spoon here,' and with that, he remembered, this attractive Indian woman who had bought one of the flats off Homecroft, had deftly squeezed the teabag and thrown it away. Fucking hell, what does time do, eh? He read the headlines and subheads again.

Mother of all bombings.
ISIS rats start to flee.
Iraqis celebrate.

US & British warplanes unleash hell.

He rolled a cigarette, smoked it all while drinking his tea, folded the less lurid of the two papers and pulled the shutter down.

She has to know, he convinced himself, as he thrust the newspaper through her letter box. Of course, it was going to worry her, but he supposed the time for giving her less cause for concern was over a long time ago. Fucking unbelievable, he mumbled, as he kicked away a few wrappers by his shopfront and went back in.

How many years had it been since the protests? Twelve years, thirteen? They'd all gathered at his store, 'Drinks on me', he'd said, and handed out water bottles, packets of crisps, KitKats, and brought out two Fruit Shoot bottles from the fridge. He had given one to Maryam's little boy—how old was he then, eight or nine?—and handed the other to Maryam. 'For the ride back home, darling, it's going to be a long day.' They had set out together from his store, their placards, banners, badges and T-shirts emblazoned with bright slogans.

Not in My Name
Hands off Iraq
Make Tea Not War
Lies, Lies, Lies
Say No to War
Don't Bomb Iraq

They had taken the tube to Central, their little anti-war group, Tony, Sheila, Gemma, Gemma's three daughters, Maryam and her husband Ash, and their little boy Dilawar. He had been at the front, Tony remembered, he had organised the whole thing, provided the cardboards and the paint, and then they had marched with the rest of the city, with the rest of the world, a throbbing sea of people sweeping across London, shouting slogans against the impending invasion of Iraq. Ash had carried his son on his shoulders near about Trafalgar Square, or maybe it was Parliament Street. Excited little fellow, he had raised his fist too, and answered to the slogans in his young voice, gazing around himself, his eyes wide open. How old was he then?

'It's the customers, Maryam, I would've seen you every day, darling, but business is low as it is. Some of our neighbours, I'm telling you, are total knobs, don't get me started, love, they wouldn't come in if they knew ... Don't get me started, the things they say, fucking hell, I'm so sorry, Maryam,' he muttered to himself and rolled another cigarette.

THIRTY-SIX

Maryam saw golden flames licking the top of the screen as the news presenter, a short-haired brown woman who wore bright red lipstick, read the headlines. It was as if she were looking into Maryam's eyes, speaking to her. She declared in a clipped, serious voice that the US-led campaign against the Islamic State and its affiliates had achieved a major breakthrough. 'Iraqi special forces have made rapid advances and recaptured many ISIS-held areas in the south. Aided by US, British and NATO jets, Iraqi troops have now started marching towards the last few cities under the control of the Islamist group …'

A ticker ran like a merry-go-round, showing the same thing over and over: *Biggest allied campaign in post-war history. White House spokesperson: The United States is determined to liberate the people of Iraq.* It ran to the end of the screen, the words sliding into view one after the other, as if in a tight chase, then looping back hurriedly.

She followed the words for a while, hypnotised by their white charge. She was clutching the end of the arm rest, her palm pressing against the fabric. She'd started watching the news regularly after Dil disappeared, but now, after Tony pushed the newspapers through her door, she made sure she didn't miss anything. God bless Tony.

The announcer cut to a correspondent who wore a blue helmet and a jacket that said 'Press'. He said something Maryam didn't fully register and switched to shots of debris, dust clouds, ammunition-laden aircraft, feet of dead bodies, shoelaces undone, then cut to a night-time film of the bombardment, the skies lit up by bright trains of arcing missiles, followed by incandescent flashes at invisible targets.

Outside her window, it was raining hard, a constant drum of raindrops on the tiles of her balcony, on the four flowerpots that hung by the rails, on the grass and the plants and trees in the garden. Had she put clothes out to dry in the garden? No, that was last week, wasn't it? Oh, but maybe she had hung some in the balcony. She should check. It was cold, what was she thinking putting clothes out to dry; or maybe she had done it because the sun had come out briefly during the day.

The foreign correspondent was back on the screen. He was sitting down, pointing to shrapnel on a debris-strewn street. He cut to a clip of US soldiers loading ammunition into the hull of an aircraft as if loading crates of fruit. He came back on and put a hand to his helmet as he spoke. 'Last night, we received footage from a militant stronghold in an undisclosed location, accompanied by a statement, which we have summarised for our viewers back home. It says, and I quote, "We will fight until the last invader has been driven out of our nation. We will fight unto death." We must, of course, remind our viewers that this cannot be independently confirmed.'

Then he switched to a dimly lit film of men on rooftops with missile launchers and machine guns on their shoulders. They were on the move, stopping to take positions in a rehearsed manner, then on the move again. Another close-up showed a small group huddled together; some of them had half covered their faces with black scarves and handkerchiefs.

'Just to remind our viewers, this is from two days ago, and we have had no further contact since … As you can imagine, it's a very fluid situation here. The scenario on the ground is changing fast, every day brings new developments. Senior US military officials told me earlier that, in many areas of the country, the militants are on the run. It is, of course, too early to tell whether these are, indeed, the last days of the so-called Islamic State and the end of American and British involvement here in Iraq. But as you can imagine from the deafening roar of the fighter jets above me, the international campaign is in full swing and shows no signs of stopping … A veteran Middle East analyst said it would seem that the outgoing US president is keen to bring American troops home and perhaps declare a victory … Back to you in the studio.'

Maryam stared at the last images and heard the woman with red lipstick say that they were going to speak with an expert in the studio. She felt a sudden chill in her stomach, so she stood up and walked to the window. Parting the curtains, she saw it was still raining, and a wet haze had spread across the garden, through which were visible the melancholic silhouettes of the hedges and trees at the fence. There were no clothes on the clothesline. She closed the curtains, her breathing so unsteady that it surprised her. Then she sat down and tried to calm herself. It's alright, Maryam, it's alright, don't panic.

After drinking a glass of water in the kitchen, her legs weak, she walked into Dilawar's room, spread the prayer mat near his bed and started to pray. The room was completely silent. It was well past the maghrib namaz, but she was convinced Allah wouldn't mind her inconsistent prayer times considering what she'd been going through. Just as she was about to start, she remembered she hadn't performed the Wuzu, so she rushed back to her bathroom—always her own bathroom for the Wuzu—and came back in a quieter, calmer mood. She glanced at the side of the bed where she had sat with Julian, then turned her eyes away and fixed her gaze on the images of Mecca and Medina in the top corners of the prayer mat.

In the third raqat, as she did her ruku and sajda, she cried. She cried quietly, suppressing her sobs, but letting the tears fall freely. Allah listened to the sighs of the broken-hearted, she'd often heard Ama say, so she opened her heart out and asked Allah to protect her son. 'Just keep him safe, Allah Mian, wherever he is, please protect my child. Forgive him if he has strayed.' Then she begged forgiveness for herself for last week. For what might have happened. She didn't feel shame because she had liked the touch of a man, she said to Allah. That moment would remain in her heart forever. She felt remorseful because she had allowed herself to expect a favour in return. Or maybe she was ashamed on all counts, she didn't know, but she asked for forgiveness from the depths of her heart and hoped Allah would forgive her. I have nothing to hide, you know what's in my heart, she said.

THIRTY-SEVEN

It was a cold and quiet Tuesday morning, November's seeping chill had settled on London, and the blushed, late autumn colours of brown, yellow and maroon covered swathes of Alexandra Park, thanks to the larches, beeches, oaks and field maples. Jigsaw patches of sapphire shone through the masses of clouds here and there. The air, though biting on contact with the face, had a freshness to it. Nothing could keep Julian's mind away from Maryam—from the pangs of mortification, sadness, guilt and thrill he felt each time he thought back to the Saturday at her house: her touch, her fragrance, her crumpled form on the bed, her tears, her sniffling smile at the end. He walked on in the cold, hands in the pockets of his light puffer jacket, going round and round the same curving path.

A while later, he stepped out of the park in the direction of the Sable D'Or café on Muswell Hill Broadway, in the vague hope that he could sit by himself and somehow break the racing chains of thought in his head. It didn't take him long to get to the café, and he was grateful for the warmth inside.

He sat at his usual table and watched the passers-by outside. He used to like observing the kinds of coats people wore as winter approached. A tall woman was trying to fasten the seatbelt on her child's pram while balancing a coffee in her other hand. As she turned to go round the buggy, she caught sight of Julian looking at her and smiled hesitantly. Julian stared, his mind elsewhere, his chest tight, but recovered his poise to return the smile. The woman had long legs, the deep blue jeans elegant and stylish over brown boots. She had dark hair and she was wearing a beige mohair jacket. She pushed back loose strands of hair inside her hat, checked her child's seatbelt and moved on, turning back briefly towards Julian in the café window. She appeared self-conscious, he thought. He'd made her so by seeming to stare at her; he wanted to tell her he hadn't been looking *at* her, his mind had been elsewhere.

He simply couldn't shake off the tension coursing in his head. Maryam's touch was fresh in his mind, her words alive, ringing and stinging, and his promise to her a real thing. He had uttered the words. Why had he done that?

'I believe you, so bring him back,' she had said.

He had kissed her and when he held her, she felt delicate of build and beautiful. He'd sensed she wanted to feel protected and safe with him.

--

At four-thirty in the afternoon, Julian saw a message from Alexei marked urgent on the J-Sec app. There was to be a briefing at 1600 hrs the next day. *Importance: High.* He opened and closed the message a few times, as though it might reveal something more about the purpose of the meeting, a familiar dread rising up in him. Urgent briefings were usually called when a new case arrived or a case was nearing closure. He had skipped office for two days, but knew he would have to go tomorrow.

When he entered the conference room the next day, the blinds were down and the wall-mounted screen lit. It reflected the long oval table, the trays of coffee and biscuits, and the fuzzy faces of the men and one woman seated around it. Hannah was in the far corner with a tablet in her lap. She sat next to David, on whose other side stood Ispahani behind a chair, leaning in.

When everybody had settled down, Alexei displayed a large map of Iraq showing the movement of Iraqi forces and the expanse of the aerial campaign. 'It's evident the situation has changed rather fast,' David began. 'It's also clear there's bound to be spillage as they ramp it up, as people flee ...' Julian was struggling to focus, but knew he had to stay alert. As Alexei went through more slides, he contemplated how he might slip out if he needed to.

'You know what BBC is,' David said.

'Of course—'

'Not that one. It's short for baseball card. Across the pond, they use them to put together a profile, an ID. And once they have a PID, they're likely to go for a kinetic strike—'

Indicating with a raised palm that he didn't want questions at this stage, he continued, 'The authorisation protocol is tiered and stepwise, escalated as and when required.'

It was a barrage of information from then on. How was he supposed to know about fucking baseball cards, and how did it matter to him, for fuck's sake. PID, HVI and APG ... A part of him felt relieved he didn't have full access to the classified drives, that he was family liaison ... And yet, he felt frustrated he couldn't check the new files himself, even as he suspected he wouldn't be able to find much on the shared drive. It was likely that Ispahani had kept 'sensitive files' firewalled from everybody except the boss. David probably had a separate channel with his friends in DC too, with the mysterious Oskar, but equally, it was also possible David was simply relaying what he'd been told down the phone line, following protocol.

In any case, all this about HumInt, SigInt and the like felt distant, alien somehow. Still, he couldn't help rolling the acronyms in his head, staring at Alexei as he made notes on a tablet. There was one phrase that struck him more than the others—APG. Aerial precision geolocation.

What the hell, David. We don't have a positive ID, we really don't, you said so yourself. Or maybe David was testing the theory … But hang on a moment, he thought, if he was referring to a high value individual, that was good, wasn't it?

A fucking baseball card!

Why was he sitting here, he thought, like an obedient apprentice listening to the master? He was a case officer, the human face to interact with the parents. He had been trained to spend time with the families, get inside their homes to gain insight. But look where that had got him.

Alexei brought up a fresh slide. Textboxes, maps, charts, question marks inside hooded figures, grainy photographs, colour codes, organisational structure diagrams.

'The presence of the HVI in Mosul simplifies the picture,' David said, turning to Julian. 'If the cousins have eyes on the HVI, everything else becomes secondary, I'm sure you follow me …'

Of course he did, David, of course he did. A lot of dossier-speak, the kind of BS left after multiple redactions on the way to my desk.

David took a sip from his orange juice and grabbed some nuts from the bowl in front of him.

'I suppose this is not really about our hideaway from Walthamstow,' he said, taking a long pause, looking around him. 'Oskar's people aren't interested in our boy anymore, Julian. Yes, they have this profile of him, but it's the HIVs they really want. Dilawar Ali is small fry.'

Everybody around the table looked on in silence. Julian lowered his eyes.

'Of course, we are going to wait for word from the field offices, JC. A whole ops town on the border, isn't that correct, Alexei? Apartments, offices, and Mars-grade tech, I hear. Think of all that and consider what we have. A cut-price Rory Stewart parked in a green zone hotel suite. I really should get an OBE for dreaming up J-Sec.'

—

Later in the evening, Julian went to Alexandra Park again, taking the Priory Lane entrance this time. When he was little, he used to run across the footbridge, ahead of his parents. Now he walked listlessly, past the faded graffiti on the wall to his right; turning left, he caught a glimpse of the bright colours of the prep school building ahead. He wished to sit on a secluded bench by the lake on the other side of the old Victorian theatre, which was undergoing restoration at last, but suspected the gates might be closed at this time of the day. So he went down to where the farmers' market assembled on Sundays and sat on a weathered grey bench. It was in the memory of an Eileen Wheybrew: mother, wife, friend of the park. Surely, she might have been a bit more than that. Woman, beloved, lover?

What was he to do? He felt his heart racing and put a hand to his chest. He had held Maryam, touched her, and she had looked at him with her wide, expectant eyes before pulling away. A mix of fear and regret, longing and dread came over him.

There was little doubt in the Section that her son was the 'Swordsman' for whose house he'd left the office one morning in spring, he thought, as he leaned back on Eileen and gazed at a dense stand of trees further away, curving streams of dark and red leaves under them. As per Alexei, and he had no reason to disbelieve him, Dilawar Ali was also the behind-the-scenes tech whiz who created proxy servers and put together encryptions, and God knows what else, for an IS cell in Mosul. He was both, one and the same.

He hadn't been copied on what was known as the DC Dossier, and he doubted it would be sent to him anytime soon—he wasn't even keen on it anymore—but he had heard enough from Alexei. Dilawar could be anything, but then where was he? Where had he vanished? Why hadn't he cropped up anywhere else? Was there any chance he was a missing person after all, as Maryam had insisted from the beginning? She had pleaded with him to bring her son back and he'd said yes, he would—he had promised—but there wasn't much he could do about it now, was there? It wasn't in his hands.

The data doesn't lie, he told himself, as a cold breeze washed over his face. In fact, the 78 per cent match goes to show how meticulous and diligent Alexei and Ispahani had been. Now, with the campaign intensifying …

But perhaps there was no need to be alarmed, nothing had actually happened yet. And, as David said, these things took time. The boss was simply keeping him and the others in the loop. The briefings were standard procedure, and he was family liaison, after all, so he ought to remain patient and not say anything to Maryam. She had enough on her mind, and besides, she wouldn't be able to understand any of this. It's best not to say anything to her, he decided. Maryam doesn't need to know.

It grew chillier as the evening turned dark, but he didn't move from the bench. There was no one else in the park. A blue light spread everywhere, gathered around the treetops, and he saw birds ducking and diving through it.

THIRTY-EIGHT

I've seen this before, Julian. I've seen perfectly sane, grown-up people completely lose their senses, throwing up their arms—it can't be true, it can't be true, they shout. I've seen distraught, deranged mothers and fathers swear by the innocence of their boys, shell-shocked relatives who look at you incredulously, as if you've made it all up. I remember their faces, all grey and pale. It's the colour of hope dying.

Your Maryam Ali, she's in denial, they all are. She still can't accept her boy is in an Islamist commune. I'd probably be the same if it was my child.

But it's terrifying, isn't it? All these boys and girls, gone to live in a crazy death cult. Some of them so fucking young … pimply, hormonal, angry kids! Can you imagine the havoc if they sneaked back in without us knowing? That's what keeps me awake at night. Yes, I do think of their mothers and fathers, but I've got a job to do, we've all got a job to do.

Your Maryam Ali is blinded by love. She thinks letting her son stay locked in his room is going to keep him safe, and her free to waltz around bingo joints. This is what a lot of these parents don't understand. Everything is online now, Julian, every fucking thing. Even things that are meant to be offline, out of the house, *off* screen, are brought together and made to happen online. More and more, things are born online.

Maryam Ali thinks this is perfect: her boy doesn't want to get out much, he wants to stay in his room all the time, and that's excellent. She can scoot off when she wants because he's out of harm's way, safe from the bad boys. He's alright, that boy, doesn't want to be in this group or that, he loves staying indoors, I've got nothing to worry about. I'm so lucky, let's go to that karaoke night, girls!

'She may have mentioned bingo once or twice, David—'

You get my drift, Julian. Maryam Ali locks the doors on her son, thinking he's safe because he's not meeting anyone. But what she doesn't understand is that kids aren't meeting people outside because they're meeting them inside! On the internet. Of course, she will swear by her son's good nature ... because that's what she sees. It's entirely plausible that's what he really is until he decides to take the techie job at an ISIS franchise. That's how they get him, Julian, they come to him in his room. Of course she's going to cry her heart out, say her boy has nothing to do with anything. The worms, she calls them, doesn't she? Not half bad, by the way.

What she doesn't know is that her good-mannered boy is making friends all the way in Mosul to fight American injustice! They land a coder brother from London, and he gets an erection being in charge of their internet ops. I feel for her, I'm not heartless, but she's in denial.

Now, I would prefer that it doesn't fall upon us to make a decision about Dilawar Ali, but if he's in bed with some dangerous cunts over there, what do you think we are going to do? He shouldn't be there, JC, he simply shouldn't be there. It's not in our hands anymore, it's not your responsibility anymore. I know how you feel about Maryam ...

'She's scared, naturally.'

Who wouldn't be. You must remember that, ultimately, she's not very different from other ISIS parents, a mother shattered senseless. They all are, looking at their children's photos and pencils and pyjamas every day, not moving them lest it bring bad luck! You've done your job, Julian. We knew next to nothing about Dilawar Ali, and I didn't have time for a news scandal. Muslim mother harassed by the security services.

She is unable to let go of her life with her son. She wants to hold on to the fiction of mum and son together.

'Fiction?'

You know what I mean. She wants to carry on in a state of suspension, in a gramophone loop of the song every day. It gives her comfort, obviously, but Hannah's eval was very clear. Acute anxiety disorder. You didn't think Hannah was there just to babysit her and copy documents, did you?

Anyhow, the Mosul gang we have been tracking ... Apparently, they operated from a warehouse on the outskirts of the city, but just before the start of the campaign, they moved to a library building, and as per latest intel, there's an HVI in the group. They've been moving men and weapons between Mosul and Raqqa for some time. Ispahani says the field office has found a fresh match for our boy, among others. All kinds, it seems: Americans, Brits, French, Emiratis, Saudis, Turks, even a few Australians ... It's like a mini-UN over there.

Ispahani also said that the video source code had some kind of digital stamp that had been traced to Mosul. If it comes to it, we will have no say in the matter, Julian.

I told her we will bring her son back.

Did you sleep with her?

It's quite a large group, so clearly, we don't know every single one of them and we don't have to.

'And the Swordsman is in the group,' Julian said, raising his eyes.

Of course, he bloody is. With the photos from Maryam's albums ... and the new visuals from Mosul, Alexei and Oskar's people built a 3D model which matches with the man in the video. Thanks to all the work, we do have a higher match now, 78 per cent. I say that's quite high.

'But doesn't it also mean, being the devil's advocate here, David, that there's a 22 to 28 per cent probability it's not him? Hani said 72 per cent last month …'

Why not focus on the 70 plus per cent—if that's how we want to do this?

Julian fell silent and started picking at the nail on his left thumb.

Ultimately, cases like this don't matter in the big picture, Julian. What I'm really worried about is how we minimise the damage here … There's a purpose for all this tech. If you and I know a boy from London or some refugee kid from some bombed-out hellhole is planning to blow up the Jubilee Line or the 91 bus in Trafalgar Square, we're going to do everything to put him out of circulation. It doesn't matter if they haven't done anything yet. There's no trial and error in this work, Julian. Only trial.

Julian disengaged from his thumb and looked around.

You have been a helpful personal counsellor to some parents, it's probably part of your job. You want to hear Maryam Ali's sob story every weekend, it's your call. You are in the field; you do what gets the job done. I don't want to know. I realised a long time ago we don't live in an era of feelings and ethics. When we have people—our own people, so they claim—who get a kick from piling up TNT sandwiches, what am I going to do with my feelings? Or Noam Chomsky's feelings for that matter …

We are here to deny, to prevent, to put away anyone threatening to, planning to, or with intent to take lives here, in this country—before they do it. What good is nabbing someone after they've blown up King's Cross or the Piccadilly Line you take home?

Julian looked out of David's office and noticed that the crowns of the plants in the hallway created a fence-like effect. It was as if he was sitting inside a locked orchard. He couldn't recall anybody in the office talking about ethics or morals. He was momentarily seized by the fear that perhaps his mother had said something on TV, she sometimes discussed international politics on late-night programmes, but Anne-Marie hadn't made a TV appearance lately, he reassured himself. What then had brought this on from David?

Our friends have lists, Julian. Lists of those who must be dealt with, and I say thank God for that! If somebody is on a list, no one can do anything about it, not you, not me, not my boss, not even Allah!

I bear no grudge against Maryam Ali's son, but it's not in our hands anymore. We will always have that. You and I both know far too many hormonal Brits have gone over to the other side, and they will all have to be dealt with one way or another.

Julian felt low and subdued, as if the air had been taken out of his lungs, a few questions still hissing inside his mind, but he reminded himself where he was, of his role, of the job he'd signed up for three years ago.

'I know, David, I've worked the cases,' he said plainly, looking at the table, at the glass-and-dark-wood panels, the realisation of the distance between him and the set-up where he was, gnawing at him with a biting shame.

Yes, exactly, you know how it is … Anyhow, I believe there are ten or twelve Western men in the Mosul group.

'Ten or twelve?'

You know we can't always find a 100 per cent match, Julian … Why do you think it takes forever to deal with this awful mess? But we've got to get on with it, we can't be late, because being late costs lives, real, proper lives, being late means child corpses and charred limbs. One day, you will remember what I said. Everyone doesn't come on CCTV.

Julian could hear his heartbeat in his throat. He sighed, looking down at his feet.

We can't have feelings about all this, my friend, it's not in your hands.

'I understand, it's not up to us.'

THIRTY-NINE

The screen on Ispahani's desk came alive with a quick flicker, a silverfish stab through the dark, and then it lit up. He had set up the peer-to-peer connection with the mother console at D Wing the night before.

'So, this is where we're going to see it happen,' he said, turning towards his colleagues, not so much informing them as asserting it was his screen where they were going to see it. Julian stood behind David's chair. David felt Julian's breath on his neck. Alexei walked in with an egg tray bearing six steaming cups from Angelo's Deli across the road.

'They will send the alert if and when, Hani,' David said, closing his eyes as he took in the vapours from his cup.

'It's a library near the university, they said. HVI is believed to be staying there with his family and inner circle. Some library staff and their families were last seen on the premises too, but we haven't had more information on them since then. Fucking unbelievable, he's been there all these months with his men, in and out too.'

'Does he have a name, David, this HVI?'

'Basri … Oskar's people think he has several aliases. Basri's last known sighting was in Baghdad around the time of the attack on the vegetable market. Scores of women and children among the dead, you may recall. They found children's arms mangled with vegetable pulp. Basri and gang had filled a garbage truck with RDX and shrapnel.

'Apparently, Basri detonated the bomb himself using a Nokia as a detonator. It took some time, but Oskar's team managed to trace the call to a telephone exchange in a neighbourhood near the library. It's been in the works for several months. Until a year ago, Basri was the chief of an elite ISIS division, but he was downgraded for taking his wife and children everywhere. Nice family man, probably watches *Coronation Street* on the weekends. Apparently, he prefers remote detonations to suicide vests and picks all the sites himself. D Wing have had eyes on him ever since the vegetable market attack. A disgruntled Saudi commander in his entourage probably had enough of the carnage. I'm told Basri rose to be the de facto leader of his cell because of the ease with which he carried out attacks in Baghdad and Mosul. He's always had a small team of tech bros in his inner circle. This is the sort of illustrious company our boy has been keeping, Julian.'

'If it's him, that is—' Julian started to say but then stopped.

'I know what Chapman is going to say. Go on … 78 per cent means there's a high chance it's him, but it also implies there's a 22 per cent probability it's someone else, which, in turn, suggests it may not be him … Is that where we are on the ethics meter, Chapman?'

'No need for the snarky tone, Faroukh, although I must say I'm impressed you are able to pronounce ethics correctly,' Julian said, taking a sip of his coffee.

'Yes, Hani, let's dial down the sarcasm,' David said.

'Thanks, David,' Julian said, eyeing him.

'Let's just wait and watch, gentlemen, shall we?'

They sipped their coffees in silence. There was no one else in the office, just the four of them. Julian cleared his throat when the screen flickered. The live feed was to appear on its own as per Ispahani's information. They waited as the beeping of garbage trucks filtered in from the streets, followed by muffled clangs.

FORTY

Zarrine and Saffina nudged each other, elbow to elbow, eyes talking. Neither spoke as they watched Maryam squat down in front of the TV. She never did this.

It was the News at 10, the signature tune playing alongside the brisk opening sequence. Maryam found it too loud and wanted to cover her ears, but she didn't. Her sisters sat in trepidation at the back. They worried something had come over Baji but wouldn't dare ask; each waited for the other to speak.

On Maryam's insistence, they had kept away for long periods, busying themselves with work, their children's lives and household chores. On the subject of their nephew, a fragile peace had been arrived at in their respective households: until it was fully confirmed, there was to be no dinnertime chat about Dilawar. They would not have it. Saffina's husband Jawad had now and then talked about the need to be prepared for the worst. 'It is for your sanity, Saffs, for your sister's …' he had said.

Zarrine ached to hear Dil's voice, but seethed with anger too. He had caused her sister to wilt, turned her mad almost. 'The way she looks at us sometimes, it's not normal, I'm scared for Baji,' she had said to Saffina on the way to Maryam's. 'I want it to end now, Saffs, think she's had enough, suffered enough, don't you think?'

'What we think won't matter, Zee, it's the authorities, the police, that Chapman guy who comes to see her, they're the ones who know what's really going on, who ought to tell us everything! I'm a bit scared too, to be honest.'

They had met midway, then taken a cab to Maryam's flat. Maryam had found it impossible to pull herself away from the news on TV, and after a week of watching it by herself, she'd called Zarrine. Zarrine had come alone the first day, and today with Saffina. They sat together on the sofa, looking at Maryam's back as she sat cross-legged on the floor.

--

When the orchestral tune faded away, as if dying into itself, Maryam shifted her weight, brought her hands together, locking her fingers, and let out a low moan. It was not the short-haired woman with the red lipstick today but the older white man whose large head came on after the opening sequence. He made a sombre face, held his pose for a fraction as the music faded, and started reading the headlines.

Zarrine grabbed Saffina's hand and tried to pull her off the sofa with her. Then, not knowing what to do because Maryam still hadn't looked back at them, she whispered, 'Shall I make tea?'

Saffina gave her a glare and said, 'Just sit down, Zarro, can't you see?'

Zarrine looked up as the presenter made what seemed to her like a formal, hasty greeting, then, as the screen cut to the red-and-white Breaking News graphic, he announced in an authoritative voice:

'News just in from Iraq. US and Iraqi forces have made major advances into the northern city of Mosul. Earlier today, Iraqi special forces marched into the western part of the city for the first time since 2014.'

The screen cut to a group of soldiers shouting slogans on a packed and smoky street, guns and flags aloft. A military commander in olive fatigues held centre stage, showing a V sign to the camera; he bent down and kissed the ground.

'Allah o Akbar, Allah o Akbar,' the sisters heard the chants ring.

The presenter came back with the same expression as before and resumed: 'There have been significant developments in the last few hours in Iraq where NATO and Iraqi forces have been engaged in some of the heaviest fighting since the start of the counter-offensive against the so-called Islamic State earlier this year. US sources have confirmed that Iraqi special forces have cleared large parts of the city of ISIS, and are now stationed at barricades before West Mosul, presumably the last stronghold of ISIS in the country. In some of the bloodiest battles since the US-led campaign started, hundreds of militants, Iraqi forces and civilians have been killed. And as you can see in the images, many neighbourhoods in Mosul have been completely destroyed or severely damaged. Some parts of the city have been reduced to rubble, with corpses scattered in the old city. At this point, we must warn our viewers that some of the scenes may be distressing. Unconfirmed reports suggest that, before fleeing the area, fighters associated with the Islamic State blew up many buildings, including a mosque and an adjoining building. Our correspondent, who's been accompanying a special forces unit, has filed this report ... Once again, viewer discretion is advised as some of the images may be distressing for some viewers.'

Maryam sighed, her chin resting on her palm. She felt dry in her mouth, a weight gathering, a dread rising.

'In another significant related development, Pentagon sources say that Hasan Basri, the head of the so-called Islamic State in the region, was killed today when US forces carried out a guided strike at his base on the outskirts of the city. It is believed that the library complex where he was killed was an operations centre and a munitions factory. Many of his associates are also likely to have been killed.' Maryam swallowed, put her face in both hands, her arms shaking.

The presenter took a pause, the screen cutting to a grainy shot of an explosion, smoke, debris.

'Our correspondent says that the secretive British jihadist recruiter and internet mastermind Dilawar Ashfaq Ali, also known as the Swordsman, may also be among the dead. He is believed to have been a member of Hasan Basri's inner circle. Earlier in the year, London-born Ali was allegedly seen in two ISIS videos that the authorities now believe were filmed in and streamed from Mosul.'

A rippling shiver ran through Maryam's body, shaking her, making her press her hands together until her knuckles began to hurt. She sat there in breathless silence as the screen switched to a short clip from the Swordsman video, in which a masked man is standing with a scabbard at his side, its red-and-black handle glinting. He's just standing there, eyes focussed on something up ahead.

'Born to a British Indian mother and an Irish Indian father, Dilawar Ali is a British national from East London. Earlier in the year, he went missing from his outer London home where he lived with his mother.'

Saffina and Zarrine came down, the latter sobbing.

The TV then cut to a split screen with Dilawar in one half and Maryam in the other. He's in the middle of an escalator at The Mall in Wood Green, Burger King in the background. She's wearing a black headscarf tied around her face. It was the photo she had seen in the tabloids in the summer. They'd gone to Ilford for lunch after the Friday prayers.

'Basri was responsible for a number of deadly attacks in Baghdad, Mosul and other Iraqi towns … Ali is believed to have helped smuggle American and British citizens, including women, to ISIS-held areas,' the TV presenter with the short grey hair and square jaw carried on. A fresh ticker started racing at the bottom of the screen.

The Swordsman presumed dead. London-born Dilawar Ali allegedly killed in an airstrike in Iraq … The Swordsman presumed dead …

Zarrine and Saffina clung to Maryam. They held her shoulders as her body trembled and convulsed. Maryam let out a piercing howl, brushing them aside.

'Hai Allah, save Dil, Allah save Dilly …' Saffina said, her voice choking on itself.

'Oh my God, oh my God, what the hell, Allah Mian, what have you done!' Zarrine started weeping, the words from the TV ringing, echoing, blurring, fading.

Maryam wailed, her hands raised, strands of hair hanging off her right hand. She held her sisters by their wrists and started swaying forwards and backwards, breathing fast, again and again and again.

'Ya Allah, ya Allah,' she kept saying, her face wet; tears streaming down her cheeks; lower lip red on one side; a drip of blood on her chin.

'Recite the Kalima, Zarro, recite the Kalima, Saffo, recite the Kalima for my baby. Hai mera bachcha … They have killed my son, Ama! They have killed my Dil.' She threw her head back with some force and hit the edge of the sofa, her neck twisting at an angle. She let her arms drop, her chadar was at her feet.

'Let's not think the worst, Baji, please! It's just a news report, they get it wrong sometimes, we don't know it was Dilly over there.' Zarrine started to cry again. 'You said so yourself, Baji, it's not Dilly over there, you said so yourself, didn't you? Please, Allah Mian, let it not be Dilly!'

'It's crazy, he never even went there, Baji, they're lying, Saffs, aren't they, they lie all the time! This is complete bullshit, he's a kid, he's my baby, okay! A fucking kid, what do you mean jihadist whatever, you fucking bastards, he's silly Dilly …' Zarrine slumped down near Maryam, laying half her body on her, sobbing, sniffling.

'Dilly, Dilly, Dilly …' Saffina's tears kept coming quietly.

—

Maryam became still then, tears streaming across her face, thin streams joining under her chin, her mind back at Whipps Cross Maternity, a wet little smudgy, crinkly face sticking to her chest, and those eyes, wide open liquid eyes like her own, as if copied from hers, staring at her … She knew immediately that he'd got her large eyes, *ditto*, and the hair on that boy, uff, you gave it all to our baby, eh, Ashy, trying to make up for the bald patches, she'd said to Ashfaq, who had clung close, beaming and wiping a tear. She was in a large rectangular room with just one other woman in the other corner, a tall white girl who had waved at Maryam from her bed, giving her a thumbs up.

'She's got some complications, poor girl,' Ama had whispered to her but not quietly enough.

'Allah toba, Ama, leave the poor woman alone, goodness!'

'Achha, achha, don't you get upset now, let's put some pretty clothes on this dirty boy. Nazr-e-bad door!'

Everybody had come to see her mixture baby, Aunt Sugra, Barrister Uncle Sharief of Hampstead, even Aunt Kulsum and Showki … Everybody wanted to see what her 'off-white' boy looked like.

'American and British jets carried out further strikes against Islamic State strongholds to back up the ground offensive.'

Maryam cupped her face in her hands, weeping, her head down. Then she fell silent.

'Saffo, Zarro, come on, uttho, uttho, stand up, will you? We must pray for Dilly, he deserves a farewell prayer, does he not? They never told me what he's done and now they say they have killed him. I will never forgive them! For the sake of mercy, Allah

Mian, when did he go to Iraq and Mosul and god knows where and become … and become that person! Let's pray for him, Zarro, offer Fateha, shouldn't we? If he's really gone, if he's really … We can't send him off without prayers. How can we! Come on, Saffo jaan, what are you waiting for!'

She stood up, and her sisters stood up with her, holding her arms. They looked at each other, held each other. One by one, they left the living room, performed the Wuzu, and came back with washed faces and swollen eyes. Maryam gave them scarves to cover their heads and they lined up towards the qibla to the northeast of the living room. The curtains were closed, but through a slit an oblong of light fell on the carpet. Maryam gazed at it and read the Surah Fateha for her son, taking a pause in the middle to steady her breath. Zarrine and Saffina repeated after her, their heads bowed down.

'Bismillah ir-Rahman ir-Rahim …' Maryam said, sobbed, pursed her lips, and started again.

They remained silent for a while after the end of the prayer, then her sisters held her.

'Oh, Baji, oh, Baji,' they said.

FORTY-ONE

Homecroft Street, the corner of the old Anglican church, Tony's shopfront, the garage lane further out where Dil used to smoke an occasional cigarette, all wore a washed look after the early morning drizzle. Squiggly, swirly dust motes, bits of paper and plastic wrappers had swept up to the walls and the corners, slid under bins and into gutters. The neighbourhood was quiet, its leafy parts glistening in the misty rain, and the bricky bits, where the terraces leaned into one another like hastily put together Lego homes, appeared less ragged. As the morning grew, steam escaped through slits in kitchen windows, the double-glazing cloudy with trapped perspiration, a toilet flush gurgled now and then, some hungry babies bawled, a delivery van accelerated, a grumpy driver's foot a bit too keen on the pedal probably.

Tony put his kettle on and watched it come to a boil. He rolled his second cigarette of the day. Must commiserate with Maryam, he thought, or maybe I should wait a few more days, but not too long, it's already been ten days. It's not right what happened, it's not right, he muttered to himself, as he dragged on his cigarette. Fucking hell.

Maryam was on the sofa, looking down at the creases on the fabric. Julian and David had sat on it when they first came to see her. She ran her hand over the fine wool. It felt the same as always. She remembered how Ash would watch her do it. A soft, blue-grey light spread in the living room, the corners still in semi-darkness. She hadn't turned on the lights. For some reason, she felt she didn't want to see Julian in clear light. He had come at nine and had been sitting quietly for about half an hour. He was wearing a dark blazer over a turtleneck sweater.

She wanted to shake him, grab him by his collar and shout at him: did you give them Dil's photos and details to have him killed, Julian? She'd imagined doing it every day but now she felt drained. She wanted to ask him so many things, and was going over them again and again.

In the end, she simply said, 'Who does this thing, Julian, do you know? Does someone say, go, do it now? It can't all be paperwork and investigations, you lot making case files and managing people like me. There must be someone who says, alright, let's drop a bomb on that house, no, not that one, the other one ...'

Julian had a hollow sensation in his chest, and his stomach tightened.

'I heard someone say "compound" on the TV,' Maryam continued. 'You don't get to decide, I know, or else I would've begged you to bring him home and do whatever you want with him, but please give me some time with him first. Maybe that's what I had wanted when you came to see me the first or second time ... Can't you just put him in prison?'

She stopped, curling a strand of hair around her index finger, pulling at it.

'Does David decide, or is it his boss, his boss's boss, or is it the prime minister? I know it doesn't matter but someone somewhere must know, someone who thinks about it all and makes a decision. Alright, boys, let's do it. Who does, Julian?'

'Maryam ... I know anything I say will never be adequate or proper, or ... I can't imagine what you must feel, I really can't.

How do I say this … I am just very, very sorry for your loss, I wish I could've—

'Who decided, Julian, you must know … You know, don't you?' She heard her voice rise.

'I don't know what to say … Maryam … I suppose people many rungs above us, way higher. They know best, I'm told, but I'm not so sure anymore. To be honest, I am quite fed up myself.'

Under no circumstances was he going to tell her the details.

'Oh, are you … fed up? Were you fed up before or after they killed my son?'

'I'm truly sorry, Maryam. I wish there was something I could say that would—'

'You could've told me they were going to do it! Instead, you came to sit with me, in my …'

'There was nothing I could do. It wasn't in my hands.'

'Maybe it never was, Julian, maybe it never was, only I was stupid and sad and desperate to think—'

'I never lied to you, Maryam, never.'

'But you led me to believe—'

'For that I will always be sorry. It was never my intention, I could never lie to you or give you false hope, but I couldn't stop coming to see you, I wanted to …'

'Please stop. You just don't know when to shut up, do you … My son—' She took a deep breath and stopped talking.

'I was never told, Maryam. I am so sorry. That's all I wanted to—'

Maryam was looking out of the window, the garden was wet, water dripping from the plants and the hedges. She turned to him and said in a cracked voice, 'Maybe you have been honest with me … At least you have been honest with me … Are you thinking of quitting?'

'Honestly, I wish I could just quit, but that's not how it works. I can't turn up and say I'm going to stop coming from Monday. But yes, I'm thinking of asking to be moved. Perhaps I can try to do some good somewhere else …'

'Good luck with that … Can you put Dilly in jail though …' She stopped. 'Do you spend enough time with your mother,' she said, as if remembering something.

'We try to …'

He looked at their reflections in the shiny darkness of the TV screen. He dreaded what she might ask next. Hannah was off the case, and he wondered if he could arrange for her to spend some more time with Maryam. It would do her good, keep her calm.

--

Of the forty-eight people in the Mosul library complex, they would probably recover some partial skeletons, a few bits and pieces, some burnt torsos, some scorched muscle, some incinerated entrails, a roasted heart or two, some ashen hands, a gnarled foot here and a twisted elbow there, teeth, twinkling in the ash mounds, a Toy Story box of body parts. Julian had heard Ispahani talk about the debris plainly, or perhaps with some feeling, he couldn't remember, but this is how he had imagined it to be. Perhaps Alexei had said something about the dignity of human lives, to which Ispahani had said, but what about the trains and the cafés and stadiums they blow up—he couldn't recall clearly because he'd felt dizzy on seeing the footage run over and over on several office screens, and he'd excused himself, gone to the bathroom, then walked past David's house plants, the tall cacti in glass staring at him, gone down in the lift, then out into the lane that went nowhere, at the front of which stood the weathered busts of Victorian men. Hands on his hips, he'd tried to shake off the scenes he had watched all morning.

--

Sitting in Maryam's living room, Julian wondered whether this thing was recent, Maryam saying the same thing over and over, or had she been like that for some time? From the beginning, from the time Dilawar disappeared? Perhaps she'd been like this all the time she had spent waiting for him.

'I know you talk to your mother, Julian, you're the kind of person who talks to his mother.'

'I guess so …'

'I wish people talked more to their mothers. I wish more boys talked to their mums, and mums to their boys. It's not bad, mothers and sons talking.'

--

It was a coalition strike in which Basri was targeted along with his inner circle, they had said on the TV. They didn't say anything about his family, but Julian suspected they had been in the library, the families of the library staff too.

'Guided strikes from an F-35, followed by Spearhead British drones,' David had said.

'Deployed to take out the VBIED factory behind the library gardens', the J-Sec internal memo said.

'The munitions on the 35s can melt metal in a matter of seconds,' Alexei had chipped in, a boyish thrill escaping his eyes.

--

'What have you thought, Maryam, what are you going to do now?' As he said this, Julian was unable to expunge from his mind the dust-coated, torn corpses of men, women and children faintly visible in the debris, nor what Ispahani had said to Alexei. 'Even the bones will have evaporated, let's just go home … Not much we haven't seen before.'

Maryam looked at his face, remembering hers next to it, and sighed. 'I don't think I can live here anymore, or maybe I don't want to. I've always loved it, you know, but now my heart has left this house. It cannot rest here. I know Dil's breath still lingers somewhere in the corners and the doorways, probably Ash's too, but I can't bear to hear them anymore.'

'Where will you go then, Maryam? Where will you live? I am just—'

'Why, have all the Premier Inns burned down? I've got my pension, my savings.'

'Premier Inn?'

'I've got other options too, don't worry. I could crash with Saffo for some time, maybe at Zarro's after that, though she's going to do my head in. Then there's our old house, that loft has been vacant for years. It's probably mouldy with piles of boxes and newspapers and cardboard, Ama is a hoarder, you know, but I'm sure it can be made liveable.

'Oh, there's also Aunt Noorie's in India, in the hills, Mussoorie.'

'Did your family go there?'

'I went with Ama–Aba when I was small. Aunt Noorie's husband was in the army then, Brigadier Beg. He told everyone he was a general. I could go for a short time, you know, they have a pretty, filmy bungalow, white fence, flower beds in the lawn … I'm sure Aunt Noorie will have me, I could cook for them, you know, earn my keep … I know cooking.'

Julian watched her. 'Erm, how shall I say this … Maryam, you could stay at my house for a few days,' he said.

Maryam looked up at him, a faint smile playing on the corner of her mouth. 'Are you asking me to move in with you, Julian? What will your folks think?'

'I mean, you could stay for some time, there's plenty of space. My parents wouldn't mind at all,' he lied, Anne-Marie's words ringing in his head: 'Don't be ridiculous, darling, you can't ask that woman to stay at my house. You can't be serious, are you!'

They let the silence fill the time for a while.

—

'I watched it over and over, Julian. I tried to stay away, but I couldn't. I found it on two other TV channels later. The dust and the smoke and the blurring sky. I don't know how I felt or maybe I didn't feel what I should have felt watching my son blown up into smoke and ash ... I'm still not sure he was there, so maybe I didn't grieve him as I should have—as I wanted to. You took that from me, didn't you, you took my grief away from me. Or maybe I'd already grieved him, had been grieving him all along, you know, like people mourn cancer patients or something ... Is that possible?'

Was she saying she was ready to face it when the time came?

'That's not what I think, though. Do you remember I once told you about giving birth to him—how that felt? I have thought about it often and I think I have a better idea of it now, maybe ... It's as if I've been mourning my conception of him all this time. Maybe that's what I wanted to say then and I'm never fully sure ... but I feel having a child is living with a lifelong conception of them. Yes, they become their own people, they become who they are, etcetera, all that's true, but what's also true is that we, the parents, the mothers and the fathers, we always have an idea of them, of what they should and could grow into—what we want them to be. I probably started mourning Dil the day he vanished, leaving me early in the morning like that. It was a negation, a refusal, the beginning of his end. When you all came home that day, maybe deep down, part of me already knew my son was dead.'

'I don't know what to say, Maryam ... I'm truly sorry, and I'm very sad for you.'

'Dil isn't going to come back, is he, what with 78 per cent of him being dead, and I don't know how to look for the 22 per cent of him that isn't a terrorist. Can't you bring something of him? Why can't you bring anything of him?

'He has left a burn hole in my heart; it simmers and it will simmer all the time I have left in this world. I can't do anything about it. I'll always think I couldn't keep him safe, couldn't protect him from the ghosts who took him from me. My heart shattered the day you called him by that name, and now it's a constant wound. I will have to live with it, with this forever injury, because I'll always be his mother. I will be known as his mother until the day I die, maybe even after I'm gone.

'I still want to live on, though. Is that bad? I know I'll have to live with this debris, but I'm also who I am. I still want a little bit of my own life, what's left of it anyway. Is that wrong? I feel I'm also Ama's, and Saffina's and Zarrine's ...

'To answer your question: no, I don't want to live here ... I should've known the day you and David walked in.

'Why can't you put Dilly in jail, though? Do you not understand?'

'Yes, I understand, Maryam ... I do. But where will you go, where will you live?'

'I told you, a bedsit somewhere. There are plenty of homeless people in London.'

'Why not come home with me for a few days, stay until you've decided?'

'Alright, alright, but only for a few days, just for a few days.'

FORTY-TWO

Maryam looked at her reflection, considering her face, the faint circles under the eyes, the fine lines. She yearned for a long night's sleep.

She had packed all her clothes, even those she wasn't sure fit her anymore but liked. She had also filled three large bags for charity and put them in a corner, each tied at the top with a string. Saffina was to take them away in her big car and hand them in at the Cancer Research shop; her and Dil's clothes would hang in the store one day, she thought, maybe in the window too. She didn't want to pursue this thought further, so she turned to look at the garden; the curtains were fully open, the light sweeping in; she had no fear of people spying on her. Everybody knew, everybody had read the papers, everybody had a TV. She had wanted to break hers.

She looked at the canoe-shaped flower bed in the centre of the garden. It never disappointed. It was nearly Christmas, and the cold had started to collect in the corners despite the radiators, but some pink roses remained steadfast.

It was three weeks since the news about Dilawar had been shown on TV, since she had seen the smoke and the dust and the scatter rising in the air.

What brought back the pain every day was that nobody had come to offer Fateha, no one from the extended family had turned up with food because that's what relatives do when someone dies: bring cooked food. None of her aunts and uncles came to offer condolences, no one recited the Quran at her house, no one blessed her son's soul. No one said, 'May his soul rest in peace', let alone 'Allah grant him a place in Jannat'. She thought of this every day, and it brought home the pain. Saffina and Zarrine came, of course, together and separately, their husbands came too, but not their children. She had wanted to see the children, Zarrine's son Zak in particular, and hoped she would be able to do so soon. The sisters didn't offer any excuses for their in-laws, and Maryam was grateful. She didn't need to say it to them, she felt, as she tried to imagine the conversations in their households. Mothers-in-law, husbands, brothers-in-law had to be taken into account, worried about. That was life.

Ama came and held her. She sat down and remained quiet for a long moment, holding Maryam's hand. Then she stood up and kissed her grandson's photo. She held Maryam again and sobbed like a baby before losing her breath. Ama walked with a stick, but that day she had left it home. She stayed for three nights. Then Zarrine took her home.

The winter roses suggested to her there was never going to be a Christmas dinner at her house, with both the boys gone. She had done it for them mostly. She liked it too, but they liked it more ... Reminded Ash of his mother Lauren and Cork; and Dil got his presents, many, many presents. It occurred to her that the thought of having the dinner this year, having Saffina and Zarrine and maybe even Julian, had been preposterous to begin with—wishful thinking really, a silly notion. It also occurred to her that it didn't matter now, whatever it was.

She glanced at the suitcases and the charity bags and the bits of rubbish scattered in the bedroom and was filled with a sense of tedium. So many things to do before she left. She had spoken with Uncle Sharief about the flat, and he'd agreed to deal with the paperwork as long as someone else did the leg work. All he had to do was deal with the bank and the estate agent, but she would ask Zarrine to help him anyway. She was bound to drive him mad, serves him right, though. Or maybe she could ask the Finchleys to sort out the whole thing, they were good with money and property and suchlike. And Aunt Kulsum had been the only one to phone her and say Magfirah. She had apologised for not being able to visit because of her bad leg.

—

She turned back to her reflection and spoke to herself ... You weren't really thinking of moving to Julian's house, were you, staying with him? You must've gone mad, Maryam Ali, full bonkers, what's the matter with you! You were thinking of going to stay with the man who might have helped kill your son? Alright, one of the people responsible for it. Of course not, she thought, of course not, although she suspected she may have been tempted by the thought when he mentioned it, or maybe tempted wasn't the right way to describe it—the thought had entered her head, and she may have contemplated what it would be like to live in his house in Muswell Hill. That was all, she said to herself in the mirror, that was all. There was nothing more to it, there's no way she was going to move in with him for even a day! What would people say! And Ama, Allah toba!

Zarrine had agreed to take Dilawar's books, old DVDs, trainers, computer, printer, and the games. There was a donation programme for the underprivileged at her mosque, which Azy looked after, so they were going to put everything in the trunk there. Doubt they would say whose things they were.

But Dil was killed by Americans—what's Julian got to do with it, she wondered, her mind not in her hands anymore. Well, yes, technically he was killed by the Americans, but who provided the photos, the info, who told them, she wondered, leaning on one side, still watching her face in the mirror. How could you even consider living in that man's house, Maryam?

Well, because it really wasn't him, he had nothing to do with it, it was way above his pay scale, he'd said. He was only family liaison, after all, only a part of the team at his office … Then there's the other thing, you can't not think of that, Maryam! You nearly had sex with him! Who's to say he won't try to get close again if you're in the next room, for god's sake. But did he really try to take advantage of the situation? Is he the kind of man who would do that? Well, first of all, he is a man, and a young man at that, and it's clear he fancies you, have you forgotten the way he looks at you! Of course, he wanted to sleep with you, you silly cow. Have you forgotten how he drooled? Poor man … brought him to the edge, didn't you, then left him standing like a lonely pup.

But there was no way she was going to stay at his house, not even for a few days. What would his mother say? She would know, wouldn't she … But they might meet sometimes.

She was going to go to Ama's and stay there as long as she wanted to, forever even. That's what Ama had said. Ama loved her. Then she would plan that trip to India and maybe go to Aunt Noorie's in Mussoorie.

She would also go on Haj one day, once people stopped recognising her, not that anyone would spot her in the massive crowd in Mecca. But first she would go to the old house and sleep in the loft room for a long, long time.

Acknowledgements

First readers, Aamer Hussein, Mohammed Hanif, Aliya Nazki and Rebecca Servadio, thank you for your wisdom and encouragement.

My brilliant agent Clare Alexander took an instant liking to Maryam and her sisters, giving me the courage to keep going. Matilda Southern-Wilkins has been a great support throughout. Thank you, both.

Ellah Wakatama gave the manuscript the time and attention only the finest readers in the world can give. Thank you for the notes, Ellah.

Mary Mount sent characteristically sharp and valuable insights. I'm grateful, Mary.

Matt Connors was kind enough to share his insights about some crucial aspects. Thanks, Matt.

I'm grateful to my publisher Karthika V.K. for believing in my work, for her patience with the fiddly edits, and for letting me take risks. If we don't take risks in our fictions, we might as well give up. Ajitha G.S., my extraordinary editor at Context, made the book better. Thank you.

Kamila Shamsie for sending the most astute and uplifting note when I needed it most.

Tahmima Anam for her solidarity and clear-eyed brilliance over the years.

Dearest Faiza Sultan Khan and Samar Attaullah for the gift of soul tonic.

Nimra Bucha and Mohammed Hanif (only man to feature twice in the same acknowledgements) for the silver-jubilee friendship.

Basharat Peer for being there when it mattered most.

Raheel Khurshid and Zahid Rafiq for warmth, shelter on hard days.

Anjali Capila, Ashish Paliwal, Yasar Khan and Pranav Capila for their presence.

Goldie Osuri and Bobby Banerjee are all-weather mates. Love to you both.

Aditya and Katy Chakrabortty, Shurobala and Asha, for their enduring love and affection.

Thank you to Ami, Abu, Sumana and Shariq. A special thank you to Nael 'Bhai' for bringing unbridled joy to life.

My mother Zehra has been a source of formidable courage and energy. My sisters Nighat, Tabasum and Nazima, and my brother Shuja give me more love than I deserve. My gratitude to Abba for holding the fort. I miss you all.

I wrote this novel during a difficult period. I'm not entirely sure I could have done it without the love and strength of my family. Mehvish, Shayan and Laila jaans, all my love is for you.

London
Autumn 2025